T0277979

Blame My Virgo Moon

Blame My Virgo Moon

FREJA NICOLE WOOLF

WALKER BOOKS

This is a work of fiction. Names, characters, places, and incidents are either products of the author's imagination or, if real, are used fictitiously.

First US edition 2024

Library of Congress Catalog Card Number 2024934268
ISBN 978-1-5362-3530-2

SHD 29 28 27 26 25 24
10 9 8 7 6 5 4 3 2 1

Printed in Chelsea, MI, USA

This book was typeset in ITC Usherwood Medium.

Walker Books US
a division of
Candlewick Press
99 Dover Street
Somerville, Massachusetts 02144

www.walkerbooksus.com

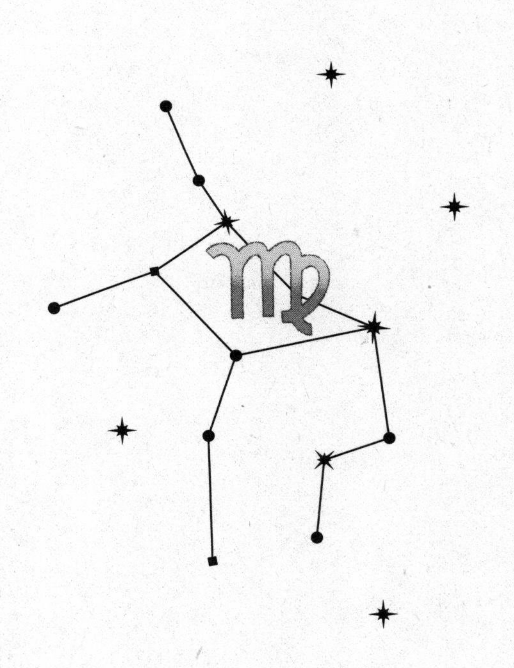

Prologue of Wondrous Joy Forever

I HAVE A GIRLFRIEND! Therefore, I am automatically better than anyone who is tragically single, like my friend Zanna. People in relationships can do cute activities together, like going to the cinema and ice-skating outdoors and, um . . . doing funny accents?

Okay, maybe not so much that last one. Although my girlfriend, Morgan, is Irish, so you never know. Either way, what can single people do? Lie about and weep, I suppose, or learn piano. I don't have time for that: my days are packed with dizzying romance and gushingly gorgeous moments! Yesterday, I laughed out loud, just for the sake of it.

"Quiet, Cathleen," bristled Mrs. Warren. "This is an English mock exam."

But what would a teacher know of love? I will not be quiet!

As Virginia Woolf once said: "There is no gate, no lock, no bolt that you can set upon the freedom of my Instagram-perfect lesbian relationship." Or something similar to that anyway.

True, it is a LITTLE sad sack of satsumas that we didn't celebrate our first Valentine's together. (Morgan doesn't "subscribe to heteronormative capitalism.") And she still hasn't watched *Frozen* with me. And she also called Taylor Swift "a little mainstream." (Yes, FOR A REASON?!) Hmm . . . But these are creases we can iron out, right?!

Because at last, after fifteen long and difficult years, I'm as happy as a Leo—which is very happy indeed, given how easily impressed Leos are. Anyway, back to me . . . I am very content, and it's literally my birthday! For once, a day that's all about me.

Aquarius
SEASON

1
Not on My Wasp

My favorite color has always been orange. So why is the theme of my On Fleek Fifteenth *yellow*?! According to Siobhan, who oh-so-graciously organized my party for me, "yellow is basically the same as orange anyway." But it's really not. I currently look like an electrocuted bumblebee in my stripy top, blond hair curling in every direction!

I'm also wearing yellow rain boots, which is never a good or fashionable thing to do. I look like my parents in their sad vegetable patch in the garden. But I literally had *no* choice: thanks to this party, there isn't a yellow shoe to be found in all of Kent.

Everyone's taken the yellow theme very seriously, and Siobhan's vast open-plan living area looks like a wasp's nest. There's Alison (with her latest boy-craze, Tall Adam), Habiba (with her boyfriend, Imaran), and the ever-glazed Lip Gloss Lizzie (with her boyfriend, Gloss-Guzzling Lawrence), all in sunny ensembles. Kenna seems to be holding a boy hostage behind the standing lamp, and even my best friend, Zanna, is arm-wrestling with Posh Josh O'Conner.

(I do mean literally, by the way. Zanna doesn't "do" romance.)

Basically, my birthday party looks like one massive speed-dating exercise. In yellow. The only person without someone is me! Morgan better have an ÜBER-Gucci excuse for being late. She knows how important tonight is! Aquarius Season may be the time to be selfish, but there are limits. Even for a Gemini like her. We've spent AGES revising my bespoke friendship plan so she can befriend my friends—I made a PowerPoint, which is more effort than I put into my schoolwork! Zanna, who actually *made* the PowerPoint while I dictated the important bits, told me as much.

Before I can digi-catapult any angry-face emojis my girlfriend's way, Siobhan comes marching over in a tight-as-Tweedle-Dee-and-Dum yellow dress and glittering heels that practically double her height. Tragically, Rich Elizabeth is with her, with an enormous yellow bow in her hair like she's been gift wrapped. They're both dripping in eye-scorchingly dazzling gleaming gold jewelry.

Siobhan is obscene for Alexander McQueen and she's designed the party in homage to the SS99 No. 13 Collection. Which includes having her ex's Lad Friends dress as robots and spray-paint guests black and yellow on the back patio. People have deliberately bought white dresses from charity shops in town to participate and are now lining up to be vandalized! Siobhan says it's going to be "very memorable." She's not wrong . . .

Siobhan also has a new boyfriend: the golf-obsessed,

polo-wearing Dale Collins, who is currently handcuffed to her by the wrist— Wait. *What?!*

"Christ on a bike, Cat! Where have you been?" Siobhan demands, slotting a key into the cuffs and setting Dale loose. He scampers to the bathroom, looking relieved. "Me and Elizabeth had to go into the *backyard* to look for you, and you know I hate nature!"

I blink at her. "I've been standing here the entire time, Siobhan."

You'd think I'd be the center of attention, considering it's *my* birthday, but apparently not. I suppose there's a good chance I just blended into the honeycomb bunting.

"Well, happy birthday, chicka!" Rich Elizabeth bedazzles away, air-kissing my cheeks. "I don't know anyone else born on February sixteenth, so it's, like, very *In Vogue* of you. What prezzies did you get? Daddy bought me a Porsche for my birthday in January. I can't wait until I'm old enough to drive it!" Then she opens a cooing convention in honor of Siobhan's dress. "And this truly is Beaut-McFruit, Siobhan. You look amazing!"

"I always dazzle in yellow," Siobhan agrees, tossing back her hair, which is so shimmeringly shiny, I'm wondering if she's actually had it laminated. "Well, every color, actually, but yellow especially. This dress is from the brand-new McQueen collection, so I HAD to debut it tonight. Honestly, you'd think I'd planned the whole party around it!"

She fake-laughs with Elizabeth as my eyes widen, because now that she says it, I'm absolutely sure that's exactly what she's done! But before I can say so, Elizabeth goes, "Wowzer's trousers, is that Brooke the Crook?"

We look around. A Brooke Mackenzie sighting is a rarity indeed! She's suspended so often, she apparently missed the whole of seventh grade without anyone noticing. But sure enough, Elizabeth is right. Brooke is crooking about by the snack tables, gangly, redheaded, and freckled.

Brooke is not the caliber of crème Siobhan would invite, especially without a budgie-smudge of yellow in sight. She's actually wearing green! Is she trying to get herself meat-minced?! Siobhan is rather a dress-code Tokugawa, so this is a McDisaster!

"What is BROOKE doing here?!" Siobhan gags. "She hasn't even been spray-painted!"

"Maybe she came for the free food?" I suggest. Honestly, Siobhan should be pleased: some bowls are practically untouched. I get that a theme is a theme, but is it any wonder nobody's tried her lemon-peel salad?

Sadly, Siobhan's having none of it.

"Brooke?" she barks, marching over. Me and Elizabeth watch with googly eyes. "You're not following my dress code. You're welcome to be spray-painted on the patio, but otherwise, you're going to have to leave."

Alarmingly, Brooke just sticks her hands in the pockets of her shorts and sways back and forth on the heels of her bright red Converse.

"Wow, Siobhan, so harsh!" she chimes. "Maybe I just don't want to look like Pikachu?"

Rich Elizabeth giggles, I wince so hard I poke myself in the eye with my straw, and Siobhan's face turns two whole beetroots redder. Siobhan does *not* like to be laughed at—something

that caused havoc during her stand-up routine at the school talent show last year.

"ENOUGH!" she explodes furiously. "Do not reference something as nerd-soaked as Pokémon here! This is an invite-only event and, now that I think about it, YOU weren't invited. Fact! So hitch up those ridiculous shorts of yours and LEAVE!"

Brooke's smile fades as everyone in the room draws breath—and, in the dingy corner, Zanna catches my eye and draws a line across her throat with her finger. An unhelpfully visual reminder of Siobhan's capabilities. But then like a low-budget horror movie, the front door crashes open, and silhouetted against the glow of the porch light is . . .

"Morgan!" I gasp.

Now, I like to think I have *some* dignity, despite Zanna once telling me that I have "about as much dignity as a donkey in dungarees." Really, I should be fumigating. Morgan is two hours late! However, she's also goose-level gorgeous and divine. She wears glasses with über-cool green frames and has pale blue eyes, as well as the most adorable constellation of freckles across her nose. Her thick, dark hair is thick and dark, and she has the dreamiest Irish accent. I don't stand a chance!

Rushing over, I pepper her with kisses and jump into her arms like I'm in a Hollywood Movie. Then, once we've made sure her shoulder isn't dislocated, I drag her inside.

"Hey, everyone," says Morgan, but the atmosphere is about as well hidden as a Pisces's unrequited crush, and she tenses at once. "What's happening? Why so quiet? I feel like a vegan who's just walked into a cannibal convention."

"Nothing's 'happening,' Mogs," snaps Siobhan. "Apart from YOU being five decades late! I'm just telling Brooke she has to leave because she's not wearing yellow."

Morgan snorts a laugh. Then her smile freezes. "Wait. Are you actually serious? Siobhan, it's a birthday party. Who cares about the theme?"

I almost choke. WHO CARES?! Siobhan's themes are ULTRA-serious. For her recent witch-themed Halloween, she locked her little sister, Niamh, in an actual cage for three days and only fed her gingerbread, just to get into character. She's even been blacklisted by the National Trust for bringing a bow and arrow to a deer park for her Cupid on Valentine's Day Date.

I try to tell Morgan with my eyes to let this one go, but then, oh horror of horrors, Morgan actually smiles at Brooke! "Green looks good on you," she says. "It's actually my favorite color. Are you a Libra? I'm getting a vibe . . ."

Brooke gasps. "Girl, I literally *am* a Libra!"

Siobhan is not used to being overruled. She goggles in disbelief, then claps her hands. "Enough! SILENCE! This is MY party and MY house and rules are RULES! Morgan, stop talking about Libras. Brooke, you need to go!"

Brooke opens her mouth, but Morgan holds up a finger. "Don't go anywhere, Brooke," she says, stepping up to Siobhan. Gooseberries, we're in a Western! "Forgive me if I'm wrong, Siobhan, but isn't this Cat's party? Surely, it's up to her if Brooke should go."

I gargle in shock. Does my girlfriend *want* to see me strung up like a fresh salami?! You don't defy Siobhan Deidre Collingdale! She's the Queen of Queen's and has the eyelash extensions

to prove it. Rebellion is definitely *not* on the checklist of Siobhan Conversation Topics from slide thirty-one of my PowerPoint.

I flap my lips about in panic. "Um, I . . . Well, she's not, um, she isn't wearing, you know, um, yellow, I guess? But, well, er, you know, party! Right? Ahem . . ."

Even Brooke, who I know for a fact is bizarre enough to have uploaded a Blu Tack sculpting tutorial onto YouTube, looks confused. I grin around the group like an absolute noodle-brain (which I am) but Siobhan doesn't waver for a second.

"Exactly," she pounces. "Not wearing yellow—you heard. Brooke can leave!"

Then Morgan does the craziest thing. She opens her leather trench coat (which is so cool, it could easily put me in a cool coma) and reveals a yellow tank top. Then she grabs it with both hands and rips the bottom half clean off.

As I swoon at the sight of Morgan's pierced belly button, everyone else goes silent (except Ariana Grande, who carries on wailing like some sort of heartbroken ghost through Siobhan's nightclub-size surround-sound speakers).

"Oh, *gasp*," Rich Elizabeth says.

Morgan ties half her top around Brooke's neck, then steps back to admire her handiwork.

"See?" she says as I gaze in astonishment. "She's in yellow. So, is there still a problem, Siobhan, or are you going to admit that this has nothing to do with dress codes and everything to do with snobbery and prejudice? Not everyone can afford a whole new outfit just for some lavish party."

"Don't be absurd!" Siobhan exclaims as I consider whether being strung up like a salami might actually be better than being

here for this conversation. "Prejudiced against what? Redheads?! I have red-haired friends! My cousin even *married* a redhead! Anyway, if you're not invited, you don't have to buy anything! And Brooke was NOT invited. CASE CLOSED!"

Then she reaches across and yanks the scarf off Brooke's neck. Unfortunately, Morgan's got a bit of a knack for knots, so Brooke jolts toward her, yells, "Oi, get off me!" then grabs the golden jug of cranberry juice and throws it all down Siobhan's yellow dress.

Even the patio spray-painting falls silent. Brooke drops the plastic jug with a clatter. Siobhan's yellow McQueen dress is DRIPPING with red, and liquid dribbles down her legs onto the shining floorboards.

Then, oh my Aphrodite above, I see Brooke's lips curve into a smile.

"Damn, Siobhan," she says, nodding to the stain. "Would you like to borrow a tampon?"

It's like a stick of dynamite just went off in Siobhan's knickers. (If she *was* wearing a tampon, it would shoot right out of her.) "GET OUT!" she shrieks, face contorting with apoplectic rage. "GET OUT RIGHT NOW! OH MY ACTUAL WOODEN CLOGS, MY DRESS! MY FREAKING SQUEAKING DRESS!"

Brooke doesn't need telling twice. Or indeed fifteen times, since Siobhan is now just yelling "GET OUT!" repeatedly. Brooke runs so fast, you'd think the house was on fire—and it soon might be if Siobhan gets any angrier. Girls in yellow cluster round, a flustered hive of support, but Siobhan has transformed from Queen Bee into Empress Wasp.

Kenna Brown, Siobhan's Most Loyal Leo Disciple, buzzes to

Siobhan's side while Sporty Habiba Qadir fans the stain energetically with a napkin. I stare at Morgan, wondering what in the name of Aphrodite's Sacred Goose just happened.

"Um . . . happy birthday, by the way?" Morgan says. She even throws in some tragic jazz hands as she says it. I may as well have stayed in with Mum.

•★.✦˙★•

After Siobhan's been carried upstairs on a makeshift stretcher, I retreat to the backyard and sit with my head in my hands. What was Morgan thinking?! This was supposed to be the first time we'd all get along. Why does she have to be such a savior?!

Zanna Szczechowska crosses the lawn and perches beside me on the wall. "How's it going, my useless blond friend?" she asks with her usual Slavic sarcasm. "At least your girlfriend showed up . . . eventually."

"Yes, she did," I reply, still bent double. "And it was a disaster. Didn't you see ANYTHING that just happened?! Siobhan is never going to let Morgan sit with us at lunch on Monday now!"

"What gave you that impression?" Zanna asks.

I sit up and frown. "Possibly the way Siobhan yelled at her, 'NEVER LOOK AT ME AGAIN, YOU GREEN-HAIRED FREAK' and then Morgan went home early?"

"Ah," says Zanna. "Yes, that's not very encouraging." We sit like silent salamanders for a few moments. Then Zanna says, "I think you need to have a conversation, Cat. Morgan was super late to your pottery-making date last week . . ."

I sigh in sad agreement. "All she had time to make was the handle for my mug . . . But, Zanna, the handle is arguably the most useful part!"

"And it's also arguably not," Zanna retorts. "And I don't buy her excuse, that she had a friendship crisis. Like, in my opinion, her friends aren't nearly interesting enough to have actual crises. And she didn't show up to Alison's Valentine's Day disco at all!"

I roll my eyes. "Because she doesn't take part in hetero-normative capitalism!"

"Does she take part in prioritizing her girlfriend?" Zanna says, raising an eyebrow. I sit there with a frowny face, and eventually Zanna just nudges me. "Sorry, okay? I want to like your girlfriend. Whoever you date, don't worry. I'll be here." She sighs sadly. "Good grief, I need a life . . ."

Gooseberries galore. Is she trying to make me feel worse?!

Then Zanna says, "Seriously, Clown, it's going to be fine. We'll handle Siobhan together like we always have. She'll have other two-thousand-pound dresses. Anyway, it's your birthday. Let's go back inside and dance. The floor will be nice and clear with everyone upstairs."

I am reminded that sometimes Zanna isn't the worst person after all. She could even be the best person, actually. A true Polish paradox. We head back in, arm in arm, and dad-dance all around the overturned tables and chairs until the neighbors arrive, asking if we need them to call us an ambulance.

WHAT YOU NEED TO KNOW ABOUT SIOBHAN DEIDRE COLLINGDALE

- She is a Scorpio, not to be confused with a scorpion. Although now that I mention it, she did once put stinging nettles in her dad's slippers when he told her she was being "unrealistic" asking for a private jet for Christmas.
- The *B* in her name stands for "Better Than You," but it's silent because: "Even if you know you're better than everyone else, you should be modest about it." —Siobhan, at her primary school graduation
- No, she hasn't noticed that her boyfriend is called Dale Collins while her surname is Collingdale. So, for safety, we call him Dale the Pale instead. We really hope this isn't why he started using fake tan.
- She likes to talk about clothes, money, "necking," clothes, Kate Middleton, hair, fashion, clothes, and also clothes. In eighth grade, she actually opened a clothes bank—Siobhanchy—at the local food bank when she was trying to impress a twelfth grader, Socialist Simon. He went official with Leftist Lakshita in the end, but Siobhan still gives styling lessons there: "Chiffon with Siobhan."
- She's not afraid of anything! A COM (Creepy Old Man) once wolf-whistled Lip Gloss Lizzie on a night out, and Siobhan still has his tooth. In fact, she had it beaded onto a friendship bracelet.
- She has more mood swings than an actual mood in an actual swing, but you should probably blame her Gemini Moon for that.

2
Head Girls Galore

Even though my disastrous birthday was yesterday, today Mum decides to make everything worse and bake me a horrendous cake. Not a good idea at all when you're internationally respected as the Worst Cook Ever. She even tries getting creative, which, considering she's a banker, is as risky rainclouds and unfortunate as it sounds. She scribbles an upside-down triangle with arms and claims she's drawn Elsa from *Frozen*.

"She's your favorite princess, isn't she?" Mum asks.

"Not if she looks like that." I grimace. "Where's her face?"

Then my thirteen-year-old eco-evangelist sister, Luna, approaches the island counter. Our house, the iPhone Box, is modern and open-plan, with so many floor-to-ceiling windows, I sometimes think we might as well forget the house completely and live in the backyard. Everything is visible from everywhere: an absolute hide-and-seek tragedy. I did try to burn it to the ground last year (accidentally . . . I think) with hair straighteners, but woe alas, my parents redid EVERYTHING the same. If anything, the glisteningly new voice-control shower makes it even MORE futuristiculous and infuriating than before.

Luna says, "Did you make Cat's cake vegan?"

I roll my eyes. If Luna becomes more vegan than she already is, she'll start growing grass out of her armpits. But Mum beams away and says that of course she did. I suppose I should be relieved. The less for me, the better.

"Why have you drawn the Bermuda Triangle on it though?" Luna asks, and I snort.

"Oh, Luna, honestly!" Mum chuckles. "It's Elsa from *Frozen*—can't you tell? Anyway, who wants the first slice? It's a completely new recipe I got from Fran."

Luna and I exchange fearful glances. I'm about to ask if Fran could have just made the cake herself. She may have given birth to my absolutely tragic ex-boyfriend, Jamie Owusu, but she's great in the kitchen, whereas the only recipe Mum could successfully follow is one for DISASTER.

Luckily, at this precise moment, the doorbell rings, and the expression "saved by the bell" takes on a whole new meaning, practically spiritual, in fact. I cannonball to the door and there, on the gravel pathway, is Morgan with an enormous bouquet of bright pink roses.

My Wildly Aquarius Instincts instantly urge me to dance about like a dallying daffodil in tap shoes: my über-groovy girlfriend has SHOWN UP AT MY HOUSE uninvited, with flowers. Surely, mature adult relationships don't get much better than that?! I am being wooed to Wuhan and back again. It's really very exciting.

Thank Aphrodite that my Mercury is in Pisces to hold me back though, because I am *definitely* still displeased from last

night. I fold my arms and fix Morgan with my most aloof look.

Morgan says, "Why are you doing that with your face?"

So my expressions clearly need work, but I am still aloof at heart. "I don't know, Morgan," I reply, cool as mozzarella. "Maybe because I'm slightly annoyed about yesterday? What were you thinking, ripping your top up like that?! You know Siobhan thinks damaging clothes is a crime against her spiritual essence! And you were so late as well! Like . . . *so*. You know? So, so, so—"

"Yes, I get it," Morgan interjects. "So. Look, I know the party didn't go as planned . . ." Definitely true. It was *planned* to be a beautiful kumbaya night of soul-bonding, and instead ended with Siobhan locking Dale in her closet for saying that Morgan seemed cool. "And I'm sorry I was late. I had to rewrite my psychology essay. Mum accidentally deleted it when ordering sports bras, which is . . . pretty miraculous, to be honest. How do you delete a file when doing a basic online order?"

"Well, she is over forty," I assure her, and Morgan shrugs in agreement. "But, Morgan, Siobhan was really trying to be friendly. And that's shockingly rare for a Scorpio."

Morgan doesn't look convinced. "Friendly?" she repeats. "Cat, she was literally throwing someone out as I arrived! I know Brooke's got a bit of a reputation, but she still deserves respect. I think she was really upset."

I snort a laugh. "Morgan, the only thing that upsets Brooke is CCTV! Alison says Brooke is the reason the *Antiques Roadshow* won't come here anymore! When she found out Kenna knows sign language, she said 'Me too' and gave her the finger! And

according to Habiba, her dog is actually a fox with a black spot spray-painted on."

"Babe." Morgan slides her arms around my waist, which would be perfectly romantic if she weren't holding a bunch of roses. The thorns go right through my leggings. But brief pain aside: gorgeous! "Didn't people say I was banned from Starbucks when I showed up? That wasn't true . . . as that private detective Siobhan hired wrote in his report."

I cough awkwardly. "I'm still very sorry about that. She said she wanted to check you were 'worthy,' but I really didn't realize she'd actually . . . !"

Morgan puts a finger over my lips. "All good, babe. But what I mean is, how do you *know* Brooke is really so bad? She might be cool. I'm only saying give her a chance."

I let out a nervous laugh. "Steady on, Morgan. Soon you'll be telling me you've asked her to sit with us at lunch next week!" Morgan doesn't laugh and I gawp back. Sappho-NO. Siobhan will KILL us! "You . . . You didn't do that, did you?"

"I don't want her to feel left out after the party!" Morgan implores as I groan and deflate like a leaky air mattress. "Besides, I need to buddy up more because guess what? I'm thinking of running for Head Girl. Maja talked me into it. How would you feel about that?"

Relieved is how I would feel. (The current Head Girl is Zariyah Al-Asiri, who's never quite forgiven me for nearly killing everyone at her charity cupcake sale. In my defense, that rat poison looked *really* similar to chocolate sprinkles.) But I am also excited!

"Morgan!" I gasp, grabbing both her hands. "You're going to be Head Girl?! That's amazing! Would that make me, like, First Lady?!"

Morgan smiles. "I guess. Although you're *my* first lady already, so . . ."

Oh my giddy Greek uncles, my legs instantly turn to seaweed. We begin a smoochathon right there on the doorstep and we only pause because Mum comes elbowing about, annoyingly offering me a vase for my flowers. Can't she see I'm busy?!

We escape upstairs and do a lot more kissing there, which is as groovy grapes as it sounds, rolling all over my bed. Well, we roll *off* the bed onto the floor at one point, but apart from that, it's all very wonderful. Morgan roughs up her hair, then smiles down at me like Aphrodite herself, and my insides disintegrate. My girlfriend is truly, truly beautiful and she smells of dark cherries. How in the name of Hayley Kiyoko can I stay mad?

"I would be mad," says Zanna on Monday at break. "If my girlfriend showed up two hours late to my birthday, then got into a fight, I'd be very mad. I can't believe you've forgiven her already."

"Yes," I reply. "But, Zanna, you've never *had* a girlfriend. Or even a boyfriend for that matter. You cannot understand the complexities of a mature adult relationship like mine. She got me flowers! Really nice, expensive ones. I checked with Dad, and he says expensive flowers always make everything okay."

"I'd rather have the money," Zanna replies.

I smile warmly at my inexperienced sapling of a friend. "Of course you would, Zanzibar, I believe that of you." We are in

the school library studying our French verbs. Which means that Zanna is painting my nails and I am telling her about my amazing afternoon with Morgan, who is soon going to be Head Girl and highly, highly important. Every time the ick-dripping librarian, Miss Bull, glances over, I hastily cover what we're doing with my textbook.

Mrs. Bullock has had a vendetta against me since the beginning of time. Well, since she caught me stealing Escape keys off the library computers for my "There Is No Escape" art project anyway. She's basically a bullfrog in a beige cardigan and keeps glaring at me like I'm doing something I shouldn't. Which I am, but it's still very annoying.

"Perhaps I should get a boyfriend," says Zanna, applying a second coat to my pinkie finger. "Then I can be a relationship guru as well. What would you say then?"

"I'd ask if he'd recently had his eyes tested," I tell Zanna, and she intentionally spills polish onto my hand. I think I'm being rather hilarious though.

Then Zanna pauses her painting. "Good grief. Is that Siobhan?"

I'm about to ask Zanna if she needs *her* eyes tested, as I don't think Siobhan has ever set foot in a library. She once said that reading is for "ugly loners," which didn't go down well, considering she said it to Miss Jamison, our English teacher. But I look over my shoulder and see that Zanna is correct! Siobhan is with Kenna, over by the printers.

"Siobhan!" I call. "What the fandango are you doing here?!"

Siobhan whirls round, glaring. "Christ on a bike, Cat! What is this—Prime Minister's Question Time!?" The printer churns out a few sheets of paper, which Siobhan swipes, nearly slitting

Kenna's throat in the process. "I'm running for Head Girl, if you must know," she announces, flapping the papers at me. "I needed to print out some forms. Trust me, you wouldn't catch me in this nerd cemetery for any other reason."

Kenna signs excitedly at Siobhan as my stomach drops like a wingless pigeon.

"It's going to be so much fun!" Kenna squeaks out loud, which is not true in the slightest. Plucking out my eyelashes with a pair of tweezers would be more fun than this will be. "Maybe Cat can help design your campaign posters?"

Siobhan splutters. "Politics isn't *fun*, Kenna! I'm only doing this because there's no other obvious candidate. I practically run this place anyway; I may as well make it official." Then she frowns and looks back at me. "Although that's not the worst idea. Cat, you can do arty stuff. It's pretty much your only talent."

I want to tell her that's not strictly true—I'm also a very good kisser! But I'm not sure that would help much with Siobhan's campaign, and I'm too busy being flustered to say it. Staring at the wall in horror, I try to read the posters pinned there to calm my panicking brain.

JOIN THE ARABIC SOCIETY TODAY!

AUDITIONS NOW OPEN FOR THE SCHOOL PLAY!

NEED HELP? ASK ABOUT COUNSELING SERVICES AT RECEPTION

(Counseling is the *least* I'm going to need.)

Siobhan can't run for Head Girl as well as Morgan! I'll have Head Girls galore pouring out of my ears until after Easter, when they elect them, then for the whole of next year, I'll have to put

up with either Morgan or Siobhan hating that the other has won.

I'm so busy being sucked into a wormhole of despair, Zanna answers for me. "Cat might have a problem . . ." she begins warily.

Zanna may have made the understatement of the millennium. Anne Boleyn getting arrested for high treason in May 1536 had less of a problem than I am having now. This is a Marie-Antoinette-baking-brownies-level disaster! How will I ever keep the peace?!

"What," snaps Siobhan, nostrils already flaring, "could possibly be more important than supporting your best friend in a vital political campaign?!"

"Cat can't," says Zanna. "Because—"

"Because I'm going to be super busy with *this*!" I cry before Zanna can spill the bamboo and truly roast my rhubarbs. Leaping out of my chair, I slap my hands onto the poster wall.

There's a pause. They all stare like stick insects.

"You're in the Arabic Society?" asks Kenna doubtfully, and I look at the poster.

Gooseberries. There's no way I can pull off that one.

"Um, no," I stutter, sliding my hands to the next poster. "I'm doing this! Um, yes, I'm auditioning for the school play. So I'm afraid I can't help much with your campaign, Siobhan. Um, sorry?"

Over Siobhan's shoulder, Zanna hangs her head in her hands.

Group Chat: The Gang

Siobhan, 7:35 p.m.:
Kenna has signed up TWENTY-TWO new supporters for my campaign. What have YOU guys done?! You've had TWO ENTIRE HOURS! GET MOVING!!!

Habiba, 7:37 p.m.:
Babe that's not fair, Kenna's been to a DEAF SOCIAL! They're not Queen's students, they can't even vote!!! I got five signatures at tennis, that's #GOALS!!!

Siobhan, 7:38 p.m.:
DID FIVE VOTES HELP HILLARY CLINTON???

Habiba, 7:39 p.m.:
Who??

Zanna, 7:39 p.m.:
Oh boy

Siobhan, 7:40 p.m.:
NO HABIBA THEY DID NOT. I WANT TWENTY-FIVE SIGNATURES FROM YOU ON MY DESK TOMORROW. QUESTIONS?

Zanna, 7:41 p.m.:
You have a desk?

Pisces SEASON

3

Frilly Hunting Hunt's Up Day

It's officially Alison Bridgewater sea— I mean, PISCES Season: the end of the zodiac year. According to the great starry sky and my handy-pandy *Bible to the Stars*, I should wake up feeling that all my wisdom has cultivated. Or was it culminated? Honestly, it could be candelabra'd for all I know, because I don't feel wise in the slightest!

I walk to school feeling sick to my stomach—and not just because Luna is squirreling on about adding kale soup to the lunch menu as part of her Vegan Meals Initiative. I have to audition for the play today! Unfortunately, I do have to go; Siobhan decided that a friend in the drama crowd could "nail a key demographic," so she made me sign up on the spot.

"Maybe I should just explain to them about my Virgo Moon," I tell my sister desperately. "It's where *all* my anxiety comes from.

It's out of my control, Luna! Not even Siobhan would make me do this if she understood the true burden of a Virgo Moon . . ."

"I wouldn't worry," Luna replies. "You'll probably only be playing a tree or something. Everyone else would have to die in a plane crash for anyone to give *you* a serious role."

"Thank you, Luna," I snap. "That's so helpful."

"Although you're taking a risk . . ." Luna muses. "Beginning something new on the brink of the Vernal Equinox. Really, you're asking for trouble."

My eyes widen. "On the brink of what?!"

"We're reaching the intersection of the celestial equator," Luna informs me, which doesn't sound dandy at all. "One of two points a year where day and night are equally long. It's a time for endings, not beginnings." Then she frowns. "Although actually, I might be getting confused with the *Autumnal* Equinox. In which case, it's the perfect time to be doing this."

I'm positively hair-yanking from stress by this point. Since when did astrology get so complicated?! I grab her by the shoulders. "Which is it? I have to audition today, Luna!"

"Stop shaking me!" Luna protests, breaking free. "I'm not a rattlesnake! I can't remember, okay? But you could take one of my crystals for good luck."

I glare at her. "Are you serious? Do I *look* like I'd believe in all that rubbish?!"

With Luna's Lucky Green Aventurine firmly in my hand, I peer through the door into the drama studios. There aren't many people, so that's good. But I can see Miss Spencer—who I once overheard Mrs. Warren call "an excitable young thing," and who

teaches drama and dance—already springing about the place like a runner bean, clapping her hands like an overstimulated otter. Yikes on a yo-yo.

I try to reason with myself. It's only a school play. It can't be that bad . . .

Then I hear Miss Spencer say, "I'm so excited! *Romeo and Juliet* is hands down one of my FAVORITE plays! Now, everyone take a script . . ."

Le gasp. *Romeo and Juliet*? That's Shakespeare! I decide it really *can* be that bad after all. This cannot be the place for me, no matter the equinox. Did I really think this would be better than helping Siobhan paint a few posters?! I back away from the door . . .

. . . and moonwalk right into someone, and nearly skin out of my sweater. "Gooseberries!"

I whirl round and find myself slap-bang-staring at Brooke the Crook. Her blue eyes are wide and amused, glittering like there are dolphins inside her. One half of her shirt is untucked and her tie looks, well, backward. Her hair is falling all over the place and doesn't look like it's seen a brush in seven million years. Morgan must be joking if she thinks a gold-blooded vixen of school society like myself can be friends with Brooke!

"Um, Brooke!" I yelp. "Are you here for the play? I was just leaving, actually . . ."

"Of course I'm here for the play!" Brooke links her arm with mine and barrels through the doors with me still attached. "Miss Spencer, Cat's auditioning for the play!" she announces. "Isn't that cat-tastic? I'm friends with her girlfriend now."

I begin to splutter in protest—mainly at Brooke saying "cat-tastic"—but Miss Spencer has already cartwheeled over to greet

us, looking more excited than a Tic-Tac-on-tacos sandwich. Before I know what's hit me, Miss Spencer has: with a printed script. It hurts. As I rub my arm, she rages on about golden opportunities and blossoming talent and it's too late now.

I sit with Brooke and pray to Aphrodite that none of Siobhan's informers are about. Chatting in the corridor with Brooke Mackenzie?! She'd have my teeth for cupcake toppings! I scan for likely snitches, and of course, Rich Elizabeth is here . . . She's a drama queen in more ways than one. She'll probably be high-heel-shoed right into the role of Juliet.

Luckily, Miss Spencer immediately launches into the auditions so Brooke doesn't have the chance to chatter at me. She's very oddballs bizarre and keeps smirking to herself, like she's giggling at her own internal voice-over . . .

Quite aside from Siobhan finding out about Brooke, what about Morgan finding out about me, doing this? Two of her Triple M Friends are here: Maja and Marcus. Maja gives me suspicious eye, which is rather Eeky-McFreaky. I really, really, *really* wish I'd thought this through. Like, even a little!

"Cat!" Miss Spencer yaps, and I jump in my seat. I glance over my shoulder but, unfortunately, I am the only Cat here. "You're up!" Miss Spencer beams, giving me two thumbs up as I drown in a brief wave of dithering dizziness.

"Um, about that . . ." I splutter, crumpling the script in my sweaty-spaghetti hands.

Before I can successfully excuse myself, Brooke leaps to her feet. "Me and Cat can audition together, Miss! Her girlfriend really stuck up for me over the weekend, and the last time someone did that, I was in court and it was literally their job, so it really meant so much. Helping is really the LEAST I can do!"

I stare at Brooke like Kate Bush looking in your window-oh-oh. What in Moomintroll's biscuit box does she think she's doing?! To my utter shock and horror, Miss Spencer gasps in delight. "How wonderful! I'd love to see that, girls! Go ahead!"

"But, Miss, I didn't actually—!" I begin, but Brooke has already grabbed my hand and teleported us to the front. She swipes my script and flips to a page in the middle as I hop about like a bunny on a pogo stick.

"You read Juliet," she says. "And I'll read Romeo."

"Brooke!" I hiss. "I really don't think—"

"It was the lark!" cries Brooke, and I'm so stunned, I actually go silent. "The herald of the morn . . . No nightingale! Look, love, what envious streaks?" Then Brooke does the craziest thing. She dives for the umbrella stand in the corner, where all these old props are lounging about like eleventh graders, and draws a full-blown SWORD.

I've no idea what envious streaks are, but I *am* more than a little anxious at Brooke having a weapon! She babbles passionately through several lines, then pokes the sword right at me. I squeal in fright, then realize it's Juliet's turn to speak and I *literally* have a knife to my throat. I grip my script with shaking hands and scan the page. Clearly Shakespeare was some sort of froth-mouthed fool because none of it makes any sense!

Then Brooke traces my collarbones with the sword. My life expectancy is literally plummeting like dropped fruitcake, so I open my mouth to say something, anything . . .

"Um, yon light is n-not daylight!" I stutter. "I know! Um, it's

a meteor the sun exhales, like, I mean, *to be* the night's torch-bear, and light the way to, um—Mantua?"

And I've done it. My first-ever lines of Shakespeare.

"Let me be put to death!" shrieks Brooke, whirling the sword. I yelp and duck as the blade slices the air above my head, then my ankle cracks and I fall to my knees! Brooke points the sword to my throat and carries on threatening death (Romeo's? Juliet's? *Mine?*) as I shiver all of my timbers at once.

Juggling the script, I blurt out, "Be gone away! Um, it's the lark that sings out of tune . . ."

My heart is hammering like a blacksmith competition. There's something about sweets, something about toads. I'm dropping words and lines all over the place, but can you blame me?! I'm practically speaking Ancient Greek! Or is this Latin? Then Brooke swipes the sword away and I practically somer-sault to my feet to avoid total decapitation.

"AND NOW I WOULD SAY THEY CHANGED VOICES TOO!" I squeal. "SINCE ARM AND ARM DOTH US A FRILLY HUNTING HUNT'S UP DAY." Brooke dives toward me and I sidestep her, whirling like a Frisbee. Then we're both yelling about light, Brooke chasing me gallivantingly around the stage.

Finally, she drops the sword with a clatter, grinning like a pixie. I feel like I've just had an out-of-body experience. Then I remember I'm standing in front of an entire class of drama nerds having just butchered their literal king and, unfortunately, I'm very much *in* my body.

"Ta-da!" I go.

Everyone looks absolutely shell-shocked. Maja keeps leafing

through the script, like she's trying to work out what I was actually reading. Posh Josh O'Conner is frozen mid-sandwich-bite, too stunned to notice hummus dripping into his lap.

Well, I knew I wasn't amazing. But you'd hope for at least a clap!

Then Miss Spencer springs to her feet and, to my ultimate bafflement, her face is absolute fireworks.

"Girls!" she gasps, clasping her hands together. "That was absolutely marvelous!" She pirouettes to face the group. "When I say I want energy, that's what I'm talking about! Such passion! Incredible work, girls—I'm so impressed!"

Impressed?! I don't want Miss Spencer to be impressed! I want her to think I'm so rubbish, I could only play a tree or rock. Speaking of which . . . I reach into my pocket and feel Luna's lucky crystal.

Then I blame Luna. LUCK?! I'm almost headless, *and* I have to sit through snooze-fest auditions for the rest of lunch. Shakespeare must have been boring as beeswax. Probably a Taurus.

WHAT YOU NEED TO KNOW ABOUT ALISON BRIDGEWATER

- She's very good at being artistic and says things like "I'm very interested in the Baroque." I think she's serious as well. Her bedroom is covered in postcards of Renaissance and Art Deco and postmodernist paintings. She wants to go to art school and I think she should absolutely Van Gogh for it.
- She's very good at crying. Absolutely everything makes Alison weep, whether it's seeing a bird pat another bird on the back with its wing (sixth grade), treading on a dandelion by mistake (seventh grade), or me trying to beatbox (eighth grade). Okay, so that last one was more crying *with laughter*, but is there really a massive difference? It's all because she's a Pisces anyway.
- She's currently into . . . Tall Adam? Hmm. Maybe that was last week. She has mentioned Brown-Haired James a few times. Or was that Off-Limits-Because-He's-Siobhan's-Ex Chidi? Sigh. It's hard to keep up . . .
- She truly believes *Alice in Wonderland* is actually called *Alison Wonderland* and none of us have the heart to tell her.
- I absolutely am over my crush on her, which is good as she's too boy crazy for me. Since Boyfriend Uno, she's dazzled through SIX relationships, and I don't fancy joining the support group because it's in the boys' changing rooms.

4

A Very Complicated Game of Musical Tables

I'm very ready to forget all about Brooke the Crook once my horrendous auditioning is over. So imagine my absolute aghast-edness when I'm walking through the playground at lunch the next day and Morgan calls, "I just heard what you did for Brooke!"

She's leaning gorgeously and recklessly against a garbage bin, which sends me into utter swoon-buckets of swooning. I scurry over and kiss her cheek.

"Hey," I say, already Dopey-McSoapy. "What are you doing here?"

"I was looking for you," Morgan says, linking her fingers through mine as my body turns to jelly. "Brooke told me at break how you auditioned with her for the play? That's so sweet of you, after our conversation over the weekend."

I do a sort of grin-grimace. Hmm. I *could* tell Morgan that

I absolutely did not audition for Brooke's sorry sake, but who would that help? Morgan looks happy, so maybe it wouldn't be *so* bad to . . . you know. Slightly play along.

"That's okay!" I chime as Aphrodite face-palms. "Like you said, we don't want anybody to get left out. Which was *obviously* why I was auditioning." I hasty-laugh. "Anyway, why don't we talk about something else? Like, um . . . Uzbekistan?"

I really am very smooth. I'm basically a marble! Morgan nods slowly. "Um . . . For sure. Or we could head to the cafeteria? I wondered if you wanted to get lunch together."

I gasp. "Like a lunch date?"

"More like a campaign meeting, actually," Morgan replies, full of enthusiasm, and my excitement splats to the floor like a wet tissue. "I really want to run through one of my ideas with you. What do you think of a buddy scheme? You and Brooke would be a great example. Imagine how it would break down the cliques?"

Then she distracts me by doing something very swoony and vulnerable: she takes my hand!

"It would really have helped me when I was new here. Like, before I had you?" She smiles and I become a goo factory. "It was difficult, finding friends. My last school was . . . not great, and I'd love to think I could change that for other people."

Still hand in hand, we drift through a group of gawping sixth graders. I don't blame them: this is Kent. A real-life lesbian sighting is rarer than, I don't know, a Scottish person. And that is really rare.

In fact, it's about as rare as I would like conversations about me becoming friends with Brooke to be. But how can I say

"ABSOLUTELY-NOTOLUTELY" when Morgan Delaney is finally being vulnerable with me?!

"It's a great idea, Morgan," I tell her eventually. "And hopefully you will have many other ideas as well—who knows which ideas you shall end up actually using?"

Aside from being a goo factory, I'm also an idea factory, so I assure Morgan of my creativity. I've written three entire fan fiction novels about Elsa marrying Rapunzel, after all. One commenter even said that my writing was "of shocking quality"!

Strangely, Morgan doesn't seem convinced, but she doesn't get a chance to say so because we walk into the cafeteria and spot the entire gang AND Lip Gloss Lizzie's Girl Brigade occupying the table in the very middle of the room. There's Alison, Zanna, Habiba, Kenna, many various boyfriends, and Siobhan using a sixth grader as a footstool.

"Is she allowed to do that?" Morgan murmurs.

"Um . . ." I go as Alison spots me. So much for Morgan's campaign meeting.

"Cat!" she calls, then her eyes flicker to Morgan, and her smile freezes. Morgan quickly drops my hand. Alison gathers herself though, hopping up in a heat wave of curly dark hair and brown eyes. "And Morgan is with you!" she says, which is more a statement of fact than a welcome, really, despite her sunbeam. "Why don't you *both* come sit with us?"

"Well, actually . . ." begins Morgan, but I regrip her hand with conviction. This is what we wanted after all: the perfect second chance for Morgan and my friends! Lunch has been a very complicated game of musical tables recently, as I dither between sitting with my girlfriend or my girl friends. Some days,

I've had to eat two entire lunches to avoid upsetting anyone. Which I'm not *complaining* about—two lunches means two desserts—but even so!

"We'll just buy our food!" I chime as I yank Morgan toward the sandwiches.

To stop Morgan from feeling left out, I buy the exact same sandwich as her, which is wonderful in theory, but Morgan buys a sandwich with *tuna*. Ironically for someone called Cat, I loathe fish. Seafood should remain in the sea—far, far away from my taste buds. Oh, the things we do for love!

The first thing that happens when we sit down is that Siobhan says, "Hello, Mogs. Nice to see your clothes are in one piece today." So we're already off to a bad start.

Morgan doesn't even say hello back! Just opens her sandwich while we watch her like silent salamanders. Or perhaps awkward alligators.

I laugh manically. "Me and Morgan were just talking about . . ." Then I trail off, because cringe-jingling galore, I actually can't remember! I blink at my girlfriend, but she's being about as useful as a white crayon. My throat bubbles in panic and my eyes dart to her unwrapped sandwich. "About fish!"

Morgan frowns. Across the table, Zanna shakes her head in despair and Siobhan's eyes widen like she's swallowed a live anchovy. Luckily, I still have Alison onside, who will do literally anything to avoid an awkward silence. She once panic-sang "Good as Hell" by Lizzo in the middle of an English mock exam.

"Wow!" says Alison, beaming between Morgan and me. "That's . . . so unusual!"

"Not really," I blurt desperately. This is going so badly!

Why the freshly battered fish-fingers did Morgan have to buy tuna?! When I try to think of words, all I see is aquatic life-forms swimming about. "We talk about fishing a lot. It's a passion of Morgan's!"

"It is?" asks Morgan, but I flap my fins at her to hush. I've totally got this.

"We are thinking of going fishing on Salmonday. I mean, on Saturday!" I blunder on. "If any of you would like to join us, let me know! It's great for, um, team building!"

"Fishing?" repeats Lip Gloss Lizzie. She's sitting in Gloss-Guzzling Lawrence's lap, who looks equally confused. Goldfish-level confused, actually. "Good for team building how?"

"I would love to go fishing!" announces Habiba, startling us all. "I always go scuba diving when I'm visiting family in Morocco—"

Luckily, Siobhan interjects. "Don't be so BASIC, Habiba! There's nothing Instagrammable about fishing; it's for trout-brained old men. Besides, I'm going to be über-occupied on Saturday, writing my Head Girl Manifesto with Kenna."

"Oh . . ." says Kenna, like a nervous minnow. "Siobhan, I did actually mention—remember my cousin's wedding . . . ?"

Siobhan glares at her. "Mamma mia, Kenna, can we stay on topic?!" Then she turns to me, completely ignoring the manic fish-gutting signals I'm giving her to SHUSH UP RIGHT NOW. "Can you help with the posters, Cat, or not?" she demands. "I can't imagine some loser-convention school play would take up *all* your time. Alison is doing some!"

From the look on Alison's face, I think that's the first she's heard of it, but I am equally floundering and useless. This is not

how I wanted Morgan to find out! I glance to Morgan, squeamish as a squid. She's giving me a very unimpressed raised eyebrow. I bury my nose in my tuna sandwich, which is a whole hammer-headed trauma in itself.

"You're running for Head Girl, Siobhan?" asks Morgan nonchalantly as I close my eyes in silent prayer to the Great Piscean Sky.

"Obviously," retorts Siobhan, tossing back her cod-brown hair. "Why?!"

"Well, I'm running, too," Morgan replies, smiling sweetly. "Didn't you know? So if Cat's going to be helping anyone, it's me: her girlfriend."

I slowly look up from my sandwich. Everyone is gawping at me, and probably not just because I've got mayonnaise all over my nose.

"So . . ." I mumble, meek as a mackerel. "Is that a *no* to fishing on Saturday?"

After the cafeteria debacle, I'm not in the swimmiest of spirits and neither is Morgan. She's clearly still offended that Siobhan asked her to "name her price," and Habiba's comment about campaigning really only being fun "if you have lots of friends" seemed to put Morgan off her lunch. She didn't even finish her tuna sandwich! I can't blame her—it is tuna—but it's still rather sad scenes. Lunches (and all meals, in fact) should never go unfinished.

"Um," I say as we're walking out of the cafeteria. Over my shoulder, I wave a quick goodbye to Alison, who is gazing after us with apologetic eyes. "Are you okay?"

Back on the playground, Morgan gives me the frowniest of

frowns and doesn't hold my hand, either. My hand just flaps about, unheld, like a popped balloon in the wind.

"Not really," she says after a split-fin moment. "I just don't see this working, with me and Siobhan and everything."

Right then, the bell rings. "Oh," I say as the emergency firefighters inside my heart rush for their engines. "When you say *this* . . ."

But then, like bad timing in human form, the Triple M's show up: Marcus, Maja, and Millie. They are Morgan's dusted, trusted, cool-encrusted inner circle. Morgan gives me a breezy smile, which may as well be a force-ten-gale smile, given how flustered it leaves me. My Virgo Moon is breakdancing rings around me, in really obnoxious sunglasses, as the worry grows and grows. How can she stand there and smile after saying *that*?! "I'd better head to class."

As she disappears with her friends, I stare at their backs like some sort of abandoned porcelain doll, one eyelid twitching in horror. Because did I hear her correctly and absolutely perfectly?! Morgan Delaney just said, *I just don't see this working*. Like a Norwegian ghost, I feel my body draining of color. Because gooseberries a'wilting.

Does "this" mean *us*?!

Chat Thread: Zanna Szczechowska

Cat, 11:10 p.m.:
Omg, Google has over NINE BILLION results when you Google 'my partner doesn't love me anymore' . . . ZANNA WHAT DO I DO???:(((

Zanna, 11:11 p.m.:
Don't Google stupid things

Problem solved

Cat, 11:11 p.m.:
That's not helpful Zanna!!!!!!

Zanna, 11:11 p.m.:
You're welcome :)

5

The Pancake Says Doom!

I should have known Pisces Season would make EVERYTHING worse. Not only is it the official era of overthinking, but emotions are flying about like knickers in the wind. How could Morgan say something like that, then just head to class?! The February drizzle pitter-patters down, and I sink deeper and darker into my Piscean woes.

With my steadily growing, medically official HeadGirl-aphobia thrown into the mix, I'm numb thumbs, anxious, and silent all afternoon and through the next day . . . which becomes problematic when I'm in English class with Miss Jamison and we're meant to be reading *A Streetcar Named Desire* out loud. When Miss Jamison calls my name, I stare at the page for a whole ten seconds like an angst-ridden axolotl.

"I'll read instead, Miss," offers Zanna, trying her best to save my mortadella. "Cat can't read aloud right now because, um, she has a bad throat. She's really, really sick."

I drop the book in alarm. Why in the name of Blanche

DuBois's deeply *un*desirable backstory did she have to say that? Everyone completely loses their Mississippis!

Augustus Ming, Most Annoying Student at Queen's, who I am unfortunate enough to be seated with, squeals away that he doesn't want to catch anything, and Miss Jamison makes me move to a table in the back corner, next to a bucket that's catching drips from the ceiling. (Which is an upgrade from Augustus Ming.)

But no one will come near me for the rest of class! Marianne Weatherly actually turns my worksheet into a paper plane when she's handing—well, *throwing*—them out later.

"Sorry, Cat," she says, shielding her mouth as I clutch my eye. "I don't want to catch anything. You do look a bit sickly, to be honest."

"That's just because she uses the wrong shade of foundation," Zanna says helpfully.

"I'm not wearing any foundation!" I retort.

Zanna adjusts her glasses. "Oh," she says. Then she turns back to the front and doesn't look at me for the rest of the lesson. Utterly, utterly useless.

•★.✦˙★•

I walk home alone, brooding like a Brontë. What are you supposed to do when your gorgeous goose of a girlfriend says *I just don't see this working* and then barely talks to you? Back at the iPhone Box, I hurry upstairs for some quality wallowing time. I feel as fragile as an entire glass menagerie. My bottom lip is actually trembling! At least it's quiet at home. I can ruminate over my troubles in peace.

Then I notice that it's actually not quiet at all. The air is feathery with birdsong and I sit up frowning, wondering if a

family of sparrows has moved into my bedroom. But the bird-song appears to be coming from next door . . .

Slowly, I follow the singing to Luna's room. Then I remember that—oh, gooseberries aplenty—it's Thursday, which means my walnut-wacko sister has all her kooky friends round for guided meditation. It's as tragic and horrifying as it sounds, so I march right into her room to demand she turn the birdsong down, please, because some of us are trying to brood!

Unfortunately, I forget that Luna has a curtain behind her door and become entangled in several layers of drifty fabric, hopping about like a cat on a hot tin roof! Just as I'm about to fall over completely, someone tears the fabric aside.

"Can I help you?" a very unimpressed-looking Luna demands. "You're upsetting the energy of the room."

Beyond her I see Luna's best friend, Niamh Collingdale, in a weird turban, Luna's "prairie goth" boyfriend, Dorian, and Luna's online friend, Willow, who sadly is no longer just online and seems to be making Luna weirder, if that's possible. Willow never wears shoes, calls women "daughters of the moon," and could host an entire pagan festival in the bagginess of her endless rainbow-colored clothing. She's currently humming cross-legged on the floor with her eyes closed. Everything's shrouded in herbal-smelling smoke. There are so many dream catchers hanging about the mint-green walls, the whole of Kent could stay cozily comatose forever.

"You're being very loud," I tell Luna, which isn't really true, but I'm annoyed about Morgan, and Luna is . . . here. I glare at her, arms crossed crossly. "What are you doing?"

"We're doing pancake readings," Dorian explains before

Luna bursts an avocado of annoyance. "Do you want to join us?"

"No, she doesn't," Luna snaps. "Because she's just leaving, actually . . ."

But I am already pushing past her into the room. Sure enough, there are pancakes cooking on a portable stove in the middle of the floor. Willow has a spatula in one hand and a bowl of smoking leaves in the other.

"Sorry," I say. "Did you say *pancake readings*?"

Luna rolls her eyes impatiently. "It's fortune-telling, Cat. Like with tea leaves. But we don't have any loose tea, so we're reading from the patterns on pancakes instead."

"Only when they're cooked," adds Niamh, as if that could possibly make a difference. "Then we search for our destinies in the batter."

I stare around the room in complete bamboozlement, wondering if I've stepped through a mirror into an alternate universe. Tragically though, it seems this truly is reality. My sister and her friends are reading fortunes from pancakes. Sappho strike me down.

"Does that really work?" I ask, and Luna splutters in outrage.

"Of course it works! Do I look like an idiot?" Before I can answer that honestly, she points to her Navajo-woven carpet. "Sit down and we'll prove it. Willow, make the next pancake for my sister. We'll have to exorcize the spirit from my hair clip later."

I'm about to tell her that a pancake fortune reading sounds about as helpful as candles on the sun, but then Willow opens one eye and says, "You've been plagued by thoughts most troubling this afternoon, sacred sister? I can taste unrest in your aura."

Gooseberries galore. How does she know?! Carefully, I lower myself onto one of Luna's lentil-stuffed floor cushions. "Um . . . What does unrest taste like?"

Willow opens both eyes and frowns. "What? Well, it tastes like . . . um . . ."

"Spinach?" suggests Niamh, and Willow snaps her fingers.

"Precisely," she agrees. I'm a little put out. My aura tastes like spinach?! No wonder Morgan doesn't see a future! Willow pours some batter into the frying pan and the mixture sizzles hypnotically. Then she mumbles something in an old, probably very sacred tongue. Although it sounds rather like "Mistletoe and chamomile . . . Cornflakes and cheese . . ."

"It's her process," Dorian assures me.

Before us, the pancake begins to brown. Willow leans over, inhaling the steam and waving her heavily ringed fingers like sea anemones. I'm actually nervous. Can a pancake really tell me if my relationship is in peril?! I bate with waited breath . . .

Suddenly, Willow lets out a gasp! She falls back and throws her head to the ceiling like a banshee bridezilla. Beside me, Luna grips Dorian's hand. I almost fall into Niamh, who clings to my shoulder in fright! Willow looks possessed!

"I see something cloudy . . ." wavers Willow. I could point out that's probably the insane amounts of incense we're breathing in, but Willow isn't done. She presses her hands to her temples and her hair beads jangle. "No! Something *clear*! I see a girl, a truly dangerous girl! In the mask of someone beloved—deception most outrageous and austere!"

Someone beloved? Morgan?!

Willow leaps to her feet, engulfing me in wafts of breakfast-flavored incense. She dutifully dithers all over the room like a warbling Hattifattener. She's milking this one, a true séance showdown. (Not that the milkman stops here anymore after Luna scared him away with her dairy industry protest.)

"Two houses!" Willow wails. "A house not meant to stand! I see stormy times ahead, sweet sister—make haste and run! DOOM! DOOM! The pancake says DOOM!" Then she kaftans her way to Luna's bed and collapses carefully on a large cushion.

Stunned as a parrot in pink lipstick, I actually grab Niamh's hand. Finally, Willow's eyes flicker open. She sits up, gazing around the room like she's seeing it for the first time. Perhaps she actually is now that Luna's finally opened a window to clear the smoke. Then the strangest thing happens. They all applaud. Luna even grabs Willow into a hug!

"That was incredible, Willow!" she sparkles as I gawp like a mannequin with googly eyes. "You had a genuine spiritual experience! Look, I have goose bumps!"

"I'm so honored to have witnessed this!" Niamh joins in. And even Dorian is grinning, offering to shake Willow's hand like she's Hera, Queen of Olympus, herself.

That's when I begin to laugh.

It's the kind of laugh I deserve to be doing—like, "O-HO-HO-HA-HE-HE-HE!"—because I am older and wiser than these batter-brewing spring saplings.

What *are* these falafel-based fools on about? I'm nearly sixteen entire years of age and can legally buy novelty matches for myself. Do they really think I'm going to listen to a pancake?!

"I'm sorry," I say, chuckling like Charlie Chaplin as they stare. "I appreciate the free night at the theater—but I have homework to do. You guys are hilarious, merci beaucoup."

I turn to go, my Morgan anxieties practically evaporated, although I can feel Luna's eyes rolling all over.

"Don't say we didn't warn you," she green-thumb grumbles.

"Totes," agrees Willow. "I mean, it's the Worm Moon soon."

I freeze.

They've already gone back to worshipping Willow as the next Wiccan demigoddess, but I hurry over to gaze into the pancake again. Oh no. Sappho-NO! How did I not see this before?! The pancake is big, and round, and golden. Small darker circles, like craters, have formed across the pleasantly browned surface in an eerily familiar way . . .

IT'S THE FULL MOON!

I rush to my room and lurch toward my bookshelf, then throw open my *Bible to the Stars* to the section on phases of the moon.

It's all there. Willow is right! Something I never thought I'd say about someone who calls not wearing shoes "living shoe-free."

"The March full moon, or Worm Moon, symbolizes the changing ecosystem as winter transitions to spring, and the massive shift in our spiritual being that comes with this change. Worms, burrowing through the soil, create the foundation for massive change; likewise, the Worm Moon reminds us that immense change can be happening beneath the surface, even invisibly or undetectably."

Now, I might not know what some of those words mean.

In fact, it's all a bit science-y for my liking—and Siobhan says that science is for "salivating, speck-sucking nerds." But as I slam shut the book, stomach rumbling nervously like a brewing spring storm, I'm starting to put two and two together.

We might not be in March yet, but . . . the party, what Morgan said—it's all the moon's fault! The sky, as usual, is to blame, and I won't rest until I've rested, then figured out how to fight it . . .

Chat Thread: Zanna Szczechowska

Cat, 1:51 a.m.:
ZANNA A PANCAKE SAID MY RELATIONSHIP IS DOOMED AND IT'S ALL THE WORM MOON'S FAULT, WHAT AM I SUPPOSED TO DO???? SOS HELP!!!

Zanna, 1:52 a.m.:
Cat, it's the middle of the night, istg

Cat, 1:52 a.m.:
AND??? WERE YOU ASLEEP???

Zanna, 1:53 a.m.:
No, but that's not the point

I do need to talk to you about something actually

Cat, 1:53 a.m.:
YES!!! ABOUT THIS!!! THE MOON, THE MOON, THE PANCAKE OF DOOM!!!

Zanna, 1:54 a.m.:
Are you sure it wasn't just a bad dream?

I hate to break it to you, but pancakes don't normally speak

Cat, 1:55 a.m.:
AAAAAAAAAAAAAAAAAAAAAAAAAAAAAAAAAAAAAAAAAAAAA

6
A Divalicious Dance-Off

According to Zanna, the best way to find out what someone means is to ask them. But I disagree: surely a grand gesture would be much more fun! Who wants to TALK?!

Unfortunately, Luna says she doesn't think it would be ethical "or even legal, actually" to capture a thousand doves, even though I assure her they'd all be released at sunset the same day. She also points out that to name an undiscovered flower after my girlfriend, I have to discover an undiscovered flower.

She makes a few valid points, I suppose.

But perhaps I'm overthinking. It's not like the Worm Moon lasts forever! It's the Pink Moon afterward, all about rebirth and reexamining your relationships . . . which also sounds terrible. When we arrive at school, I'm so nauseated, I'm tempted to tell Luna I'll just go home. But then I'm interrupted by Rich Elizabeth, charging toward me like a stampeding ostrich. She looks furious!

"E-Elizabeth?" I stammer. "What's wrong?!"

"How can you even ask that?!" she demands, and before I

have time to point to my voice box, she thrusts a sheet of paper at me. "Take a look at that, chicka, then ask again. Is Miss Spencer in your pocket or something? I can't BELIEVE . . . !"

I don't even *have* pockets—I'm wearing a skirt! But I don't think Elizabeth will hear reason right now. Or anything at all, since she's shrieking like a dehydrated cobra, yanking out clumps of her frankincense-blond hair.

Then I read the paper and my stomach drops. What in the name of Benvolio's blistery feet?!

It's Miss Spencer's cast list for the play. And right at the top of the list, just below where it says *Romeo—Brooke Mackenzie*, which is shocking chandeliers enough, I see that Juliet shall be played by me, Cathleen Phillips.

William Shakespeare me down!

To say I'm surprised is an understatement. I think I'd be less surprised if my parents gave up their jobs in banking and became professional boatbuilders! Although they're actually rather likely to do something as clownishly ridiculous as that, so that isn't saying much.

I don't want to be Juliet! I can't even remember more than three French verbs—how am I supposed to memorize a script?! Panicking like Piccadilly Circus, I avoid everyone for the rest of the morning—even Morgan. She'll probably only want to talk about this candidate announcement Mr. Drew is forcing upon us after lunch. Siobhan mentioned she had "something planned," which could mean anything from a speech to human sacrifice!

If it's a sacrifice, at least I can volunteer as tribute.

Unfortunately, come assembly time, Morgan says "Hello"

into the mic just as it crackles, and so this loud, bowel-like sound rips through the room like a panicked skunk. Everyone laughs and I snap out of my angst iceberg to concentrate: Supportive Girlfriend Mode, where are you?!

Morgan clears her throat. Feedback squeaks again and people wince. There are a few suppressed giggles. I try to smile encouragingly.

"OUCH," goes Loudmouth Jasmine McGregor with her huge, enormous mouth.

I glance around, looking for the gang. Siobhan will be furious if they don't show up! I'm sitting between Zanna and Alison. Kenna is at the front looking trembly and alone. But where's Habiba? Where's Lip Gloss Lizzie? Perhaps they fell into the bathroom mirrors?!

"So, I'm here to tell you, um . . . I'm running for Head Girl!" Morgan's voice takes me by surprise. It feels like she's been shuffling Post-it Notes for about seven million decades. All that laughing seems to really have rocked Morgan's mojo. "Hope I can count on your support . . . I've got some great ideas . . ."

Mr. Drew, standing off to the left with his northern arms folded, clears his throat disruptively and says, "We will be sharing the candidates' ideas at a later date."

"*Another* assembly?!" scoffs Brooke from somewhere.

"Um, THANK YOU, Miss Mackenzie," says Mr. Drew.

"Yeah," says Morgan. "Cheers . . ."

The mic crackles. Then it happens again: blowing raspberries like a chorus of Bart Simpsons. People giggle away and when Morgan talks more, it's rushed and breathless as she fights for attention. Jasmine and the Foghorn Brigade are hooting like coots on a hen night!

"I want to do this differently," Morgan rambles. "I don't want to show off and strut about the place like . . . any old Head Girl; I want to be that listening ear, you know? And take your suggestions seriously, so we feel like we're all on the same team. So . . . Yeah. Thanks."

Then she walks back to her seat in the front row just as the mic full-on belches and Jasmine shoots off another enormous quack-laugh. No one else is applauding, but Mr. Drew does a boring, teachery slow clap as he returns to the front.

"Thank you, Miss Morgan Delaney!" he says, which gets a snort of disapproval from Maja, presumably because using "Miss" is far too mainstream. "Now, we have one other candidate to declare . . ." He narrows his eyes, scanning the hall. "Siobhan Collingdale?"

There's silence. I OMG-gasp. Has Siobhan not shown up?! Does that mean she's dropping out of the race?! YYYYYES! Hummus hallelujah—she's changed her mind! Of course, being Head Girl would be far too losery and nerdsome for someone like Siobhan. She's already Queen of Queen's—who needs a title? She must have decided—

The lights suddenly fade. People murmur. Alison lets out a frightened whimper and grabs my hand.

"Just a power outage!" calls Mr. Drew. "Nothing to worry—"

He's cut off by loud music, pulsing from the speakers up on the walls. A voice going, "HEYYYY, BROTHER . . ."

Is that Avicii? What the mighty hoopla is going on?!

A spotlight hits the stage. A silhouetted figure in stilettos is there, hands on hips, back to the audience. She spreads her arms wide . . . Then the strobe lights begin flashing.

Mr. Drew is waving his arms about, shouting things, but nobody cares about Mr. Drew anymore. The music is PUMPING! People jump to their feet and clap. Then the figure spins around . . . It's Habiba! And she's got pom-poms.

Up go the curtains. All very operatic. The ENTIRE CHEERLEADING SQUAD is waiting behind them, huge glittery pom-poms at the ready, and as the beat drops, they all begin to dance, jumping up and down like there's no tomorrow.

There literally might not be, once Mrs. Warren finds out about this, but I think everyone is too excited to give a gooseberry. People whoop and hand-pump and—WOW-CAKES GALORE—there's literally a full-on synchronized dance routine happening. Zanna grabs my hand and I'm pulled to my feet, although I quickly shove my hands in my pockets—if Morgan sees me being enthusiastic about Siobhan, we're finished! But then the ceiling opens and I'm gasping; tinsel and confetti rain down upon us and people are jumping to catch it!

While Zanna is spitting out silver confetti, the mighty doors to the hall open behind us and—oh, Scorpi-OH—in comes Siobhan, carried by four Lad Friends on a literal throne. Well, I actually think it's a desk with a chair taped on top, but she's thrown a glitzy blanket over it, so it looks rather divalicious.

Siobhan is dressed in white satin, a headdress draped across her hair. The crowds part and she sails to the stage, where Habiba and the cheerleaders have frozen mid-pose. Siobhan climbs off

the throne and joins them in position. People are screaming like she's literal Beyoncé! Then Siobhan throws off the gown to reveal a sequined blazer and shorts.

BOOM goes the music, then Siobhan is dancing, too.

Just as I'm on the verge of passing out from sensory overload, I notice Morgan standing in the very corner, absolutely frozen. Even Marcus and Millie are shimmying their shoulders, but quickly stop after an ice-blond death-glare from Maja.

Morgan looks utterly defeated. It's stuck-in-traffic tragic.

I try not to all-out dance . . . I just boogie a little sadly, like Dad at the disco, with great shame in every swing of my hips. Eventually, the vogueing ends and Siobhan tosses back her hair, marching forward to grab the mic like it's life by the throat.

"GOOD AFTERNOON, MY LITTLE WORKER BEES," she says, which is actually quite insulting if you think about it, but everyone just hollers back like Pingu on a porcupine. She whips out a cue card and begins, "My message is clear and blackhead-free. Head Girl is not for the fainthearted! You can't just hand the role to some paper pusher with a loyalty card to Specsavers—you need PASSION, EXPLOSIVES, and ENTHUSIASM . . ."

Habiba leans forward to whisper in Siobhan's ear.

"Um, I mean PASSION and EXPLOSIVE ENTHUSIASM." Siobhan glares at a grimacing Lip Gloss Lizzie (her PR manager, who probably can't type very well with those huge, manicured nails). "Anyway—vote Siobhan!"

And with a flash of her perfect teeth, she's done.

"Any idea who was stronger?" I ask Zanna as everyone applauds not just with their hands, but with their feet, too, until

the ground is vibrating and a worrying amount of dust is trickling down from the ceiling. "I'd say it was quite close!"

Zanna gives me a raised eyebrow.

"Fair point," I sigh.

Siobhan is clearly feeling rather Boomtown-Rats victorious after the speech, because she takes us all to Lambley Common Green for a celebration picnic after school. We lounge around dipping pita bread into hummus while random taggers-on chant "HEYYY, BROTHER!" on loop in the background. Which is about as annoying as it sounds.

"That was the coolest thing EVER!" some random girl is telling Siobhan for about the seven thousandth time.

"Yes," Siobhan agrees. "It was."

They take selfies, which Siobhan uploads instantly to her already-jam-and-peanut-butter-packed Instagram Stories, and with a sigh, I open my own feed. We're required to like anything Siobhan posts within a two-minute timeframe, else we're blocked for two days. But Morgan has posted, so I open that up first. At least she's not deleted her socials and gone into hibernation. Where did she flee after assembly?!

Then I yelp so hard, I almost hiccup. A selfie at the skateboard park with BROOKE THE CROOK? WHY WOULD MORGAN POST THAT?! On a platform ANYONE can check!!! If Siobhan sees this, she's going to go absolutely—

"WHAT THE FREAKY FLORAL BEDSPREAD?!"

"It's not what it looks like!" I shriek, leaping to my feet and diving for Siobhan's phone. "It's photoshopped! It's a really realistic illustration by, um . . . Picasso!"

Siobhan yanks her phone out of my reach. "Picasso doesn't DO realistic, you uncultured artifact! Did you already know about this abomination?" Siobhan snatches my phone from my quivering hand and digests what's on the screen.

Oh, goose-juices aplenty. I'm an Aquarius deceased.

"Cat, tell me something," Siobhan says eventually. Kenna, Habiba, Zanna, and Alison peer over Siobhan's shoulder at the screen and turn three moon-shades paler. Which is practically translucent in Zanna's case.

I frown as I think. "I used to have a life-size poster of Taylor Swift stuck to the ceiling above my bed so I could wake up gazing into her beautiful blue eyes?"

Siobhan looks momentarily baffled. "Wow, you are an utter freak. I actually meant, tell me: Am I not known for being sympathetic to each charity-case loser at school? Do I not always try to see the best in people, even when they're the absolute epitome of idiocy?!"

"Um . . ." How honest does she want me to be?

"So why," Siobhan continues, nostrils twitching, "is Morgan, your TRAGIC girlfriend, ASSAULTING me with pictures of Brooke the Crook?! Is she sad friends with her and WHY was I not informed about this sooner?!"

I gulp down my helter-skelter panic. "Um, I wouldn't say they're friends. Morgan is, um, trying out this buddy scheme idea for her Head Girl campaign!"

Gooseberries galore, I might be a genius. I told a lie that's actually believable! Much better than when I told Mrs. Warren a clown had eaten my homework as a party trick. Morgan talked

about a buddy scheme already! So it's really very believable that Brooke would be her guinea pig.

Literally, with those two enormous front teeth she has.

But Siobhan doesn't sound any happier. "What sort of desperate attention-seeking nonsense is that?! I would bet a hundred pounds of someone else's money she's doing this just to pulp my poodles. She's going to WISH she had a buddy to save her blistery backside once I get hold of her!"

Then she hurls the phone across the grass, into the rubbish bin on the sidewalk, with perfect aim. She really *has* been practicing her netball lately . . .

"That was impressive!" I admit.

Zanna clears her throat. "That was your phone, Cat."

Five minutes later, I collapse back onto the grass with literal bin juice in my hair. Siobhan makes me sit nine feet away. I fully blame Brooke and I text Morgan to imply this, but she doesn't reply, so I just sloth about, stressed to the absolute west. And to the absolute east as well.

Chat Thread: Morgan Delaney

Cat, 4:45 p.m.:
Couldn't find u after assembly :(

You went off with Brooke instead???

Morgan, 4:51 p.m.:
Well I knew where you'd be

How's Siobhan's picnic?

Cat, 4:53 p.m.:
Very nice, thank u, lots of hummus

But I miss u, wanted to check u were okay :(

Morgan, 4:55 p.m.:
So you think I've lost already huh?

Thanks for your support

Cat, 4:56 p.m.:
THAT ISN'T WHAT I MEANT!!!

There's plenty of time to turn things around!!! :)

Morgan, 5:05 p.m.:
Enjoy the picnic

7
More Confused Than Pingu

My master plan to get out of making Siobhan's posters might have spiraled ever so slightly out of control. Over the weekend, I have to admit to my parents that I'm actually starring in the school play, and back in school on Monday when everyone's given a script, I have to admit it to myself. I've also made a brand-new enemy in Rich Elizabeth. Literally brand-new given how often she replenishes her wardrobe.

But despite the pancake's prediction, all is not doomed: Morgan hasn't broken up with me yet! Take that Worm Moon!

And if she can't get along with my friends, I have decided that I shall get along with hers. Maybe not in classes! Or at lunch. Or on social media. But . . . somewhere. And tonight, that somewhere is the patio garden of a very Smoky McFolky late-night café.

I need to not get distracted by how truly beautiful Morgan is though. Mmm . . .

She really does look very slinky and divine tonight in her

leathery trench coat, green extensions clipped into her hair like . . . well, like green extensions clipped into her hair. Which is very cool and groovy. But what's *not* cool and groovy is that neither Morgan nor her friends thought I would enjoy an LGBT stand-up poetry night! I literally had to ASK to be invited . . . something a girlfriend should never have to do.

To make up for our lunch-date-gone-wrong last week, I offered to sit with Morgan's friends at lunch. Which was rather generous of me, considering her friends are all skateboarding weirdos on wheels who listen to K-pop, while I'm the crème de la crème of school society in really nice shoes. Millie usually sort of smiles at me, but Maja and Marcus clearly don't like me—I've no idea why!

"So, what time are we meeting this evening?" Maja said to Morgan, making ice-blond eye contact with me the entire time. "I've already planned a sick outfit so it's going to be, like, lit."

"Lit?" I repeated, frowning. "Like, literary? Morgan, where are you going?"

"That's . . ." Morgan closed her eyes. "No, that isn't what that means, babe. Although actually, it's going to be literary as well. We're going to an LGBT poetry night in Sevenoaks."

I stared at my so-called girlfriend. "And you didn't invite me . . . ?"

Morgan at least had the decency to look awkward. She went a bit Pink Moon pink, like a real-life speechless apricot, but then Maja bobbed in, "We didn't think it would be your thing. It's probably going to be, like, hard-core intense. Like, intellectual, you know?"

I waved my arms about. "I literally am obsessed with poetry!"

"You like Mary Oliver," Maja said with a snort. "That's easy

reading compared to this. Like, girl, Pihla Kruus is going to be there. As in THE pansexual anti-capitalist poet of Finland. And didn't you once tell Morgan that *Pingu* had a confusing plotline?"

"Because they're penguins!" I protested. "They all look the same!"

"That's not very inclusive to the seal," said Marcus, and the two of them burst out laughing like goths at the goth circus.

Luckily Morgan noticed I was not SCROL-ling (Scream-LOL-ing) along. She put her hand on my knee. "Of course you're invited, babe. I'm sorry, okay? I'm still not used to, like, including you with my friends. But I'd—*we'd*—love to have you there."

Maja and Marcus stopped cackling then. I smiled very smuggy indeed.

So, fast-forward, I'm now sitting under the stars with my hand practically BOLT-GUNNED to Morgan's knee. It's all red umbrellas and wooden picnic benches, very scenic and summery, and I meet Maja's eye and sunbeam right at her ice-blond bob. She rolls her eyes and looks grumpy. But that could just be her face.

We've had two "performances" so far and it's quite weird. But I'm no way giving Maja and Marcus the satisfaction of being even slightly right, so I'm pretending to understand everything like a true LGBTQIA. (The *I* stands for INTELLECTUAL, by the way, because that is what I am. I mean, I make Sappho references!)

Meanwhile, the Triple M's goon about like depressed vegans, like they wish I wasn't there. Which would make three of us. Finally, there is a break, so I can focus on showing Morgan that I am absolutely cool enough to go out with.

"I'm actually not worried about the play, actually," I say out

of the blue. "I'm very confident in front of people, actually. I could read some of MY poetry, actually, Morgan—that's how confident and capable I actually am, actually."

Morgan bites into her falafel wrap, frowning a little like she's worried I'm having a brain malfunction. "You're gonna be fine as Juliet," she assures me. "It's me you should be worried for. I've got to beat Siobhan for Head Girl and I get this really mild impression that she doesn't like losing."

"Is it true that she tried to get *babooning* added to the dictionary just so she wouldn't lose a game of Scrabble?" asks Marcus, leaning in like he's actually interested in my answer.

I hesitate. "Well, possibly. But it's actually a very useful word! How many times have you wanted to say you saw a boy babooning along somewhere, but then you couldn't because *babooning* isn't a real word?" Then I gesture round the garden. "Anyway, how can you complain about making up words here?!"

Maja just snorts. "Girls like that *never* lose," she says, then she fixes me with a very chilly stare. It might just be her bob kicking in, but Maja looks like she has über issues with yours truly. "They have everything handed to them on a platter."

"Well, Siobhan does have a lot of fancy serving dishes," I agree. "But that's because her mum is an event organizer. It would be a waste not to use them."

Morgan rolls her eyes. "Not a literal platter, Cat. Maja means that she's rude and entitled and probably thinks she should be Head Girl by default."

I open my mouth to protest. But then I stop myself, just like Disney does every time it nearly confirms Elsa is gay. Siobhan *is* rude and entitled . . . but she's also really good at hair

care! She lends us her VERY expensive clothes (once she's "finished with them for the season," anyway). She protects us from Jasmine McGregor (who once tried to "bounce Kenna Brown to the moon" on the school trampoline!). And she taught us all where to punch a man where it REALLY hurts! (With a somewhat unnecessary live demonstration.)

Not to mention she dumped Kieran Wakely-Brown for my sake after he spread some VERY untrue rumors about me. I cannot help but ponder . . . if Morgan and her friends were Lad Brigade, too, all this complaining about my friends would be much more uncool than Morgan and Maja seem to think.

I mean, I wouldn't dump my friends for a *boy*friend . . .

I don't think they will listen though. In the end, I just let them baboon on about Pihla Kruus, who is apparently on in five. And also on another planet, by the looks of her Instagram! I watch one of her performances with my headphones as the M's all intellectualize without me, and she mainly seems to dance around and scream things, like some strange Celtic fairy.

Then the maddest madness happens. Brooke Mackenzie comes clattering up to our table with her huge leather satchel.

"Hey, GANG!" she sparkles. "Guess whose mum forgot to lock her jewelry box?! I could afford a taxi to come with you after all!"

Morgan and the others whoop as I gaze on in disbelief. I suppose they think Brooke is joking! But whatever she's doing, why is she doing it HERE? And how in the name of Mary Oliver's olives could Morgan invite her but not me?!

Alas, there's no time to be insulted. As Brooke chatters on with Marcus about graphic novels, I become fully occupied

dodging being in the background of all the selfies Maja is taking with Morgan, then with Brooke. If I'm spotted on Instagram hanging out with Brooke, I will be in DEEP Danish pastries with Siobhan! And from the way she fully embraced the Hansel and Gretel theme for Halloween, that might not actually be a metaphor . . .

"Cat, what are you doing under the table?" Morgan calls to me. "I've ordered food for everyone—do you like ketchup? Plus, I want a picture with all of us."

"Um!" I am quite literally planking the patio. A ground-level low moment. "Just a second, I'm looking for my . . . pet centipede!"

The chatter above dies down. "Your what . . . ?" Morgan asks.

I bite my lip. What in the name of Walt Whitman's wallabies am I going to do?! I can't take a selfie with Brooke the Crook! Then—thank Sappho times a million—the mic crackles and someone says, "All right, people, it's the moment you've all been waiting for . . ." and Morgan forgets all about taking selfies. Aphrodite be praised!

"It's Pihla Kruus!" the host squeals as I scramble back into my seat. Pihla, who is dressed in a floor-length yellow sundress with literal daisies woven through her hair (in March?!), drifts onstage with less enthusiasm than Zanna at a Valentine's Day dance. Everyone still cheers like chimps on banana milkshakes though.

"WOW!" gasps Brooke. "She's, like, Morgan-level cool!"

"Oh, shut up," snorts Morgan, but I can tell she LOVED the compliment. I glare at Brooke very severely indeed. Not that she notices.

"The poem is called 'Shades of Yellow,'" says Pihla, eyes glazed, and then she begins. Very slowly. With a gap of at least five seconds between every word.

"Goldenrod.

Saffron.

Citrine.

Flax.

Xanthic."

I stare in astonishment as she guffs on, a true manufacturer of confusiontude. Eventually, I lean over to Morgan and whisper, "Morgan, what is going on? Is this a poem? She's literally just listing weird shades of yellow!"

"Um . . ." Morgan is honest enough to look *slightly* confused. But she's also glancing cautiously at Maja, and I could roll my eyes to Jupiter and back again. How can Morgan, who is bold enough to wear corduroy in front of Siobhan, care what Moody Maja thinks?

Maja hisses, "It's not *about* the colors . . . It's about what they *mean*. Isn't that obvious?" Then she rolls her eyes and goes back to listening. She really is pretentious for someone who brings a thermos flask on a night out. What is she—ninety-three?!

Tragically, I may be ninety-three by the time we reach the end of this "poem." Pihla is still kruus-ing on:

"Laguna.

Hunyadi.

Sand.

Tuscany.

Dijon."

On and on, she goes. I suppose it's to be expected—she is a writer. But she's genuinely challenging Mum for Most Boring Banana of the Year! In fact, I'm getting rather sleepy . . . I lean back in my seat, the waves of yellow washing over me like sunshine . . . then I wake up with a jump. Gooseberries, did I fall asleep?!

"Moccasin.

Chartreuse.

Mikado."

She's still going. I can't have been asleep *that* long. How many shades of yellow can there be?! I eye Morgan and hope she didn't notice. I need to perk up! At least we have food for vital energy maintenance. I munch some onion rings off the tray.

I'm not the only one bored as a plank. Brooke is on her phone! Then I frown, noticing the pink glitter case. Wait a tooth-picking minute . . . That's not her phone—it's mine! She must have nicked it while I was sleeping, and now she's browsing the gang's group chat!

"Brooke!" I hiss, leaning on the table to try to snatch it back.

Only, I don't lean on the table. I lean on the tray, which is slightly on the *edge* of the table. With true magnificence, the tray flips, catapulting eggplant salad and onion rings across the room as I crash to the floor like a giraffe on ice skates.

Pihla Kruus falls silent—but I can't even celebrate because I am lying on the floor with ketchup down my favorite top. Humiliations galore!

"Wow, Kitty!" Brooke exclaims. "I never knew you could be

such fun?!" Then she picks up the eggplant salad and Frisbees it across the room after the tray, where it lands right on some lady . . . who's wearing a fully white pantsuit.

Then all hell breaks loose. Or heaven, if you're a bit peckish.

White-suit lady's girlfriend grabs a smoothie and tosses it over Maja, who lets out a truly undead-sounding shriek. Someone throws a spoon, but it misses us and hits someone on our *other* side. Then food is flying from every direction. People are jumping under tables like a pet-centipedes prison break is going down, and even Pihla Kruus is screaming in very nonpoetic terms that there's barbecue sauce on her saffron sundress.

That's when I see Brooke aiming a mustard bottle and jetting down the poet herself with yellow. Which, despite toning well with her performance, Pihla doesn't seem happy about. Security rushes over and I wave madly at Morgan, who is gazing around the canary-colored carnage in disbelief.

"Christ," she says. "Cat, what did you do?!"

I stare at her. "ME?! Morgan, look at Brooke!"

Morgan glances around just in time to see Brooke being flattened by two members of staff. My savior girlfriend gasps and hurries over, screaming yellow murder at them, and just when I think my luck in exposing Brooke's true colors can't get any worse, I am hit in the face with a plateful of fried food. This is one Frieday night I will never forget.

Chat Thread: Zanna Szczechowska

Zanna, 9:58 p.m.:
hey loser, can I get some advice

as u can tell from me asking u, I literally have no one else

Cat, 10:25 p.m.:
Not sure you want advice from me Zanzibar :(my life is a DISASTER!!!!!

Zanna, 10:27 p.m.:
Oh . . . what happened?

Cat, 10:35 p.m.:
Got kicked out of the poetry night for starting a food fight

Everyone angry armadillos

BROOKE IS SO ANNOYING IM GOING TO DIE. She took my phone when I was asleep and then I slipped trying to get it back and that's what started the fight but Morgan is INSISTING she wasnt reading my texts so im having to "let it go"

Thank goodness I am an Aquarius and being fake comes naturally!!!!!!!!!

Zanna, 10:41 p.m.:
Right . . . a lot going on in these messages

Firstly, sounds like Brooke started the fight not u

Cat, 10:43 p.m.:
THANK YOU

Urgh Zanna :(I knew you'd understand!!!!

Zanna, 10:44 p.m.:
Morgan being silly as fruit rn if u ask me

Literally EVERYONE knows Brooke is bad news

Remember when she locked Claustrophobic Robyn in the PE locker?

Cat, 10:45 p.m.:

I heard she still sleeps in her backyard :(

Zanna, 10:45 p.m.:

Morgan would be like, "it was aversion therapy" tho lmao

Cat, 10:46 p.m.:

LOL

Would that actually work though?

You know how Luna has that kiwi allergy? :)

Zanna, 10:48 p.m.:

CAT, NO

CAT

DON'T EVEN

8

Show Up for Siobhan

Pisces Season is ruining my life. I've already cried today for no reason, and it's only eight o'clock! Well, not *completely* for no reason. My girlfriend's friends now hate me even more than they did already, and Siobhan is forest-fire furious because she saw my clown-size feet in the background of Morgan's selfie with Brooke on Instagram. *And* because Brooke sent her a selfie from MY phone, grinning like Harley Quinn on holiday. WHO DOES THAT?! Siobhan was, according to Kenna, "totally apoplectic" for over forty-five minutes.

Anyway, my friend and my girlfriend are now openly out for each other's blood, and I am like the sheep carcass they are scrapping over.

To make things worse, Siobhan's broken up with Dale! Apparently, she wants to fully focus on the campaign, and he's "too clingy . . ." Which I suppose is true, given he was often literally handcuffed to her. But Siobhan has never handled breakups well. She's going to be foul as over-fermented fruit today, so things could definitely be peachier.

"Well, Willow did say that you're doomed," Luna points out helpfully on the walk to school. "She's not often wrong. She told me I was going to have a fight with Dorian last Wednesday, so I ghosted him all day to avoid it. But then he called me, all angry that I'd been ignoring him, and we had a massive fight. See? Just like Willow predicted!"

I predict that Willow will wake up tomorrow as clueless as she's woken up today.

"Maybe it's about the play?" I suggest hopefully. We had our second rehearsal yesterday and it did *not* go well. "Because I don't mind the play being doomed! In fact, I'd totally support that."

"We don't need a mystic pancake to tell us that you onstage is about as sensible as banana-skin shoes," Luna says, unfazed, and I scowl. "Just avoid situations of conflict. That's what my horoscope for Pisces Season says. We're supposed to be breaking away and exploring more spiritual ways of living. Pancake fortunes are just the beginning!"

Now, there's something to worry about. But maybe Luna isn't completely wrong . . . Even if her desire to wear dried fruit as jewelry is. Maybe if I simply trust in the Tranquil Piscean Life Philosophy, stay lagoon-level relaxed, and keep away from the Head Girl campaigns, everything will be as fine as Morgan's glow-in-the-dark hair extensions and I can overpower the disastrous moon cycle completely.

Only I arrive at school and find Siobhan on the playground, standing on an upturned box with an enormous bright red

megaphone. So much for avoiding yet-to-be Head Girls. Everyone's gathered round and Kenna is handing out *Show Up for Siobhan* pamphlets.

"Passion! Empathy! Patience! Respect!" Siobhan announces through the megaphone. "These are the qualities I plan to learn in order to fulfill my duties as Head Girl. You already know me as a loyal and well-dressed friend to everyone. Except you, Jasmine."

"YOU HAVE SWIMMER'S SHOULDERS!" Jasmine bellows, and Siobhan grabs Kenna's handbag and launches it through the air toward Jasmine, who only just manages to duck in time.

"I have been described by our vice principal, Mr. Drew, as highly entitled," Siobhan continues as Kenna scuttles off to retrieve her bag. "But he's wrong. Despite my grace and charm, which has moved many of our teachers to tears, I don't have any titles at all! Now the time has come for that to change. Soon, I intend to be titled as Head Girl!"

Everyone cheers and claps. It's all rather impressive. But then—oh, gooseberries aplenty—another familiar voice calls out. "And what are your policies, Siobhan?"

The clapping slows and I feel my throat closing. Morgan has pushed her way to the front of the crowd with her Triple M friends. She turns to face us. "Head Girl should not be a popularity contest. I'm running to propose actual changes to school policy, like a vegan lunch option." Next to me, Luna inhales her tongue. "I also want the bathrooms to be gender neutral, so that everyone feels comfortable using them, not just the Barbies and their boyfriends."

Luna looks like she might be about to swoon. I grip her arm

to save her from collapsing and Siobhan clears her throat thunderously into the megaphone. "Well, duh?! Obviously, I have policies, Mogs. What sort of Morgan—sorry, *moron*—do you think I am?!"

Everyone laughs, even Jasmine McGregor, who hoots loudly, echoing round the playground like some sort of hooting coot in flight. Morgan glowers as Siobhan spreads her arms wide, beaming into the crowds like she's Kate Middleton herself.

"Then why don't you grace us with some of your wonderful ideas?" Morgan retorts, hipster hands on hipster hips. "Let me guess: Bring a Designer Handbag to School Day?"

Siobhan's eyes widen and she crouches to sign something at Kenna. "Don't be ridiculous, Mogs," she replies hastily. "That's the worst idea I've EVER heard, and I've heard Jasmine McGregor trying to audition for *The Voice* before."

"YOU WORE YOUR BRA INSIDE OUT IN SIXTH GRADE!" Jasmine bellows, and Siobhan grabs Kenna's bag and torpedoes it at Jasmine again.

"IT WAS A STYLISTIC CHOICE!" Siobhan yells, and for a moment, she looks worried. Which is unusual for Siobhan, who once attended a judo class for a date. Then her eyes light up again. "I have one really great idea, actually," she says, lifting the megaphone. "I have a plan to eliminate loneliness at Queen's as thoroughly as I eliminated Habiba's corduroy collection . . ."

"You did what?!" Habiba gasps.

"Or, Alison, like I eliminated your ex's ex," Siobhan explains dutifully, "so you could date him instead!"

"You did *what*?" murmurs Alison.

"HEY!" bellows Jasmine McGregor. "That was ME!"

"I'm planning to make . . ." Siobhan winks at me. "A BUDDY SCHEME!"

"YOU'RE WHAT?!" I yelp louder than a loudmouth as I elbow Luna's face in shock.

"For too long, losers with no social skills have had to suffer in silence," Siobhan continues grandly, and Augustus Ming nods in tragic understanding. "But not everyone is a lost cause, resorting to green hair extensions in place of a personality! I will make it my personal duty to make Queen's the ULTIMATE friendship factory!"

YIKES IN YOKOHAMA. Did Siobhan just STEAL Morgan's idea?! The idea that *I* told her about? Oh, Aphrodit-EEK, this is not good.

Morgan's face drops so far, it basically falls off completely. "You absolute . . . !" she begins, her hands in fists, and I go pale. They look like they're about to fight! Visions swim round my head of Morgan beaten to a pulp in a hospital or Siobhan ruining her perfect nude manicure, so I open my mouth and—

"HELP ME!" I yell. "I'M FAINTING!"

Everyone goes silent. Siobhan lowers the megaphone. Morgan loosens her fists and frowns. Well, at least it worked.

"You don't look like you're fainting," points out Siobhan after a full five seconds of me standing there totally upright.

"Oh, sorry, um . . ." I glance between Siobhan and Morgan, then dutifully dither about and collapse dramatically to the ground. I'm just wondering why people aren't rushing over to help when Luna crouches down and empties her water bottle onto my face.

"Oh, thank goodness." My sister smirks as I sit bolt upright, shocked and dripping. "Looks like you're totally awake again."

• ★ • ✦ • ★ •

"That was so embarrassing to watch, Cat," says Zanna when we're once more sneak-manicuring in the library. "Who says 'I'm fainting' to cause a distraction, then doesn't actually faint until someone tells them to? Siobhan is probably going to disown you over this. Have I ever told you that you're absolutely useless?"

"Yes, actually," I reply. "You wrote it in my birthday card."

"Well, I'm telling you again," says Zanna. "You're absolutely useless. How are you actually real? If you weren't sitting before me right now in your orange foundation, I'd think you were a hallucination."

Orange foundation?! I swipe my handheld mirror from my bag and start scrubbing foundation off my (admittedly fairly orange) face.

I've just about had enough of my extremely annoying friend, but before I can push her off her chair or anything, like she deserves, the library doors open and Morgan, Brooke, and the Triple M's stride in like a low-budget Avril Lavigne tribute group.

Gooseberries, I can't see Morgan now! How am I going to explain that I gave her idea to Siobhan? So I do what any self-respecting person would do in this situation. I dive into Zanna's lap, then try to cover myself with her blazer.

"What are you doing?!" hisses Zanna. "Cat, everyone can see you! Your enormous blond hair literally has its own gravitational pull!"

"Shush!" I hiss back. "I can't handle this conversation right now!"

"Cat?" calls Morgan, and we both freeze. "Are you hiding in Zanna's sweater?"

I hastily extract myself. The Triple M's are all frowning at me (which is basically their favorite thing to do). I flush crimson. "Um, hiding?! No! Why would you think that?! I was searching for, well, beetles." I nod quickly. "There are a lot of them about, and they really will nest anywhere, so I was just . . . checking. For Zanna."

Brooke is still sparkling away with her bright blue eyes, like she's thoroughly enjoying my suffering. Gooseberries galore, does she have to be absolutely everywhere?! Morgan crosses her arms. There's probably a good chance that she isn't buying my beetle story. "Why did you give my idea to Siobhan?" she demands.

I briefly wonder if I really am too old to wet myself.

"Well . . ." I begin.

"She's not denying it," interrupts Maja.

Morgan scoffs. "So, it's true?"

"No!" I splutter. "I mean . . . possibly? But, Morgan, I was only trying to explain to her why you're always with Brooke! And she thought it was a rubbish idea anyway! Why would I suspect she'd take it?!"

Morgan smacks her forehead exasperatedly. "Because she hates me? And—for the record—I don't like her, either! So you should probably stop pushing us to roast marshmallows round the campfire together, because it's not going to work. And

actually, I hang out with Brooke because I like her. At least I can *trust* her."

I gaze at Morgan in shock, and what she said seems to hit her, like a toilet plunger to the forehead. My eyes fill with tears. For a moment, I think Morgan is going to come over and tell me she didn't mean it . . .

But then she marches over to the printer without so much as a lesbian goodbye.

Even Zanna feels the sting enough to gently link her fingers through mine and squeeze my hand. Morgan must be serious if she's bringing marshmallows into this. Maja looks me up and down like I'm a comedy banjo player, busking in the street with no shoes on. Then she snorts a laugh and the group edge-queens away after Morgan.

"See you in rehearsals, Kitty!" says Brooke. "Elizabeth still loathes you for getting the role. She refused to do a monologue from *Cats* in drama because she said she couldn't perform a play named after the 'worst person ever.'" She lowers her voice. "I think she means you! Anyway, see you later!" Then she pixie-sprinkles off, red hair bouncing.

This is not even "under the surface" like the Worm Moon warned me. I'm literally doing Shakespeare while in a Capulet crescendo of conflict! All I want is to be the sheath to Morgan's happy dagger. But with each moon that passes, it looks less and less likely that me and Morgan will even make it to Strawberry Moon summer.

Chat Thread: Habiba Qadir

Habiba, 4:00 p.m.:

Hey babes!! Got any horoscopes for Geminis? For Charlotte from netball. She's totes a two-faced cow, but I'm pretending to be her friend so LMK!!! Xx

Cat, 4:09 p.m.:

Hello yes I have one!!!

Gemini's house of public image is strong in Pisces Season, meaning career success is incoming. Tell her to drop out of school and GET A JOB! Also, rose-colored glasses should be coming OFF, so if Charlotte wears glasses, tell her to clean them! That way she can see her TRUE DESIRES more clearly xxx

Habiba, 4:10 p.m.:

TYSM babes! Haha, rose-colored glasses coming off? Good luck ;) xxx

Cat, 4:11 p.m.:

Wdym??x

Habiba, 4:11 p.m.:

Well Morgan's a Gemini!!!! #AppleOfHerGeminEyes . . . #FORNOW ;) xxx

Cat, 4:14 p.m.:

Bit late for that Hababy :(

I think her glasses are in PIECES on the floor

Habiba, 4:15 p.m.:

Aww . . . Good luck!!!xxxx

#BePositive !!!! :)

Here if u want to talk!!!

Cat, 4:17 p.m.:
Yesssss pls

Can we call?

Cat, 4:19 p.m.:
Habiba?

Cat, 4:25 p.m.:
Habiba :/

Cat, 4:44 p.m.:
Thanks

9

The Princess of Swan Bog

Morgan doesn't even text me after school. The audacity! I go on Instagram so I can share some heartbreak quotes for attention. But before I can even post my seventeenth one, I see Morgan is posting stories. She's at the park, skateboarding with Brooke Mackenzie again! Has she no shame?! She looks like she's enjoying herself. It's very, very upsetting.

On Saturday, Mum and Dad decide to build a greenhouse in the backyard, which is an absolute joke, considering our entire house is made from glass already. I watch from my enormous see-through wall (window) as they clown up and down the lawn together with large sheets of glass, like a slapstick comedy waiting to happen.

Then, thank Sappho, I'm saved by my phone.

"Zanna!" I gasp at once. "Thank goodness you've called. My parents are being utter idiots as usual and everything is still weird with Morgan! Why is my life so hard?!"

"Um," says Zanna. "Sorry about that. I wanted to talk to you about something, so if we can loop back to you in a minute . . ."

It's not like Zanna to ask my advice. Wincing as Mum spins a wooden beam around and whacks Dad on the back of the head, I say, "Zanna, if this is about eating raw broccoli again, I've told you already. You are welcome to do it in your own home, but I am never going to agree that it's okay."

"Well, it is okay," says Zanna. "But it's actually not about that. I actually wanted to—"

"Morgan says it's fine though," I continue, watching in awe as Dad drops a power drill right onto a sheet of glass, which shatters instantly. "She says Marcus is always eating raw vegetables. Luna can *never* find out—she's already started making tea from cut grass!"

"It's not about the raw broccoli," insists Zanna. "Although I'm glad Morgan is on my side. Anyway, Cat, I just wanted—"

"I wish Morgan was on *my* side," I sigh, miserably collapsing onto my bed.

Zanna sighs impatiently. "Look. Phases of the moon aside, I think you should just talk to her about everything. But if you can't, maybe take her on a cute date? Get dinner or go rowing together and she'll forget all about you betraying her buddy scheme to Siobhan. You'll be groovy. Actually, that brings me back nicely to what *I* wanted to ask—"

"Zanna!" I gasp, sitting bolt upright. "You're a genius! That's exactly what I need to do! I'll take her on a date this weekend, somewhere really romantic . . ."

"It *is* the weekend," Zanna reminds me. "Today is Saturday."

I almost drop my phone, because for the love of Olaf the Snowman, Zanna isn't wrong. I've got less than a day to think

of something wonderful, before the moon turns pink as Dad's nose and I'll have to suffer another WEEK of Morgan malfunctions at school!

"I'd better get planning! Thanks so much, Zanna."

"But Cat!" protests Zanna. "I still haven't—"

I hang up the phone and dive for my laptop like a person struck by divine inspiration. Hmm, hmm, and hmm again. What would be the perfect date to win back Morgan's heart? Or *keep* Morgan's heart, as I haven't technically lost it . . . yet.

"Is that a pedalo shaped like a swan?" asks Morgan.

"No," I inform her proudly. "Morgan, that's a *Pedal O'Delaney*." At her blank stare, I clarify, "Because you're Irish, see? It's not just a pedalo. It's a *Pedal O'Delaney*."

"Yes, I get the joke," says Morgan. "It's just that my name isn't *O'Delaney*, is it? It's just Delaney, so the joke doesn't really work. You're just saying pedalo and then my name."

"Well, maybe we should just call it a paddleboat!" I declare as a nearby swan takes flight. Unfortunately, it also showers Morgan with lake water, so she's already looking damp and annoyed and we haven't even got into the boat yet.

We're in a park on the outskirts of Lambley Common. So much on the outskirts that it's actually another town and we had to take a bus, which I think is rather adventurous and romantic. Even if there were some weird Lad-o-lot Lads on the bus who kept asking for our phone numbers. To Morgan's horror, I gave them the number of my evil Gemini cousin, Lilac, which is great revenge for her signing me up to a South Dakotan cult.

The lake itself is huge and, according to the sign, 5.9 feet

deep. When I told Luna where I was going, she asked if I'd written a will. But there are a few pedalos already on the water, some even with children on board, so they can't be *that* dangerous. There's an island in the middle, covered in willows. *Sehr romantique* indeed! And you can't lose, organizing a water-themed date during Pisces Season. What could possibly go wrong?

I can't help noticing Morgan asking for an extra life jacket before climbing into the large floating swan. But then we pedalo out onto the lake and when I anxiously glance at my girlfriend, I see that—Aphrodite be praised—she's almost smiling!

"So?" I ask after a moment's bobbing. "Are you impressed?"

Morgan smirks. "That you managed to navigate an online booking system *and* use public transport without help? Very."

Okay—Morgan is in a good mood! Perhaps now is the right time to *Talk*?

"Morgan . . ." I begin. "About your idea that I may have given to Siobhan—"

"Let's not," Morgan interrupts. Then she takes my hand, gazing round the lake. "It's really beautiful here. I'm glad you thought of this. Honestly, the last thing I want to think about right now is Siobhan."

Score! We don't even have to get serious! I'm so smug, I may as well take up a career as a smuggler. For a few blissful minutes, we drift around the lake and everything is perfect. I really am very brilliant and wonderful. Especially when far, FAR away from all moody goths, Norwegian poets, and redheaded criminals. Morgan will never doubt me again if I'm able to orchestrate such excellent dates! Who knew a buoyant bird made from plastic could work such watery wonders?

Then Morgan says, "What the fresh heck? Is that Brooke?"

I am very tranquil, so I don't open my eyes. "No, Morgan, this is a lake. A brook is much smaller. More like a stream. I fell into one, remember?"

"No," says Morgan. "Cat, it's Brooke Mackenzie. She's on a pedalo!"

My eyes shoot open. WHAT THE FISHY FLIP-FLOP?! Praying that Morgan just has a smudge on her glasses again, like when she thought she saw a ghost in our kitchen, I sit up in the pedalo. But alas, the only thing smudging my vision is Brooke's offensively orange hair, powering toward us.

"This can't be happening . . ." I murmur, and Morgan grins.

"I know, right? What are the chances!" Then she stands up in the pedalo, which is very sexy and reckless. Something I'd enjoy a lot more if she wasn't waving for Brooke to come over. "Hey, girl! What are you doing here?! I thought you were banned from this park!"

Brooke's swan collides into ours, rocking us rudely. I almost drop my sunglasses! "I was," Brooke explains as I regain my balance. "For putting olive oil on the monkey bars in the playground. But then my mum started dating Pedalo Bill, so he put in a good word for me!"

"Sweet," says Morgan as I goggle in disbelief. Is she intentionally mishearing half of what Brooke is saying?! I'm beginning to think Brooke could gun down the Royal Family in front of us and Morgan would say it was chill. "Good for your mum. Me and Cat were just going to explore the island. Wanna tag along?"

WANNA WHAT?! I make rapid throat-cutting gestures at Morgan, but Brooke is already agreeing, sparkling about swan

nests by the willows, and then Morgan is pedaling off after her while I sit in unglamorous silence. Gooseberries galore! Can I not enjoy one afternoon of swan-themed romance without Brooke crooking about?!

Brooke leads us right into this boggy mud-patch by the island. "Baby swans are cute, but not as cute as baby ducks," she flaps away. "I just love that baby ducks are yellow?! It's one of my favorite colors, actually. I painted my whole room yellow once! Mum went ballistic because we were only staying there on holiday, so we had to repaint it blue again . . ."

I can't believe this. If yellow is her favorite color, WHY did she wear GREEN to my party in the first place?!

On and on Brooke goes, like a jabbering jack-in-the-box. It's exhausting! But Morgan seems to be having a great goose of a time, cooing over the nests. "Cat!" she simpers in a very uncool, un-Morgan-like way. "Come and see! They're so cute . . ."

I roll my eyes. I'm lying back in the tail of our swan, wishing I could just doze off. Morgan is snapping pictures on her phone and I glance at Brooke . . . who is loading unhatched eggs into a khaki tote bag. Wait—what?! I sit upright so suddenly, the whole swan rocks, and Morgan has to grip the bird's neck to steady herself.

"Cat!" she exclaims. "Watch it!"

I point at Brooke. "Look what she's doing!" I hiss, and Morgan glances round. But Brooke's just sitting in her boat looking totally innocent again! In fact, she raises a hand to wave. Morgan swivels back to me, shrugging in confusion.

"She seems to be waving?"

"Not that!" I insist. "Morgan, she was—"

"Guys, there's another nest here!" Brooke calls, and Morgan starts pedaling, jerking me back into the tail. I fall with a thud, then sit up, blowing a blond curl out of my eyes. That's IT! I'm going to watch Brooke as intensely as Luna watches the household recycling bins. If she tries sneaking another egg, I'm going to catch her red-handed! And redheaded, too.

"Wow, look!" Morgan gasps again, and I do. I look very suspicious.

I see Brooke reaching for another nest. "Morgan, *look*!" I hiss, and I jab at her. Only, Morgan is standing up, so I actually punch her in the back of the leg. Her knee buckles, and Morgan screams as she topples out of the boat and into the water.

I'm so shook up, I'm basically a maraca. Did I just push my girlfriend into the lake?! Brooke stares at me and I stare back, like a staring competition. Which I lose because I'm suddenly eyelash-fluttering and very flustered indeed. Oh my gooseberries. Oh my ACTUAL cashew-nut milkshake! WHAT HAVE I DONE?! I leap onto my knees and gaze into the water. Morgan's flapping about in the mud, baby swans squawking around her.

And that's when I hear honking. Fearfully, I look over my shoulder. Mighty Aphrodite! A huge swan is advancing toward us, wings spread like battle-axes. Are swans known for being very protective of their young?! We may be in deep trouble—5.9 feet of trouble, to be exact.

"Morgan, take my hand!" I squeal, reaching into the water. Brooke is pedaling manically toward us, THE SWAN IS COMING, and then just as Morgan takes my hand, there's an enormous *thud*—Brooke's swan colliding with mine—and I'm sent lurching

forward. More specifically, my forehead is launched right into Morgan's face.

"JESUS!" Morgan shrieks as her hand slips from mine and I am dizzied over onto my back in a highly inelegant fashion, the Princess of Swan Bog. My ex–ballet teacher would be weeping from shame all over again if she could see me now.

Suddenly, everything is blurred. There's a white blob, growing bigger and bigger, and for a moment, I think Morgan's face must have broken my skull and I am dead and this is an angel, descending from Heaven to whisk me away to Aphrodite's Lesbian Palace . . .

Then things swing back into focus and I see it's actually a swan, torpedoing toward us at terrifying speed. I open my mouth to scream. "GOOSEBERR—!" And that's when the swan crashes into the boat and sends me toppling back into the water.

What an absolutely web-footed woe-fest.

10
Ready to Be Romeo'd

And that's how I gave my girlfriend a black eye. The swan is fine, but I am not fine at all. Not only am I traumatized by the whole encounter, but I'm expected to pay for the broken pedalo as well! Thank goodness I still have those sneaky photos of Evil Cousin Lilac's bank card on my phone . . .

I try to stay calm. I mean, how bad can my situation really be? Do girls usually break up with you if you accidentally head-butt them in the face? Unfortunately, my internet sleuthing only reveals that this isn't actually a common problem, so I'm not sure where we go from here.

I do know one thing though. Brooke the Crook is RUINING my Amazing Aquarius Life. She's worse than the Worm Moon! How can Morgan not see that she's a car crash in human form?! So much for that useless horoscope about Geminis losing their rose-colored glasses. I think Morgan's glasses have been smelted onto her skull with a blowtorch! And it seems the only person with a pink-tinted aura of perfection is Brooke . . .

I spend all morning complaining to Zanna about how truly horrendous Brooke is. "BEING REDHEADED DOESN'T MEAN YOU HAVE A WILD AND EXCITING PERSONALITY!" I rage. "When will books and films learn?"

"Probably when they learn to stop casting identical white guys in literally every superhero movie," says Zanna. "So never."

I groan very deeply indeed. Mr. Derry, who is passing us in the corridors, widens his eyes in alarm, probably thinking I'm a hippo. "If I see that pixie nightmare girl one more time," I tell Zanna, "I may actually explode to death. What do I have next?"

"You have a rehearsal," says Zanna, smirking. "With Brooke."

I do not look amused, because I am not. I think if I were any less amused than I am right now, I would have to be a clown killer. But Zanna clearly doesn't share my unamused moods because she just sniggers away like the demon-breeder she is.

• ★ • ✦ • ★ •

When I walk into the drama studios (shockingly on time), Rich Elizabeth and her glossy drama-queen friends—Eliza, Ella, and Un-Alliterative Abigail—instantly start giggling like a gang of Goldilocks impersonators. Elizabeth says, "Cute shoes, chicka!"

"*So* cute," agrees Eliza, and Elizabeth smirks.

"Actually," Elizabeth drawls, "I don't want to be mean, babes . . . But they'll probably have more personality onstage than you will!"

"Lay off, Elizabeth," Maja chips in, emerging from the gothic shadows with Marcus. For a moment, my heart leaps—Morgan's friends will protect me! Then Maja goes, "Cat doesn't need bad vibes from you to mess this up. She'll do that fine on her own."

Then everyone is snorting and sniggering and I'm getting redder by the second. Only Marcus has the decency to actually smile at me, so I shuffle over to him. We stand there in silence and gay solidarity. Marcus says, "Don't worry about the others. Lots of people wanted to be Juliet, is all. No one's too chuffed it went to a non-drama student."

"But—but that's not fair!" I stammer. "I'm very high drama! And also, it's not like I wanted to be Juliet?! I didn't mean for any of this to happen! I auditioned by mistake!"

Marcus stares at me for a long time. Then he just shakes his head. "Yeah, you're still not getting it," he sighs. "And I am too gay and tired to explain it to you."

"Explain what?!" I ogle in panic to where people are handing five-pound notes to Rich Elizabeth. "You can't just say that, then stop! And why are they swapping money over there?"

"Oh, they're placing bets," says Marcus. "On how long you're going to last. Literally everyone thinks you're going to stack it and fail miserably. If you could make it to the fifth rehearsal though, that would work well for me."

I gaze at him like a dazed daddy longlegs. What was I thinking?! I can't do this! I'm no Juliet and all the rehearsing in the zodiac calendar won't change that. I swivel on my heel and head to the doors. Elizabeth can take the role and roll with it—I am OUT. So what if I have to help two opposing campaigns? Worst-case scenario, I'll just fake my own death!

Although if I do that, I may as well be Juliet after all . . .

Rushed and flushed as a red robin, I reach for the door handle. Then Brooke appears with Miss Spencer, swinging open the door with abounding enthusiasm. Right into my face.

BOOM goes my head, and I stumble back and collapse. Like a leprechaun on a surfboard, Brooke heel-skids into the room.

"Hey, everyone! Ready to be Romeo'd?!" Then she notices me, semi-unconscious on the floor. "Wow, Kitty! Are you all right?!"

• ★ . ✦ ˙ ★ •

I have the worst headache, but I'm not actually sure it's from the door. Miss Spencer sends Brooke *with* me to the school nurse, and she's been raving away the entire time. Even when I'm sitting in the nurse's office with an ice pack, gazing forlornly at Morgan's and Siobhan's campaign posters.

SIOBHAN SAYS NO TO SICKNESS. JUST STAY WELL.

VOTE MORGAN—WHO BELIEVES ALL THE SCHOOL NURSES SHOULD HAVE FIRST AID TRAINING.

UUUUURGH.

At least Morgan won't feel left out now that I have a matching black eye of my own.

"You'll be GRAND," Brooke calamities on. "You finally saw stars in the drama department, which is a first for Queen's! And you're going to be amazing as Juliet, too, Kitty, I just know it! Trust me, I've got a nose for talent. And men with a criminal record. Mum still has no idea how I found out her date was a drug dealer . . ."

"Brooke!" I interrupt at last, brandishing the ice pack at her. "Can you please calm down?! I'm actually injured over here, and you're doing my head in!"

We sit like silent salamanders for a few moments. Then Brooke says, "Sorry, Kitty. I don't mean to be annoying! I just am by nature. Just like you're really clumsy, you know? Always walking into things and falling over . . ."

"I'm not *always* walking into—" I begin, but Brooke just sighs.

"I'm actually quite jealous of you, Kitty. Everybody likes you! Well, except Elizabeth, and most of my drama class, but oh well. I'd like to be more like you, to be honest."

Brooke smiles and I goggle back, fully and genuinely confusioned. Brooke is *jealous* of me?! I'm not sure I understand. I literally gave myself an ear infection the first time I tried using a spray-on deodorant. No one is jealous of me!

"More like me?" I echo. "Brooke, are you sure you haven't hit *your* head?"

But Brooke springs to her feet, lively as a lemur, and starts opening all the cupboards and peering inside them. I'm not sure it's allowed, but I'm too concussed to care. "You've got the girl of your dreams, Kitty! And your friends. And you're so pretty. Don't say you're not—everyone thinks so! But the boy I like doesn't even look at me, even in my nicest dungarees."

I frown, removing the ice pack. "Who do you like? Is he in our year?"

"Yes," says Brooke, turning the taps on and off. She really is very random. "But he's the coolest guy in school, Kitty. He's way too popular and special to even *look* at a girl like me . . . Well, unless you talked to him of course."

Gooseberries, it's Kieran Wakely-Brown. I face-plant into my ice pack again.

"Oh, I don't know, Brooke . . ." I mumble, wondering exactly how Siobhan will execute Brooke if she finds out. She can get very possessive over her exes. "I think he's dating Elizabeth . . . !"

"He's in a band, Kitty!" Brooke plows on, and now I'm thrown because Kieran isn't in a band . . . Gosh, I really hope

he isn't anyway. He already swaggers all around school like he's Harry Styles on hair-swish pills. "He's so stylish and creative! I realized I liked him when he read out some of his lyrics in poetry class . . . He's so caring and . . . self-aware!"

Well, it definitely isn't Kieran. He literally has his own selfie as his lock screen!

Brooke gnome-squats before me, blue eyes awash with hope. "Kitty, would you talk to him for me? When I saw you outside the studios before our audition, I almost asked you, but I was worried you'd be mad at me, considering how close you are with him! But now that we're pals . . ."

Close? To a boy? Does she mean literally? Is there a boy in the room with us now? I look around just in case, but the room is empty.

"Brooke," I say impatiently. "I have no idea who you're talking about! I'm not close with any boys. I know nothing about them. It's the best thing about being a lesbian! Are you talking about Kieran Wakely-Brown or someone else?"

Brooke gazes at me, all glitter-eyed. Then she throws back her flaming hair and shrieks the most hysterical laugh, like a hyena mid–Heimlich maneuver.

"Kitty, you're hilarious! Kieran?! No way would I fancy THAT loser! I'm talking about Jamie Owusu!"

I gaze right back. Am I hallucinating? Did I hit my head and die in the drama studios and this is an alternate reality? Is there another Jamie Owusu in Lambley Common? Because surely Brooke cannot mean . . .

"I love his waistcoats!" Brooke adds.

Gooseberries galore. She *does* mean Jamie Owusu. *My*

ex-boyfriend. Pointy-shoed, cookie-dunking, guitar-sacrileging DISASTER Jamie Owusu, who once, in second grade, told me his dad was Batman, to "seem more cool." Suddenly, I feel like I want to smack my head into a door again, just to knock this newfound shocker into my brain.

Vibing on My Guitar

by Jamie Owusu

(Loosely based on "America" by Razorlight)

I'm like Buzz Lightyear,
Feeling things so deep.
Taylor Swift and Harry Styles
Mean so much to me . . .

Every day,
I'm vibing on my guitar . . .
Wa-ha-hey!
Notice me, Taylor Swift . . .
We could slay,
Vibing on our guitars,
Can I call you Tay?

11

The Skinniest Legend of Lambley Common

Jamie Owusu was my boyfriend for about three weeks last year. He was there and it was Libra Season. Mistakes happen, okay?! Once I became official with Morgan, I asked if she felt jealous of him, and she laughed until she cried. That is how unthreatening he is.

Since our breakup, Jamie has pursued his love of music with horrifying passion. His mum, Fran, is best friends with Mum, and Jamie often comes round on Saturdays when they have their so-called sewing group and shares his many woes. At least he can write about them in his terrible songs now. But then he went and started a band. As if the world isn't suffering enough already!

"It's me, my man Lucas, and our mate from skateboarding class, Ryan," he informed me one Saturday, nodding earnestly. "We're the Skinny Dippers."

We were drinking hot chocolate in my room, but when

Jamie said that, I literally spat mine all over my wall. Which took some explaining to Dad later, who walked in and thought I'd had a terrible accident thanks to Mum's chicken korma.

"Did you say the *Skinny Dippers*?!" I repeated in disbelief. I couldn't believe my eyes, ears, or celestial energies. This was too much.

Jamie said, "I've always admired birds, Cat. Not women—I'd never call a woman a bird, because that's disrespectful. But the dipper bird . . . That's a special one."

"Yes, but, Jamie . . ."

"There's a family of them in my backyard," he explained, stroking the body of his guitar. "I'd sing and play with my instrument and they'd come watch, so it felt only right to honor them. They inspired me to keep going, even when I had doubts about my music."

"Are you sure that's what they were trying to do?" I asked.

Apparently he called them the "Skinny" Dippers because they're "the skinniest legends in Lambley Common." I was absolutely gobsmacked when he told me the Chalky Lamb Pub had booked them for a gig, which (according to the posters Miss Jamison took down from the library) is next week. Although I have a sneaking suspicion that Jamie may actually have paid *them*, since he unexpectedly sold his *Gilmore Girls* box set.

The fact that Brooke thinks Jamie's cool is hysterical! I'm totally speechless, which is a bit awkward when Morgan and I are taking our romantic walk home from school. It's very important this walk goes well, so I've made Luna walk ten steps behind.

“Mum still blames Gwyneth Paltrow for the divorce,” Morgan is saying. “I miss eggs though. Like, what’s Easter without eggs? But Mum is adamant that the Delaney family is completely boycotting them.” There’s a pause. “Cat?”

“Sorry.” I grind to a halt in the middle of Lambley Common Green. A few feet behind, Luna stops, too. She rolls her eyes impatiently. “Morgan, I found out something shocking today—”

“If this is about earthquakes on the moon being called moonquakes, I already read your Instagram Stories,” Morgan says, brushing my hand brushaliciously. “All forty-five of them. But I really don’t think it’s that shocking—what else would they be called?”

“No, Morgan, it’s not about that! Although that *is* completely mind-blowing. Or is it moon-blowing? No, this is about Brooke Mackenzie. I found out who she fancies and you’ll literally never believe who it is!” I give a dramatic pause.

Luna starts moaning, “Can you just tell her, please? I have loads of homework, Cat. I don’t have time for dramatic pauses.”

Ignoring my sister, I announce, “JAMIE OWUSU!” and Luna lets out a long, frustrated groan. “She thinks his waistcoats are cool. Isn’t that the most tragic thing?”

I wait for Morgan to start losing her mind. Luna is flapping her hands, trying to get my attention and mouthing, “I NEED TO GO,” but I pretend not to notice. She really is so self-absorbed! Can’t she see we’re having an important conversation? Then, to my shock, Morgan says, “Aww, isn’t that cute? They’d be an adorable couple. We should set them up!”

My eyes widen. “Morgan, did you hear me? I said *Jamie Owusu*. My ex!”

"Yeah, isn't that perfect?" she says as I spiritually transcend my body. Luna checks her watch, then lets out a whimper. I suppose she's as horrified as me. "You could talk to him since you guys still hang out! Cat, would you? I'd really love it if you would."

I'd really love it if Jodie Comer asked for my hand in marriage, but some things just aren't likely to happen!

"Cat will think about it," Luna says, cutting between us and grabbing me by the wrist, "while I am thinking about all the algebra I have due tomorrow . . ."

But Morgan steals back my hand. It's deeply romantic and I go giggly.

"Maybe she can think about this, too," she says, then she kisses me deliciously.

"UUUUUURGH," I hear Luna going, then she's on the phone. "Mum, I NEEEED my own keys! PLEEEEASE? I've got deadlines and Cat's just snogging her girlfriend!" There's a pause. "No, I won't take a picture! MUM, GROSS?!"

"Okay," I sigh as Morgan slides her thumbs into my belt loops. "I'll think about it." Then we kiss some more as Luna rages on, beneath a pink and beautiful sunset.

•★.✦˙★•

The next morning, Mum strides into my room like she hasn't a care in the world, which she definitely should have, judging by the state of this bizarre new cardigan she's wearing. It looks like a load of seaweed caught in a fishing net. She says, "What a beautiful day! Where does the time go? I can't believe it's almost April!"

I can. I've felt every soggy moment of Pisces Season! If I'm

not crying about Morgan, I'm crying about the school play, or the Head Girl campaigns, or the fact that Mum still thinks it's okay to call me Cattykins in front of my friends. Does the humiliation never end? I'm in a highly stressful phase of my life, and Mum barreling into my private space like she's auditioning for *The Sound of Music* is exactly what I do NOT need.

"I'm not awake yet," I inform her.

Mum tears open my curtains. "You have school, Cat! Fran and I are having brunch in Sevenoaks, so it's chippity-chop and speedy spaghettis this morning—I'm on a tight schedule! Caroline's coming, too, so it's a proper Bitch 'n' Stitch group outing."

"Mum!" I groan, covering my ears. Why does she talk such nonsense? It's properly annoying avocadoes. "Please stop calling it that. It's a sewing group. You don't gossip about anyone anyway! Except me and Morgan. Which is also really embarrassing." What could be worse than Morgan's mum joining Mum's sewing group? Well, it could be my ex's mum also being there. Which she is. A truly knit-worthy nightmare.

"Fran tells me Jamie's band has their first gig soon!" Mum plows on. "I hope you'll be popping along to show some support. Take Morgan! She likes music, doesn't she?"

I could tell Mum that nobody who likes music should be subjected to the Skinny Dippers, but she's still under the astonishing delusion that Jamie's actually talented. I bury myself in my pillow to avoid talking to her, but Mum, who couldn't catch a hint if it was glued into the palm of her hand, sits on the end of my bed and takes my hand. What in the name of Zsa Zsa Gabor is she doing?

"I know it must be difficult," says Mum earnestly. "Seeing

other girls chase after Jamie when it didn't work out for the two of you. Jealousy is natural, especially since Jamie's so cool and musical now. He must have so many young ladies interested!"

I stare at Mum like she's speaking Swahili. And she may as well be, for all the sense she's making. How is it possible to be so deeply, deeply wrong?

"Mum," I inform her, very slowly so she understands. "I am not jealous. The only person who fancies Jamie is Morgan's annoying new friend! She's the most annoying person in my life after you, in fact."

This seems to catch Mum's interest. Which is very unfortunate since I'd actually just like her to leave. "And what's so annoying about this girl?" she asks.

I may be desperate, but am I really desperate enough to confide in my own mother? She ogles away though, so I cave. "She's just always . . . there! Like, who crashes a date?! But Morgan doesn't seem to care. It's very Gemini and annoying of her. Not that you'd understand."

I put my pillow on my face again. But Mum sighs one of her parenting sighs, and I worry I am in for a life sermon. "Do you remember Donna? She came to our sewing group right after her divorce."

I lift my pillow. "Thatched-Roof Hair Donna?"

Mum snaps her fingers. "The very same! Well, Fran kept inviting her along because she was lonely, but we didn't really gel. Donna wanted us to join forces with the widows' sewing group, Weaving 'n' Grieving, but I wasn't keen! They're all older women, so you never know, well . . ." Mum lowers her voice. ". . . *how they'll feel about lesbians.*"

"STOP WHISPERING 'LESBIANS'!" I exclaim. "It isn't 1856!"

"Well, I'm never sure how comfortable you are, darling!" Mum chuckles as I attempt to smother myself to death. "You didn't like it when I put that bumper sticker on the car."

"That's because it was MY FACE printed onto a rainbow flag!" I splutter, lifting the pillow again. "Siobhan still has a picture of it on Instagram . . ."

"Anyway, my point is," continues Mum, as if there is ever a point to anything she says, "I solved my little problem with a lovely spot of matchmaking! Do you remember my work friend Neal?"

I frown. "Tesco Meal-Deal Neal?"

"That's him! Well, I introduced Donna to him, and what do you know? Donna disappeared once she had a flashy new man in her life. So you never know, love. Maybe introducing this friend of Morgan's to Jamie could solve two birds at once!"

She finally leaves me to get dressed after that. I'm going to be late for school and it's all because of her! And because I fall asleep for another twenty minutes, but mainly because of her. I slowly and carefully do my makeup in the mirror, which is a very therapeutic distraction from Mum and Luna shrieking that we have to go. Because what if, by some miraculous coincidence, Mum has actually had a half-decent idea?

Could offloading Brooke the Crook onto Jamie actually fix my Delaney Dilemma? To quote Carly Rae Jepsen: maybe. And with the Pink Moon blossoming on the horizon, they'll both be perfectly ripe and desperate for love! I may be the sparkiest matchstick maker since Emma Woodhouse . . .

POTENTIAL SHIP NAMES FOR BROOKE AND JAMIE

- Jookie
- Brie (Larson . . . *Sigh.*)
- Jamoke Hokey Pokey
- Bray Me (???)
- Joke. Hmm.

12
Daring to Go Delaney

Absolute scenes at break time, despite my developing master plan. Me and Zanna have just had French and I am explaining to her, at great length, that I really don't think it's fair I got another detention. How was I supposed to know it was an interactive whiteboard?!

"Maybe because you've been in that classroom multiple times a week for almost five years, and it's never not been an interactive whiteboard?" Zanna suggests. "You really should have stopped drawing when Miss Ward said 'Stop' for the second time."

"But Zanna," I explain patiently. "How am I supposed to know she meant 'stop' in English? It could be French for 'good job' for all I know!"

Zanna pauses walking. She lowers her glasses to take a good, long look at me. "We have exams in a few months and you still don't even know the French for 'good job'? Cat, I really worry you are too clueless to survive in the adult world."

"It's lucky I'm only fourteen, then," I say.

"You're fifteen," Zanna reminds me, and I scowl. Gooseberries! Why is Zanna so often right? "Also," she continues annoyingly, "I still need to tell you about something. But I don't want Siobhan to know, else she'll totally hijack it, so can you keep a secret?"

We're approaching the picnic tables now, so Siobhan is likely not far away. I say, "Oui, oui, mon petite fleur . . . J'ai can, er, keep une secret. See, Zanna?! French! J'habite so talented . . ."

"Cat!" interrupts Zanna, scowling herself for once. "Can you please just listen? I'm actually having mad anxiety about this, and I really need—"

But she's cut off by a bone-tingling SCREAM. We stare at each other like startled hens, then rush around the corner to the picnic tables. We're confronted by Luna and the whole gang on their feet, Habiba holding Siobhan back by her ponytail. But it seems Siobhan's conditioner really is amazing, because her hair slides out of Habiba's hands and she charges for my sister. What has Luna done?! (Apart from all the annoyingness, of course.)

Then Zanna nudges me and points, and I notice Niamh has climbed into the branches of the nearest tree. Ah. Siobhan begins jumping, lunging for her sister's feet.

"ARE YOU ACTUALLY SERIOUS?" she yells. "MY OWN BLOOD! YOU BACKSTABBING, TREE-SNOGGING, TOAD-LICKING ***TRAITOR***!" Siobhan rushes for the trunk like she might actually climb it herself! An admirable venture, in her McQueen heels. But my death-wishing sister, bold as the ozone layer, grabs Siobhan by the shoulder and drags her back, then stands there, face-offing in a true Scorpio showdown. Up above, Niamh's holding a stack of green-colored paper, and a few sheets drop like falling leaves from her shaking hands and bluster to our feet.

Zanna crouches and picks one up. It's a poster with a (particularly dashing) picture of Morgan with the tagline *Dare to Go Delaney*. Aphrodite in a nightie, this surely can't be what it looks like . . .

Niamh is campaigning against her own sister?

"Firstly, Niamh's never licked a toad," says Luna defiantly. "It was a kiss, and it was a frog. And secondly, just because we're supporting Morgan for Head Girl doesn't mean we don't love you, Siobhan!" she continues, death wish clearly expanding by the second, and my eyes widen in Aquarius aghastitude. "It's not personal, it's about veganism. Morgan is going to take our Vegan Meals Initiative to the headmistress!"

"MORGAN WILL BE TAKING YOU TO THE *SCHOOL NURSE* ONCE I'M FINISHED WITH YOU!" Siobhan rages, swiping some posters from Luna's grasp.

She spins around and throws them all over the gathering crowd. (Which is actually *spreading* Morgan's word, technically speaking, but I decide not to risk my life by pointing this out.) Jasmine McGregor hoots away about suing if she gets paper cuts.

"HOW COULD YOU DO THIS TO ME?!" Siobhan shrieks up at Niamh, crushing two posters in her fists. "I'VE EATEN *ASPARAGUS* FOR YOU!"

"Didn't you wrap them in bacon?" Luna murmurs, but

Niamh finally drops down from her branch and stands before her sister.

Habiba, Siobhan's self-appointed media manager, holds up her phone.

"Siobhan, listen!" Niamh says, Celtic rings clattering as her hands tremble. "I'm sorry. I didn't want you to find out this way, but it really is just about the lunches! Think of all the animal lives we'll save . . . We could be eating asparagus every day! Isn't that what we all want?"

There's a moment where nobody says anything. I grimace at Zanna.

Siobhan's eyes narrow and Niamh backs slowly toward the trunk. "I'm going to open an entire sausage factory," Siobhan hisses. "And I'm going to NAME IT AFTER YOU!" Then she swivels on her heel and marches back to the picnic tables, where Habiba and Kenna flock around her like protective worker bees.

"This is going to be fun," Zanna says, beside me.

I look at the poster in my hand. *Sacré jaune*.

• ★ . ✦ ˙ ★ •

And that's how Niamh came to move in with us. She showed up at the iPhone Box half an hour ago with a suitcase full of kaftans and a bamboo-infused Indonesian blanket. Luna is telling Mum it's either here with us or Niamh will have to seek asylum in the German embassy.

"They have really good policies on climate change over there," Niamh explains tearfully as Luna strokes her hand. They're wearing matching khaki-green hair scarves and look like they grow their own food for fun. Which they do, actually.

"Well, I suppose it's not a problem." Mum sighs, agitatedly tapping her foot. "But I'll have to call your mother. I can't have her worrying!" Then she calls Miriam Collingdale and spends almost two entire hours discussing the latest episode of *Gardeners' World*.

Morgan rings me up when I'm being productive later in the evening (lying on my bed and watching "Best of Melissa McCarthy" compilations on YouTube while texting Zanna that I am MUCH too busy with important goings-on and weird vegans moving into my house to talk now). Morgan says, "Hey, babe," which is always a very gooey experience. "You good? You've been very quiet today."

"I am perfectly splendid, Morgan," I chime, deciding to skip the whole Niamh saga. She will find out soon enough anyway, if Habiba's livestream was as detailed as Zanna warned me. The last thing I want is to give Morgan ANY excuse to dislike Siobhan more. Even I must admit, throwing her sister out of the family home doesn't exactly shower her in sunlight. More importantly, I have to discuss my amazing mistress plan for Brooke!

"Actually, I have groovy news!" I say. "I think I can help Brooke. Jamie has a gig next Thursday. Maybe we could take Brooke along and introduce them? But Morgan, I have a very important condition."

The line crackles. "It's not a medical condition, is it?" Morgan asks. "Has your fungal infection from last year come back? I still can't believe Zanna did a whole presentation about it in biology."

"No, Morgan, it's not—" I blink, startled as a star-crossed

lover. "Wait. Did she actually?! I'm going to kill—" I take a deep breath. "For the last time: it wasn't an infection; it was a bruise. And no, my condition is that the next time we hang out, it's just us. I want us to have a cute and normal date. It's nearly Aries Season, so we should be able to tell each other what we really want and I want us to make more time for each other."

I hold my breath like a puffer fish and wait. The line crackles some more. Then Morgan says, "Sorry, babe. I know I've been really preoccupied recently, and the friendship drama hasn't done us any favors." There's a pause as I process this understatement to end all understatements. "But hey, there's this new horror film I'd love to see this weekend? It could be a cute date."

Zanna won't let me watch horror films anymore—not since my screaming led to the police being called to her house that time. But that was in seventh grade, long before I knew Morgan, so perhaps I have matured enough to cope? Hmm . . .

"I'd absolutely love that," I tell her. "Horror! Exactly my thing."

Then we talk a lot about Sarah Paulson, as lesbians do. When we eventually hang up, I'm very hazy and happy. But I always am when it's just us and the rest of the world is happening somewhere else. Maybe the key to this relationship staying perfect forever is *literally* a key. To a room that no one else can enter.

Aries
SEASON

Group Chat: The Gang

Cat, 4:54 p.m.:
WELCOME TO ARIES SEASON GUYS!!!!

It's going to be RUTHLESS so remember to SAY WHAT YOU WANT! BE ASSERTIVE! Make the change you want to see *HAPPEN*!!!!!!

Zanna, 4:55 p.m.:
I want you to shut up

Cat, 4:56 p.m.:
That's really not very in the spirit of things, Zanna

Zanna, 4:56 p.m.:
I see it didn't work, then

Siobhan, 4:56 p.m.:
I WANT VICTORY, AND TO CRUSH ALL THOSE WHO OPPOSE ME.

Habiba, 4:57 p.m.:
I want Imaran to be more open with me about his #RelationshipGoals

He's been so distant lately :(

Siobhan, 4:59 p.m.:
OM-ACTUAL-G YOU ARE SUCH A LOSER.

AND LOSERS WON'T HELP ME WIN HEAD GIRL.

ARE YOU A LOSER HABIBA?

Habiba, 5:01 p.m.:
#WINNING is my whole personality babe!!!xxx

We can talk about Imaran later!!!xox

Zanna, 5:03 p.m.:
do we absolutely have to?

13

Penguins at the Disco

Dust me down and hurl me into the sunlight—Aries Season is here! If my *Bible to the Stars* is correct (and Dad reckons there's a whole ten-percent chance that it is), now is the perfect time to set important plans in motion, take on the world and ALL of its moons, and steamroller anyone who stands in my way . . . Which sounds like the perfect confirmation from the great starry sky that tonight is going to work. I shall set up Brooke the Crook with Jamie and she will finally be gone from my Amazing Aquarius Life with Morgan Delaney.

"This is so exciting." Brooke is hyperventilating. "I never go out like this, even though I'm a Leo." My eyes widen. Didn't Brooke say she was a LIBRA?! Before I can call this out, she babbles on, "Usually, I just go shoplifting. Or I'm putting trip wires all over the skateboard park. Do you think I'm wearing the right clothes?"

I blink at her. "You do WHAT?!"

Morgan squeezes my hand extra-tight. "You look great, B,"

she says, and I cough in shock. Brooke gets a nickname now? Her name is one syllable long! Also, her outfit is . . . Well, would we call a hoodie an "outfit"? According to Morgan, it's what's on the inside that counts. But I'm not sure that will do Brooke much good, either. Morgan says, "Me and Cat are gonna look after you, so don't worry. It'll be a really fun night!"

Who is she trying to convince? Anxiously eyeing the roundness of the moon and hearing echoes of the doom-filled pancake, I squeeze Morgan's hand back and silently pray to Aphrodite that Jamie hasn't planned a long set. All the Aries Season determination in the world isn't enough for my ears to cope.

The Skinny Dippers are performing at the Chalky Lamb, which is universally acknowledged as the worst pub in Lambley Common. When I told Dad where we were going, he made me bring hand sanitizer and told me not to go near the food.

"My mate Steve ate there last year . . ." he said, grimacing.

I grimaced, too. Mainly, because Dad just used the word "mate," even though he's disturbingly middle-class. "What happened to Steve?" I asked.

Dad looked right at me. "Dead. Poisoned. His whole face turned green . . ."

"David!" Mum scolded from the kitchen as Dad chuckled like some dusty old dustbin with a cough. "Don't say things like that! You know Cat's very gullible."

"I'm right here!" I protested.

"Well, nowhere is perfect," said Dad, and Mum burst out laughing. They really are the absolute worst! And I *still* don't know what happened to Dad's friend Steve . . .

Anyway, the Chalky Lamb is on the corner of an ugly roundabout. It has rickety and uneven walls, not because it's old and pretty, but because cars keep driving into it. There are three different memorial plaques around the front door, and lots of bouquets of dead flowers. And some worryingly fresh-looking ones as well . . . There are a surprising number of people slouching around, including Kieran Wakely-Brown and his Lad Friends! My eyes properly pop.

"It's Wildcat!" cheers Imaran Kalmati, waving a beer bottle at me. How did he buy that?! He's fifteen!

I scowl. "You're not supposed to call me that anymore. I've got Siobhan on speed dial!"

That shuts them up. Then Zach Collins asks Morgan if she wants to sit in his lap. Two minutes later, when he's lost his stool to Morgan in an arm-wrestling match, I sit in Morgan's lap and the boys watch us forlornly. Everything smells of beer and Axe deodorant, a truly heterosexual daydream—and a homosexual nightmare. The last gig I went to with Morgan was in London. It was sapphic and awesome and very, *very* different from tonight. Yikes.

As if to prove this further, Jamie comes bounding onto the little stage with his tragic bandmates, Loser-Fest Lucas and Unoriginal Ryan. Brooke gasps. "Wow, guys, look at Jamie! Isn't he such class?"

Jamie looks like Jamie always looks. Like a beanpole in a waistcoat, accessorized with a random guitar. But I'm trying to convince Brooke here, which might take a lot of work, depending on what Jamie chooses to sing, so I nod very earnestly and say, "Yes, totally groovy!" All very convincing.

"Good evening, Lambs!" Jamie announces with a wink at the crowd. One man instantly stands up and leaves. "Glad to see you've been shepherded our way . . . We are the Skinny Dippers . . ." There's a roar of laughter. "And we have some clanger tunes!"

"Banging tunes," Lucas corrects him.

"GET IN THERE, JAMIE, MY SON!" a Lad Friend bellows, and everyone cheers. Meanwhile, I'm wondering if it's worth mummifying myself in duct tape to avoid this. Does Morgan realize how truly awful this is going to be? Then Jamie begins his version of Madonna's "Holiday." He calls it "an ode to inclusivity." Sappho strike me down.

"We are a diverse band . . . We have someone from every nation!

I'm Black and Ryan's white . . . And Lucas is a quarter Asian!

But we still vibe . . . ! And vibes are important, o'yeah . . ."

They warble on. I cringe especially painfully when all three of them put their heads together and sing, *"WE NEED SOMEONE WHO'S GAAAAA-AY!"* Brooke actually nudges my knee and points at me and Morgan, and I have to go, "HAHAHA" without exploding.

Which would be another great way of avoiding this actually . . .

As I daydream about plastic explosives, Brooke sighs away, and Morgan gawps at the stage with what I can only assume is utter shock and astonishment. The Skinny Dippers disaster their way through three thrillingly horrendous songs. Then they do "Holiday" again by mistake. Finally it's the intermission, and Jamie comes grinning over to me.

"Cat-Attack!" He drags me into a hug and I inhale part of his pocket handkerchief. "How's my sister from another mister? So psyched you came to see me play! Think you'll be a Mini Skinny? That's what we're calling our fans."

"I have no words," says Morgan, and Jamie grins in thanks.

I nervy-laugh. "Wow, yes! Thank you for that, Jamie! You were absolutely terrible. Um, I mean, terrific?! YES! Really, really, um, unique." He looks thrilled, so before I can car-crash this conversation further, I hook Brooke by the elbow and yank her over. "Jamie, this is Brooke! She's . . . Well, she's red-haired!"

Gooseberries. Is that all I could think to say?!

Luckily, Jamie is as clueless as ever and extends a hand. "Thanks for coming, Brooke! I'm digging the hoodie. Are you the same Brooke who spray-painted all those gravestones at my church? I know about it because I volunteered to clean them! Those neon colors were especially tricky but . . ." He flexes his shoulders. "Nothing a bit of muscle can't handle."

Morgan sneezes into her drink and I go, "AHAHAHA! Oh my SCROL, Jamie, aren't you funny?! But you're definitely mistaken, that was, um . . . Definitely someone else! Brooke doesn't do insane things like that, do you, Brooke?"

"Nope!" says Brooke, then nobody says anything at all. I stare at her freckled face, dumbfounded. Brooke, who usually talks faster than Eminem on energy drinks, is absolutely silent. I want to shake her by the shoulders.

Then my phone starts buzzing. Perfect—it's Zanna! Just the get-out clause I need for this awkward-armadillo-fest. "Um, I'd better answer this!" I babble, grinning hysterically at Morgan. "Why don't you all stay here and . . . um . . . I'll be right back!"

I rush outside, narrowly avoiding a veering motorbike, and answer the phone.

"ZANNA!" I exclaim. "Thank goodness it's you. I was just in the most horrendous situation. How did you know?! It's like when you called me just as I was about to burn those used hair-spray cans. You absolutely saved my life!"

"Right," says Zanna. "Well, that was ridiculous. Who burns hairspray cans? But I'm actually calling because I need your help. Which I know is unusual—"

"Are you sure?" I grimace, leaning against a memorial plaque. "Because I'm actually trying to help someone right now and it's going terribly! You won't believe where I am!"

"Where?" Zanna asks. "I can hear rumbling. Cat, you're not skateboarding again, are you? I've told you already, Morgan can't be impressed with you if you're dead."

"I'm not going to die!" I gasp exasperatedly. "Unless it's from embarrassment . . ." I glance over my shoulder and yikes myself yellow. Brooke and Jamie are just shuffling their feet around like penguins at the disco and Morgan is nowhere to be seen! "Brooke is being totally useless! Zanna, how can someone have zero social skills?"

"Brooke?" interrupts Zanna. "You're with Brooke the Crook?!"

Gooseberries, I didn't mean to mention that! Zanna is definitely going to lecture me. "It's no biggie!" I babble at once. "I'm just helping her get a boyfriend! Morgan asked me, but Zanna, if I have to talk about boys anymore, I actually might move to Lesbos. I didn't come out for this! It's really hard work, pretending to be excited over some boring straight guy."

There is silence on the other end of the phone. Then Zanna

says, "Cool. Well, I guess you should get back to helping Brooke, then. Sorry to have bothered you."

Then she disappears. I wave the phone around. Did I lose connection? I text her, but she doesn't reply. Hmm. It's almost like I said something wrong . . . I'm glum-frowning at Zanna's chat thread and walk right into some old man's shirty back as I return to the pub.

"Watch it!" he begins angrily, then he sees me and his frown softens. "Oh, you're a wee one! Never mind, love." Then he frowns again. "Aren't you a bit *too* wee to be in here?!"

I hesitate. "Um . . . I'm fifteen?"

This catches the attention of the man behind the bar, who looks like a pug dog with enormous eyebrows. "Can't be in here by yourself if you're under eighteen, love."

"It's all good, mate," says Imaran, rapping the bar. "She's with me."

"But you're fifteen as well!" I blurt out, and all the Lad Friends go silent.

The pug man furrows his brow in an eyebrow avalanche. "You're what? Your ID said you were twenty-three! I've served you lot drinks!"

Imaran spins around. "RUN!"

Lad Friends flee toward me like wood lice from an upturned flowerpot. In pub-induced panic, I glance around for Morgan and Brooke—who's in the corner with Jamie Owusu, kissing him right on the lips.

Green grapes galore. It's enough to turn me vegan!

Chat Thread: Zanna Szczechowska

Cat, 9:09 p.m.:
Zanna?? Where did u go???

???

Are u there Zanna???

??

Zanna, 10:19 p.m.:
No

Cat, 10:21 p.m.:
Oh okay sorry

WAIT

14

The Saggy in Sagittarius

It might be a bit awkward back at school, seeing how I got everybody thrown out of the pub. Imaran's photo is being circulated all around town and even the Skinny Dippers had to leave once they found out Jamie was not nineteen, like he told them on the phone.

"It was artistic license," he explained while we were all lurking around the parking lot, his guitar in one hand and Brooke in the other. "You can't play by the rules to rule the world, Cat-Attack."

If I have to hear Jamie call me Cat-Attack one more time, I may have to rocket-launch myself into the sun. But, apart from that, the evening was a success! Morgan is very pleased with me and Brooke seems to have had a waistcoated whale of a time, although I don't know who I am judging more: Brooke, for getting with Jamie, or Jamie, for getting with Brooke.

"At least I should finally have my girlfriend to myself now,"

I tell Zanna when updating her on my chaotic Thursday night. "That's what matters most!"

"Yeah," says Zanna. "I'm aware."

"Although it's amazing the police officer actually believed Imaran's story. He looks nothing like an old lady, even in the coat!"

"Cool," says Zanna.

The bell rings and Mrs. Warren, our homeroom teacher, enters the classroom, looking about as jolly as a grave-digging grandma. Or as jolly as Zanna, since she's just sitting there, leafing through a copy of *The Bell Jar,* like Sylvia Plath in spectacles.

"Zanna," I say impatiently. "Elsa building an ice palace with magic is cool. I just gave you the absolute hottest gossip. How are you not losing your mind right now?"

"I'm fine," says Zanna.

"Well, you shouldn't be!" I elbow her. "You should be losing your mind!"

"I'm not in the mood, Cat."

"Cathleen Phillips!" Mrs. Warren rises to her feet like a Norwegian winter. Me and Zanna go quiet as garden gnomes and Mrs. Warren shark-drifts over. "Well, well, well. Why am I not surprised that when I'm sharing the bulletin with the class, it is you who considers it acceptable to interrupt me? Anything you'd like to share with us, Cathleen?"

"No, Miss," I mumble, eyes on my desk.

"No, I shouldn't think so," says Mrs. Warren. "One more interruption and I shall have you dictate your entire conversation in French. Miss Ward tells me you've missed three

homework assignments of late, so you'll be needing the practice all the more."

She's actually wrong. It's FIVE homework assignments. But since I'm not allowed to interrupt, I keep that to myself. I don't say anything for the rest of homeroom, and neither does my saggy-faced Sagittarius sidekick.

Well, Zanna may be all gloomy Tuesdays for no reason, but Brooke is completely sunny Saturdays at rehearsal. Miss Spencer, who must be some sort of masochist, lets Brooke organize the warm-up, so we all have to jog around the studios in character.

"Like a criminal!" says Brooke, and we all put our hands in our pockets.

"Like a princess!" We all put on airy-fairy smiles and drift along.

"Like a snobby old woman!" Rich Elizabeth just walks in her normal way.

But how am I supposed to focus on important tasks, like walking in funny ways, if my favorite Slav is suffering? It's very hard to be dreamy-at-the-seamy Juliet with so much tragedy taking place. Also, Rich Elizabeth won't stop glaring at me. I may have laughed, long and lusciously, at her Nurse costume, but does she have to be so rude?!

"WRONG," she announces mid-scene. "CUT! Miss Spencer, Cat said her line wrong AGAIN! The line is 'And stint thou too, I pray thee, nurse, say I,' and Cat said, 'Isn't thou tooth in praline, nurse.' It's not even remotely similar!"

"Come off it, Elizabeth," Brooke says. "Don't you have

enough lines of your own to worry about? You know, for the comedy Nurse role you landed?"

As Brooke breaks down pixie-giggling, Elizabeth's face turns beetroot ballistic. "I CAN'T WORK LIKE THIS! When people get their lines wrong, it ruins my flow."

"There's a pill for that," says Brooke, and everyone hoots away like a roomful of Jasmine McGregors (a frightening concept indeed). Even Morgan's motionless friends, Maja and Marcus, can't resist cracking a smile.

"All right, Brooke, settle down!" says Miss Spencer, although even she's tittering. "Cat, Elizabeth makes a good point. Make time to learn these lines! But your energy is magnetic! I can see you shaking with emotion—it's very powerful!"

I didn't even realize I was moving, so that's not good! I teeth-chatter my way through the rest of rehearsal, and Elizabeth only yells "CUT" fifteen more times (not including the time where she goes, "Someone just cut my throat! PLEASE, I'm begging you!").

Then, horror of horrors, Jamie shows up at the studios. He tap-dances through the double doors in his strange pointy shoes and grins right at me.

"Jamie!" I shriek. "What are you doing here?"

"Oh, you know," he says, although I obviously don't, or why would I be asking? "Just here to show support for my leading lady." Then he does this terrifying wink.

"Um . . ." I let out a strangled laugh. "That's very flattering, but—"

"HEY, BABE!" Brooke interrupts me, and she clatters over and kisses Jamie on the lips in front of absolutely everyone.

Rich Elizabeth gasps. "Thanks so much for coming! Shall we go get cappuccinos? I think there's one café in town that will still serve me."

Oh, bell-ringing Romeos galore. Jamie meant Brooke, not me (thank Sappho . . .).

"So it looks like you two have . . . um . . . really hit it off!" I say in complete bamboozlement. Mum's idea actually worked! It's a practically historic event.

"Yeah, since the gig, we've become really close." Jamie gazes into Brooke's eyes, one arm slung loosely over her shoulders, like a snapped stem of grass.

"Since the gig," I repeat. "As in . . . last night? Literally sixteen hours ago?"

"It's so nice to find someone and just click!" Jamie snaps his fingers. Once Brooke has un-dislocated his knuckle, we carry on talking. Jamie drones through their loved-up texts, how much he's been laughing, and says, "When you know, you know. You know?"

"No," I say. "I mean, absolutely!"

"I hope you find this someday, Kitty!" says Brooke, bounding off with Jamie down the corridor like an accident waiting to happen. "It really is the grooviest!"

"I HAVE A GIRLFRIEND!" I call after them. And then I kick my heels in absolute joy! Because I do have a girlfriend, and I am going on a date to the cinema with her this weekend, and everything is going to be perfect and wonderful again because Brooke won't be there! The Worm Moon has *finally* been and gone—and Morgan's surfaces remain undisturbed. I really love solving all my problems at once. Who knew it could be so easy?

At least my daily problem of who I eat lunch with is a quick fix today. Morgan has a doctor's appointment—it's been nearly two weeks, but her black eye is still throbbing painfully at night (ahem), so I'm free to just jangle about with the gang. But when I find them in the cafeteria, Siobhan chasing the sixth graders off our favorite table with a water pistol, Zanna is nowhere in sight!

"Where's Zanna?" I ask, sitting down.

Alison is drying off her seat with a napkin. "I haven't seen her, actually . . . Maybe she's at the Slavic Society?"

"I hope to Zendaya's zebra-patterned sunglasses that she's not!" Siobhan rages. "I told you all to QUIT your sad-fest so-ci-e-ties! How are we supposed to focus on my campaign if you lot insist on having lives? It's bad enough that Cat's dancing about being Shakespeare."

"Juliet," I correct her. "And I'm not dancing!"

"Thank goodness," says Habiba. "Remember when you auditioned for the dance squad?" The mere mention of this has everyone falling about laughing.

I glower. My friends really could do with slightly worse memories. But the point is, no one knows where Zanna is. After lunch, I go all around the school searching for her, like a wandering spirit with sad eyes. I even go to the library, risking a confrontation with Mrs. Bullock. Luckily, she's busy making a sixth grader cry, but she still glares me down, her amphibian eyelids swiveling sideways as I pass.

Then it's afternoon homeroom, and Zanna isn't there either. Mrs. Warren just tuts away and marks a big X in the register. After school, I call Morgan and update her on the situation.

Which is a welcome distraction from Luna and Niamh doing "scream yoga" next door.

"Listen, babe," says Morgan over the sound of a knife on a chopping board. She read online that eating pineapple heals black eyes, so it's now absolute pineapples aplenty. She even poured fruit juice into her bath last night, but apparently it stung in places it shouldn't, so she probably won't again. "I know Zanna is your best friend. Actually, she's probably the only friend of yours I like . . ."

"What about Habiba?" I suggest hopefully. "She ran a marathon for Islamic Relief!"

"Her gym videos on Instagram are so self-involved," explains Morgan. "And she always intentionally picks Maja last in PE. If you don't drink charcoal smoothies, you're basically wallpaper to that girl. Anyway, I know Zanna is always there for you . . . But she does have a life outside you. And that's healthy. You wouldn't want her to be some soulless follower like Kenna Brown."

Morgan can speak for herself! Say what you like about Kenna: she still left a George Ezra concert just three songs in because Siobhan got her hair caught in a zipper and required emergency assistance. She zipped right to the rescue, you could say.

"Maybe I should text her again," I muse. "Just to make sure she's alive."

"Yes," agrees Morgan. "Because being dead is literally the only reason she might not be available. Hey, do you have any red onions? Apparently, they ease inflammation."

“Hmm,” I say. “That doesn’t sound real.”

Half an hour later, with an entire onion placed onto my own black eye (which is more a faint yellow by now), I pick up my phone again. I do what any good friend would do and send Zanna clown memes. Including a selfie of myself to see if she’ll spot the difference. But time ticks on, clowns unicycle by, and still I have no word from my Sagittarius soul mate. Highly saggy scenes, with violins playing.

WHAT YOU NEED TO KNOW ABOUT HABIBA QADIR

- She's a Virgo, so technically, she's the oldest one in the gang. But Siobhan doesn't appreciate being second, in any way, so Habiba tells everyone she's a Capricorn instead. Since these are both very boring signs, I shouldn't think this makes much difference. Let's just be thankful that she's not a Taurus.
- She's the captain of the netball team and uses all her trophies as water glasses at her house. It's not the modesty you'd expect from a Virgo. It's probably because she's a *secret* Virgo though.
- Her Fitstagram has over fifteen thousand followers. And while I don't want to say that it's because she posts a lot of squatting videos . . . It's because she posts a lot of squatting videos. She even has a hashtag: #HotLikeHabibASS
- She's going out with Imaran Kalmati, which is a tragic waste! He looks twenty-nine and smokes cigars. I have no idea what they talk about, but they have to date in secret because Habiba's dad said, "If I find that hairy brute in your walk-in closet again, I'll rearrange his teeth! Capiche?"
- I don't know what "capiche" means, but it's probably something to do with the fruit Habiba is always eating. Her lifelong dream is to make her own brand of peach-based energy bars. I blame her fake-Capricorn sun for not being more ambitious.

15
An Unhelpful Maneuver in the Dark

Zanna's wuthering and dithering will have to wait. The Pink Moon will be on its milky way, and I have my Sunday date with Morgan Delaney, where I must prove that we work, no matter what phase the moon is in. It's important that Morgan is reminded how gaga-gorgeous I am, so I hurl myself toward the mirror first thing and cuckoo-clock my face to Kathmandu with concealer, eye shadow, mascara, and Lip Gloss Lizzie's most highly recommended lip gloss.

Then I imagine Morgan breaking up with me, leaving me to face December's Cold Moon alone, and cry it all off, so I have to start over again. Gooseberries! Isn't Pisces Season over?! Why do I *still* feel like I'm on some cursed roller coaster of trauma?!

"You're hormonal," Luna tells me over a breakfast of tofu-based waffles. "That's why your T-zone looks like that. I really love that you're going with your natural skin though! It's so empowering. Which I would never expect from someone as spineless as you."

I goggle her, aghast. "I'm wearing a full face of makeup, Luna!"

Luna blinks at me and Niamh hides her face in her nauseating food. "Yes, of course you are . . ." Luna says slowly. "And I was only joking. You look very . . . adequate."

I HATE HER! I rush upstairs again and add another five layers of concealer to my T-zone. Everything about this afternoon has to be high-pitch-scream PERFECT.

I look more than adequate in the end, in my divine-feminine-energy leather jacket and shiniest, lint-rolled white jeans. I even flirtatiously persuade Morgan into ordering bubble tea with me at the cinema. She looks deeply confused when I tell her strawberry is my favorite flavor *because it's pink*. Apparently, you can't taste color.

"You shouldn't be so pessimistic!" I tell her as we clatter into our front-row seats. Gooseberries, I wish Morgan hadn't taken me so seriously when I told her any seats were fine. "Pink is obviously the best flavor, Morgan."

"Well, I guess I did order lemon-and-lime because it's green," she says, then she leans over to kiss me, which is very giggly and delicious. Even if I accidentally cough one of the bubbles into her mouth. Morgan chews it thoughtfully. "Hmm. I guess pink tastes okay. Or maybe that's just your lip gloss."

Morgan smirks and I watch her with wide eyes. She must still love me if she's happy to eat food from my actual mouth!

Surely that has to be a good sign?! I wish I could shoot Aphrodite a text to confirm, but you're not allowed to use your phones in the cinema.

Also, Aphrodite isn't known for being very tech-savvy.

By the time the movie starts, my lips are basically *swelling* from the amount of kissing they have been doing. Me and Morgan lower ourselves deeper into our seats, very rosy-cheeked and romantic as the lights dim. My heart goes pitta-patter pita bread.

"How scary is this actually going to—" I begin.

"SHUSH!" someone goes, in the row behind.

Morgan takes my hand and squeezes it, instantly turning me into lemon juice. "Don't worry, babe," she whispers. "I'll be right here with you. I know anything above PG is a lot for you and I'm very grateful you're doing this for us."

I almost squeeze her hand back before I realize she's probably very slightly making fun of me. I still squeeze back anyway, and sip my pink bubble tea in suspense.

On the screen, a woman is creeping along a creaky corridor. She's just heard a bang on the other side of this locked wooden door, so of course she's walking right toward it, calling her boyfriend's name and saying, "Brad, stop messing around!"

She must be very stupid. But then she is heterosexual.

Then she's in the room, flashlight flashing about, and I slowly lift the straw of my bubble tea to my lips. The woman swivels the flashlight to the corner and "AAAAARGH!!" everyone goes, although that might just be me, because there's someone with a mask of her boyfriend's face—like, *literally* his face, ripped off his body, highly gory scenes.

"OH MY GOSH!" she shrieks. "THERE'S SO MUCH BLOOD!"

That's when I glance down and notice my red jeans. I notice this because I'm pretty sure they were white jeans when I put them on this morning. My eyes widen. I touch my shivering hand to the fabric and my fingers come away red.

"MORGAN!" I shriek. "MORGAN, THE FILM IS REAL! THE FILM IS REAL I'M LITERALLY BLEEDING OH GOOSEBERRIES, HELP!"

Then I take a deep breath to scream some more and one of the bubbles from my bubble tea shoots straight down my windpipe. My whole chest explodes as all oxygen intake ceases and I grip Morgan's shoulders in horrified shock.

Morgan curses, leaping to her feet, screaming, "SOMEONE HELP! MY GIRLFRIEND IS CHOKING!" I can't even be excited that she publicly called me her girlfriend because Morgan is right—I'm DYING! All the lights come on, the movie stops playing, people are on their feet, and I'm spluttering and wheezing away. Then someone has me from behind, holding me in ways I want no one other than Morgan to hold me, and before I know what's happening, I'm retching bubble tea all down Morgan's top.

Did I do something wrong in a past life? Am I a joke to you, Slender Aphrodite? Why do these absolutely astonishing things always happen to ME?! I must be the only girl in the world who can forget her own period *and wear white jeans the day it starts*. Luna was right about my T-zone after all! Morgan has to sprint, still soaked in regurgitated strawberry bubble tea, to the nearest pharmacy and buy me an enormous box of NIGHTTIME sanitary pads, which don't fit in my clutch bag, so I have to clown around with them lodged under my arm like a blood-sucking squeeze-box.

"Don't blame me," says Morgan. "It was the only box they

had! You're lucky the pharmacist didn't hold me there for treatment. She said I look like I've been stabbed."

I grimace at my girlfriend. Mixed with the neon green of Morgan's überlisciously cool T-shirt, the pink bubble tea has turned an unhealthy shade of red. We're currently sitting on a bench on Lambley Common Green, a short walk from the cinema.

"It's lucky that man knew how to do the Heimlich maneuver," I sigh, rubbing my bruised ribs. "I'm really sorry we missed the film, but maybe we can go back next week?"

"That might not be the best idea," Morgan mumbles. "I may not be banned from Starbucks, but I doubt the cinema will be serving us bubble tea anytime soon."

I awkwardly readjust my jacket, which is tied round my waist to conceal my . . . um . . . accident. I think about that horoscope again. Morgan's rose-colored glasses are not just coming off, but are smashed to pieces completely with a hammer! Probably by me personally.

"Am I a rubbish girlfriend?" I ask in my teeniest voice.

Morgan sighs, which isn't very encouraging. Then she takes off her green-rimmed glasses and looks right at me. Gooseberries! The prophecy is coming true, more literally than I thought! Luckily, before I can panic-babble, Morgan says, "You're not rubbish at anything, babe. Well, except at skateboarding. We're never doing that again."

I blush. "I did tell you my balance isn't the best . . ."

Morgan snorts a laugh. Then she shuffles closer and puts her arm around me. Which is necessary, as well as nice, because it's actually quite chilly without my jacket on. "Cat, I know most of our dates recently have ended with a medical emergency." I

cough apologetically. "But I'm still glad we're together. I still . . ." She shrugs. "You know."

We pause. "Still what?" I ask, nudging her hopefully.

Morgan rolls her eyes. "You're really gonna make me say it?"

"Why wouldn't you say it if you really mean it?!"

"Because . . ." Morgan traces the lines on my palm. "Because it means a lot to say that and I'm . . . Well, I'm not that great at being vulnerable. It feels like I'm taking a massive risk. Literally, when I'm with you. Like, a risk to my safety."

"Yes, all right!" I cut in impatiently. Then we swap hands, so that I am tracing hers. I wish I could palm-read. Then maybe I'd be able to tell if Morgan really is my Happily Ever After Aphrodite. "When you said that you don't see this working . . ." I begin. My heart is absolutely shrieking at me to shush, but perhaps miracles are real and Zanna was right. Talking about it *is* better. "Did you mean, like, our relationship? Because I can't stop thinking about it, Morgan."

I'm almost too scared to breathe! When I look up, Morgan is frowning. "When did I say that?"

I blink at her. "Well, I'm not sure exactly . . ." I gulp, lacing my fingers. "But maybe, roughly about thirty-one days, two hours, and fifteen minutes ago? Um, just approximately . . ."

Morgan looks completely blank for a moment, then she closes her eyes. "Thirty-one days and . . . oh, Cat. You thought I was talking about you and me? Is that why you've been acting so jitterbug lately? I *thought* you were being weirder than normal."

"I'm never weird—!" I begin, but Morgan groans.

"Why didn't you say something?! That was after the Head Girl thing—I was talking about me being friends with Siobhan. Like,

obviously. That lunch was really awkward. I felt like I was this freaky three-eyed fish, all your friends ogling me. I wasn't talking about our relationship."

"Oh," I say. Because that does make more sense. "But, Morgan, then I realized it was coming up to the Worm Moon, when important things can change beneath the surface, and I was worried. I really like you, you know? But from how you've been with my friends, I wondered if secretly underneath . . . You didn't like me the same anymore?"

Morgan studies me. Then she just sighs. "I didn't tell you this before, because I didn't want you to think I'm a massive loser. But at my old school, I *was* a massive loser. My stupid twin, Arya, was someone *everyone* wanted to know—just because she was in that toothpaste ad . . . I was so freaking hyped to move away from her and get a fresh start. But sometimes, being with your friends is like a flashback to my old and . . . *really* godawful life. That's why I get weird around them."

I nod slowly, trying to compute in what alternative dimension Morgan Delaney could be considered a massive loser. "You will always be the überest to me, Morgan. I don't care what Siobhan thinks! Well, unless it's to do with hair products. She really knows her conditioners. But apart from that! You will always be the coolest of, um, Coolsville."

Morgan tilts her head at me. "Coolsville," she repeats. "Well, I can't argue with that. Only the coolest people need to name their town Coolsville to feel cool."

I giggle. "Well, what about Überwood? Like Hollywood!"

Morgan snorts. "Babe, have I ever told you that you are so painfully innocent?"

I gasp, then slide away from Morgan down the bench. But she chases me into a kiss, then we are giggling like geese again, and it's all very perfect, her forehead pressed right against mine. I slide my hand along her thigh, just to prove that I'm not *completely* innocent, and that's when we hear a harrumph. We pull away from our kiss and an old woman is staring at us, in a horrendous polka-dotted coat and floppy brown hat, like a sad, damp dog.

"Um . . ." I glance at Morgan. "Can we help you, Miss?"

"Are you really happy to do that, in front of children?" the old lady asks, gesturing to where some beige-clad families are late-afternoon Frisbeeing on Lambley Common Green behind her.

I actually go, "OMG" with my whole mouth. Is this real homophobia?! I've never experienced it before! It's quite exciting, actually. I look at Morgan with wide eyes. She slouches back on the bench, scuffing the heels of her Doc Martens. Then she bites her bottom lip, scanning the lady up and down.

"Are *you* really happy to wear that coat in front of your husband?" Morgan replies, and the lady gasps, then she scuttles off harrumphing away as I shriek with laughter, throwing myself into Morgan's arms like a legless, bleeding clown in truest, happiest love.

Chat Thread: Morgan Delaney

Cat, 11:35 p.m.:
Hey :) I like u a lot :)

Morgan, 11:36 p.m.:
Well that's convenient. Bc I like you a lot too x

Cat, 11:36 p.m.:
Do you really tho?? :(((Like really really???

Morgan, 11:36 p.m.:
Yes, lol

Cat, 11:37 p.m.:
Would u still like me if I was a shrimp?

Morgan, 11:37 p.m.:
Babe please let's not go down this road again

Cat, 11:37 p.m.:
SO YOU WOULDN'T??? :'(

Morgan, 11:37 p.m.:
Omggggg. Yes. I would still like u if u were a shrimp. Happy?

Cat, 11:38 p.m.:
Yes :) xx

. . .

What about if I was an avocado?

16

The Trouble with My Tutu Is

My relationship isn't doomed after all, so everything is fine. THE END.

Me and Morgan video-call after the cinema until late into the night, which is very reckless and exciting. We even watch the full Pink Moon together, and I tell her about the Flower Moon, which is sprouting up next.

"And what does the Flower Moon mean?" Morgan asks sleepily. "Apart from that I'm going to have to buy you a huge bunch of roses, obviously."

It's lucky I'm lying down, because I get sappy in the knees. "It's about intimacy, actually," I tell her wisefully. "With ourselves and with . . . you know . . . other people."

Morgan smiles into the camera. "Well, I hope not too many other people. I only want to get intimate with one."

Internally, I explode into petals and butterflies.

Then I wake up, phone vibrating against my cheek. Oh my Swift-singing GOODNESS! Did I fall asleep?! I see that Morgan ended our call at 2 a.m. along with a text saying, *so glad my story sent u to sleep*, then another saying, *you look cute tho*.

Mushy and marvelous as that is, I AM LATE FOR SCHOOL. Why didn't Luna wake me up?! Probably distracted by Niamh as usual. And how selfish of Mum to go into work earlier than me! This is a genuine Kar-crashian disaster.

I also have a phone-shaped rectangle printed onto my cheek.

Groaning, I answer my phone. It appears to be Siobhan: frightening stuff for 9 a.m. . . . At least *someone* has noticed I'm not there! I slightly wish it were Zanna, but still.

"Where are you?" Siobhan demands without so much as a good morning.

I pull my duvet back on. "Um, in bed? Why?"

"IN BED?!" Siobhan banshee-shrieks into my ear with such force, I sit bolt upright and catapult my duvet to the carpet. "It's seven thirty! We're meeting for Dress-Up Day BEFORE HOME-ROOM! It's for charity and it's part of my campaign, Cat—you HAVE to be here!"

I follow my duvet, rolling onto the floor. "That's TODAY?!"

I vaguely remember Siobhan mentioning a dress-up day. But I thought that was just an *idea*—not something I'd actually have to do! Why didn't Zanna forewarn me?!

"YES, it's today, you total condiment!" Siobhan barks. She growls in frustration. "But you'll never make it in time now . . . You'd better have planned an AMAZING outfit, and it better not clash with my Poison Ivy costume or you're SO canceled! Alison will have to fill you in when you get here." There's a mumble in the background. "BECAUSE I DON'T REPEAT MYSELF, ALISON, THAT'S WHY!"

Gooseberries galore, what am I supposed to wear?! This is exactly what happens when Zanna goes radio silent. How am I supposed to remember all my comings and goings?! I tell Siobhan I'll be there soon and hang up the phone before she can shout at me more. Then I rush to my wardrobe and fling open the doors.

After I've unburied myself from the avalanche of clothes, I rummage about for anything that might count as a costume. I don't find much, except for my Rapunzel dress from when I was literally six. Then my eyes land on a crumpled old tutu.

Of course! Excitedly, I extract a pink leotard and some white tights from the pile. They're practically unworn as well, since I failed that dance audition. And to think Zanna said I'd wasted my money on the clothes! She'll be sorry now.

I tug on the outfit, tights and tutu galore, then dig out the old fairy wings from Lilac's fairy-themed party, age ten. I remember the horror in her eyes when I showed up carrying a flyswatter and giggle away. I really am very hilarious and brilliant.

Finally, I have a costume. There's no way this could clash with Poison Ivy, so Siobhan will be thrilled! I tinker down the stairs then bell down the driveway. If I literally run all the way to school, I should just about make it in time . . .

Strolling through the gates twenty-five minutes later, I whistle my way through the playground, swinging my bag in one hand. Everywhere is deserted, being so late, except for my history teacher, Mr. Derry, who stops to scratch his beardy chin as I ramshackle by.

"Good morning, Cat," he says, frowning. "That's a very imaginative outfit."

"Thank you, sir," I say, smiling proudly. "I'm just doing my bit for charity."

"Is that what this is!" Mr. Derry says, goggling me up and down. "Splendid."

He teachers away with his too-tight black trousers and notebook. Typical of Mr. Derry to compliment me with no witnesses around! I'm pretty sure half the school fancies him. I hurry on toward my classroom, updating my Instagram followers with the important news as I go. I'm almost ten full minutes late though. Mrs. Warren is going to pluck my wings off!

I jog up the stairs, tutu bouncing, then barrel through the classroom door, plastic wand in my spare hand for full effect. Right away, everyone bursts out laughing. I glance down at myself, wondering what the trouble with my tutu is . . . Then I look up and I realize that the trouble is the tutu itself. No one else is dressed up. AT ALL!

Siobhan goes pale. "OH. MY. CHUCKLE-BROTHERING. GOSH."

Mrs. Warren is standing to read the bulletin. She glares around, already steaming at the ears, then does a proper double take. It's the first time I've ever seen her look genuinely surprised. She says, "Good morning, Miss Phillips. May I inquire as to what on God's green earth you're wearing?"

I'm fully fish-mouthed. "Um . . . I'm dressed as a fairy, Miss!"

Mrs. Warren breathes in sharply. "Yes, I am aware of that, Cathleen. What I mean to ask is *why* are you dressed as a fairy?"

I look at Siobhan, who has both hands clapped over her mouth. Alison looks like she's going through brain-altering trauma. Finally, I look at Zanna. Even Zanna, who has ignored me all weekend, is lowering her spectacles in bemused horror.

"Siobhan said . . . She said it was a dress-up day!" I babble at Mrs. Warren. "For charity!" I actually pinch my arm to wake myself up, but no such luck.

Everyone looks round at Siobhan.

"I said it was the MEETING for Dress-Up Day, you absolute . . . !" She rests her manicured fingers on her temples, like her head is on the verge of exploding. "You were supposed to be at my campaign meeting ABOUT Dress-Up Day. The day itself isn't until next semester! Not even I can throw together a first-class event in one morning, you lentil."

I stare at her like I am going to kill her. Which I am. But before I can snap my wand in half and use it to stab her repeatedly, Mrs. Warren lets out a tired sigh. "Clearly, there's been a miscommunication here," she says, which has got to be the understatement of the century. "Let us not dwell and waste any more time on this ridiculous matter. Cathleen, take your seat."

I gawp at her. "Miss! I need to go home and get changed!"

"You're late as it is, Cathleen," Mrs. Warren tuts. "Take your seat, please. I won't ask nicely again." Then she returns to the bulletin and carries on reading.

I continue to gawp at her. Surely, she can't do this! I stand for another few moments, waiting for Mrs. Warren to tell me this is some twisted joke, but she doesn't even crack a smile. I take my seat, wings drooping in shame.

"Christ, Christ, CHRIST on a bike," says Siobhan at break time. "You are shockingly embarrassing, Cat. I expected a typical apology video with some fake tears—at MOST. Not for you to rock up like you're in the freaking *Nutcracker*."

"Well, how was I supposed to know?!" I exclaim. "It was very easy to misinterpret what you shouted over the phone! I panicked, okay?! This is completely your fault!"

I tried to spare myself some humiliation by taking off the wings, but they're actually too large to fit in my bag. It felt weirder to walk around just holding them, so in the end, I surrendered to my fate and put them back on. Mrs. Warren even supplied me with a note to explain her mortifying decision to the other staff:

Due to some miscommunication, Cathleen's clothes are not following the usual dress code. To avoid disruption to Cathleen's education, of which she is clearly in need, she may attend her classes. Rest assured that I am monitoring the situation. Any inquiries, my classroom can be found second to the right in English. Otherwise, we may proceed straight on until tomorrow morning without further concern.

Best regards,
B. Warren

I have an idea or two about what *B* should stand for. How is this less disruptive to my education?! I can't take five steps without someone calling me Tinker Bell! Some clown sixth-grade boy even tried to give me his tooth!

"It fell out this morning," he said, sniggering. "Can I have a pound?"

"I'll give you a pound!" barked Siobhan, cracking her knuckles, and they all ran away screaming. I suppose being in the

Queen Bee's hive does have its benefits. Even if she's the one who stung me.

Anyway, we're at the picnic tables now and Habiba won't stop cackling. I've not seen her laugh this much since Jamie changed his Instagram bio to "if looks could kill, I'd be America's most wanted." She's practically morphed into a hyena.

"This has made my day," Habiba says, breaking into giggles. Again. "I think if I died tonight, I'd die happy . . . Not that that's likely, given my high-protein diet and KILLER metabolic health. Oh, and age!" She raises her phone for another picture.

"This wouldn't have happened if you'd replied to my texts!" I snap at Zanna, who is sitting across from me, snacking on raisins like everything is normal. "You know I can't afford another late mark. *And* I didn't even know what homework I had to do this weekend—I had to check my planner!"

At last, Zanna looks at me with one raised eyebrow. Then she says, "Well, sorry, mate. I was actually busy, living my own life for once. I had a date."

I frown at her snack. "Well, you should give the box back to the cafeteria, then!" I tell her. "There are only supposed to be raisins in there."

Zanna rolls her eyes. "Wow, Cat, really?! I mean I *went* on a date. On Sunday. With a boy. And it went really, really well. Thanks so much for asking."

There is a moment of apocalyptic silence. Then Siobhan practically liquifies herself. "WHAT THE ACTUAL PINSTRIPE PANTSUIT?!" she explodes. "YOU HAD A DATE AND YOU DIDN'T FREAKING TELL US? WHAT WERE YOU THINKING?!"

"I was *thinking* that I didn't want to make a fuss," says Zanna, smirking. Then she does the most horrifying thing. She elbows Lip Gloss Lizzie, who has managed to stay oddly calm and collected, all things considered, and says, "So I just asked Lizzie to come round on Saturday and help me put together an outfit. That way, if the date went badly, I wouldn't have to tell all of you, because I'd rather go belly dancing with Mrs. Warren than do that."

We all pause to shudder. Zanna really can be the creepiest.

Then Lip Gloss Lizzie beams, lips shining. "Well, we don't have to worry about that now, do we, hun?" She clasps Zanna's hand on the tabletop. Zanna quickly retracts it, but even so. The absolute nerve! "It went really well and she's seeing him again. Right, babe?"

Zanna doesn't like to be called babe! Zanna doesn't even wear lip gloss! I am so speechless, I actually forget that I am dressed like a unicorn cowgirl for a moment. I goggle across the table at my so-called best friend, my heart aflutter with dizzy confusion.

Because of all the people Zanna should have told . . . How could she not have told her useless blond friend, her one true clown, her bestest poetry-writing pal?! I should ask Miss Spencer if Juliet can get stabbed in the BACK instead of the heart.

WHAT YOU NEED TO KNOW ABOUT ZANNA SZCZECHOWSKA

- She always wears black, like Wednesday Addams. I think this is because her Black Moon Lilith is in Leo, so she doesn't like drawing attention to herself. Zanna thinks it's because she "just likes black, to be honest."
- She has a secret tattoo that's so secret, she's actually forgotten where it is. We once spent three whole hours looking for it. We're starting to wonder if it was just a temporary tattoo and that strange lady in Camden scammed her.
- She is very sarcastic. So sarcastic, actually, that I replied "LOL" when she texted to say her grandmother had died, because I thought she was joking. I really wish she hadn't shown her dad because he's been weird to me ever since.
- She likes weird taboo things, such as music from the '90s and books where people slouch around being depressed for 349 pages. I blame her Jupiter being in Scorpio for this. And Sylvia Plath.
- Zanna can cook and do laundry, which is very impressive indeed. I'm too busy being amazing and hilarious to do those things myself.
- Zanna's dad, Matt, can repair anything but can't boil an egg to save his life. Zanna says he's too useless to ever find a new girlfriend. I think she loves him lots though. She clearly has a soft spot for useless people . . .

- I've known her since toddlerhood and she's the best person who has ever lived. No, Zanna, you cannot include that. Just listen to my dictations! No, of course I didn't want you to write that bit down. I said stop writing! STOP!

17
Tooth Fairy at the Care Home

What a miserable day to be dressed in a glittery pink tutu. I am like a tooth fairy in a world full of dentures: nobody needs me, not even my best friend. Aries Season is turning EVERYBODY into independence JUNKIES—we're not even Americans! I grate through another grim-biscuits rehearsal with Rich Elizabeth croning on, then an assembly where Mr. Drew, the vice principal, makes the worst announcement ever.

"If we can all stop getting distracted by Tinker Bell in the back there . . ." he says, which is probably a northern attempt at a joke. Everyone laughs, grinning over their shoulders at me like a tentful of clowns. "I am overjoyed to announce that we will be holding a proper debate for the Head Girl candidates."

I almost spit my drink! Which I'm actually not meant to be drinking, so I hastily hide the bottle in my tutu ruffles before I'm spotted. That doesn't sound joyous! The very opposite, in fact. Morgan and Siobhan, arguing in public. Has Mr. Drew lost his senses?

"This is the perfect opportunity to embrace the wonderful Queen's community spirit," he plows on, confirming that he has. "It's essential we conduct ourselves in an adult manner and make room for each candidate's views to be shared and respected . . ."

What an absolute joker on toast! Siobhan is more likely to volunteer at a children's hospital than respect someone else's views. I say as much to Morgan after the assembly, when we find each other in the corridor before final period (French, Aphrodite help us).

"Maybe you should tell him you won't do it," I suggest hopefully once she's finished laughing at my outfit. "Tell him you think it's a terrible idea."

"Why would I do that?" Morgan replies. "I'm the one who suggested it."

I gawp at her. "Morgan. Is your black eye swelling into your brain?"

Morgan rolls her eyes, then she takes my arm and pulls me aside. Maja and Marcus trudge ahead. They still never look happy to see me, but then they are goths. Hades himself, God of the Underworld, probably couldn't get them to smile. Unless he came out as nonbinary or something. Millie gives me a little smile. (Well, a normal smile really, but everything Millie does is little, since she's not very tall.)

"Listen," Morgan says. "No one's going to vote for me if I can't get my message out there. Not when Siobhan is . . . Well, Siobhan. She's got this in the bag by default."

"She's got really nice bags, too," I agree, sighing. "But Morgan, do you really think debating her is a good idea? You don't know

what Siobhan is capable of! You weren't here when she made that priest cry in seventh grade! He left the church because of her."

"That's where you're wrong, babe," Morgan says, flicking her eyebrows. They're really perfect eyebrows, but my stomach still twists with dread. "I know exactly what she's like. She won't prepare for it because she won't believe she needs to. That's how I'll destroy her."

"When you say 'destroy' . . ." I begin precariously, but then a shadow falls across us, and I flutter around right into Mrs. Warren and her boring-as-bread brown jacket.

"Miss Phillips. Miss Delaney. While I admire your commitment to each other, may I suggest preserving the chitchat for the lunch hour? I believe, Cathleen, you have French. I'd hate to see your sparkle dampened by another late mark."

I think she'd quite enjoy it. Mrs. Warren probably eats fairy kebabs for dinner! But we both just mumble "Sorry, Miss" and hurry away. It's only right when we're hugging (and possibly kissing) goodbye in the playground that Morgan says, "Why didn't she send you to the lost and found? They probably have loads of spare uniforms there."

I consider this for a moment. I can only conclude that Mrs. Warren is even more evil than I ever thought possible . . . or that Irish people have a VERY funny sense of humor.

• ★ . ✦ ˙ ★ •

French is very ridiculous. Not the language (although that, too, because everything, from a fridge to a bra strap, has a gender. How pointless is that?) but the class. Miss Ward makes us recite "*Je suis une fée, tu es une fée*" and so forth, until my wings are wilting.

"You've definitely brightened my day, Cat," she adds, tittering on. "How would this school cope without you? Now, for 'pixie,' we'd say *une lutin* . . ."

Never mind the school though—Zanna can clearly cope without me just fine! All through French, Zanna sits nicely and writes her verbs down like she's actually paying attention for the entire class. It's absolutely criminal! She doesn't even wait for me at the end.

I catch up with her at the gates though. I have to push through a crowd of sixth graders chanting "I do believe in fairies!" first, but I finally grab her shoulder. I actually drop my wand to do so. "Zanna! Don't you think we need to talk?" I wheeze. I'm panting quite asthmatically, so I hold up a finger. "Just . . . Just a minute, actually . . . Gooseberries, you walk fast!"

Zanna crosses her arms. "Look, Cat—"

"WHY?!" I catapult out the word. "Zanna, am I not your best friend? You're going on your first-ever date and you ask LIZZIE to help you? She can't style you correctly! You need to be chic and sexy with a sprinkling of goth. Only I know that!"

"Yes, but Cat—"

"Who did your first-ever spit handshake with you? With real spit, Zanna! Who did you call when the cute security guard finally noticed you loitering and said, 'Oi, you'?! And who did an entire online course in Māori because I accidentally clicked on 'Polynesian languages' when I was looking for Polish lessons?!" I'm practically tearing my blond curls out. "Why wouldn't you tell me, Zanna? It's actually quite hurtful."

"Oh, really?" Zanna retorts, eyes widening in disbelief. "*That's* hurtful? Well, how about trying to talk to you for weeks

and getting nowhere? Every time I call you, you hang up! And we somehow *always* seem to talk about you, your messes, your girlfriend, never about me, but then you're falling over yourself to help Brooke Mackenzie?!"

I'm taken aback. "You're upset I helped Brooke? But Zanna, I was only doing that for Morgan! You know how weird things have been. I'm trying to juggle all my friendships and relationships at once, and you know I can't juggle! How can you be mad at that?!"

Zanna gesticulates wildly. "I'm mad at YOU! It's . . . well, it's difficult to take you seriously when you're dressed like that, but YES, I AM UPSET. I've listened to every desperate detail of your extensive lesbian saga, but you can't even have one conversation with me about a boy I like! And then you tell me on the phone that it's BORING?! Well, sorry that I'm not glittery and gay and interesting enough for you. So yes, I asked Lizzie instead."

"But Zanna . . ." I gaze at her, slightly lost for words. I unfortunately end up saying, "You don't even wear lip gloss!"

Zanna sighs crossly. "Yes, well . . . I wiped it off at the train station. But at least Lizzie was actually excited for me. At least she was there. You've been unavailable for weeks."

We fall silent. It's not ideal that we're having this conversation in the middle of the school pickup line, buses (oh, Aphrodite above, protect me!), coaches, and cars screeching, students in their blazers laughing at me repeatedly . . . It's hard to concentrate.

"Um . . ." I go. "I didn't . . . I didn't mean to be like that."

"Well, you were," Zanna retorts, crossing her arms. "And I know, okay? You never mean to . . . be like you are. But sometimes

you're so self-absorbed, you don't even notice what's going on around you."

"That's not my fault!" I exclaim. "I'm a MASSIVE overthinker, Zanna. Morgan says one weird thing and I spend weeks worrying about it, then I get distracted! You know my moon is in Virgo! I can't keep track of every little thing that's happening!"

"No," interjects Zanna, shaking her head. "You can't do that, Cat! You can't always just blame the stars for your mistakes. Also—*over*thinking?! You never think at all!"

"I said my *moon*, Zanna! A moon is not a star!"

"Oh, wow. Are you ACTUALLY being serious, or just clowning as usual?"

"I AM NOT A CLOWN, ZANNA, HOW MANY TIMES?"

"THEN WHY ARE YOU WEARING A TUTU TO SCHOOL?"

But before I can dignify that ridiculous accusation with an answer, Luna and Niamh come social-justice-marching round the corner with their DARE TO GO DELANEY pin badges. Wait—what?! Morgan didn't tell me anything about this!

"Oh. My. Plant-based. Goddess." Luna grips Niamh's arm. "I can't believe this! I thought the rumors had to be a joke! Cat, has anyone taken a picture of you in this state?"

"Yes . . ." I roll my eyes. "Lots of pictures. Luna, I'm actually in the middle of talking to Zanna right now, so if you wouldn't mind, well, GETTING LOST . . ."

"It's okay," Zanna butts in, cold-shouldering me. "I'm heading home. Bye, Cat."

And I am so boogie-brained about everything we've just shouted at each other, I can't even think up the words to make her stay. Luna and Niamh discuss creating an Instagram highlight of

my chaotic moments, and I just stand there like a dying Tinker Bell, but without the clapping children and sparkly music.

Dinner with the family (and Niamh) only makes things worse. Dad won't stop chuckling and saying "What a day," like I haven't gotten the message that going to school in a tutu was an error of judgment.

Then he says, "Your uncle Hillary's seen the Facebook post I made."

This alone nearly makes me choke on the witch fingers (asparagus) I'm being force-fed. I really can't wait for Niamh to go so Mum will stop pandering to Luna's horror-show herbalist diet. "You put it on Facebook?!" I exclaim. "Dad!"

He only chuckles. "He left me a comment! Apparently, Lilac was delighted. She's even asked to have a copy printed for the family Christmas card!"

"What a lovely idea!" gasps Mum as I gawp between them in speechless horror. "Then we can look back on this moment and have a right old laugh."

I don't want to have a right old laugh! I don't want to ever remember this happened! But as usual, my plate-spinning clown family is already yo-yoing on to make sure I never live this down, not even if I live to a really ancient age, like forty-one.

"Don't be so grumpy, love!" Mum says, which is obviously only going to make me grumpier. I pick through my quinoa like it's deeply unappealing. Which it is. "We all have social hiccups! The important thing is picking yourself back up."

What an absolutely useless thing to say! But that's parents

for you. "I don't care about the tutu," I mutter. "I had a fight with Zanna today, okay?! I'm not in the mood to laugh."

"Oh, love!" Mum reaches across the table and takes my hand. She squeezes reassuringly. "Don't worry. I'm sure she'll forgive you in the end."

I stare at her in utter disbelief. Then I snatch my hand right back. "WHY DO YOU ALWAYS ASSUME IT'S MY FAULT?!" I yell, throwing down my spoon and stomping right upstairs to my bedroom. I'm sure Miss Spencer would be proud of my dramatics.

But I am not feeling proud at all. The more I think about it, the more I'm seeing how truly, crushingly right Zanna was earlier. I've been trying so hard to be an amazing girlfriend that I've ended up being a terrible best friend. And now my terrible best friend doesn't want to be friends anymore.

I drop my phone onto my bed, then stare at my ceiling. I'm still in my tutu and leotard because I'm too troubled to change my clothes.

Because how useless have I been? Zanna's been unhappy with me all this time and I didn't even notice. It's all been happening just below the surface . . .

Suddenly, I sit up, eyes wide as clown noses. I watch the way the silvery moonlight creeps across my bedroom walls. Of course! The Worm Moon has been munching away at my foundations all this time. But it wasn't my relationship with Morgan the bedbugs were after . . . It was my friendship. The pancake said DOOM and now here I am, in an abracadabra abyss of sorrow, without even Zanna to save me.

Chat Thread: Morgan Delaney

Cat, 9:50 p.m.:
Can't stop thinking about Zanna :(

Morgan, 9:53 p.m.:
Should I be jealous?

Cat, 9:53 p.m.:
Morgaaaannnnnnnn X'(

Idk what to do

She seemed genuinely upset

Morgan, 9:57 p.m.:
Babe she just feels a bit neglected rn. May take a while, but just keep in touch with her, keep letting her know you're there, thinking of her. She may not answer till she's cooled off but I'm sure she'd appreciate it

Cat, 10:01 p.m.:
Do you think I can ask her what English homework I have??

Morgan, 10:02 p.m.:
Ummm . . . Maybe not the best idea babe

That's not really what I meant

18

Who Wants to Be a Three-Eyed Fish?

Unfortunately, having a friendship crisis isn't a valid reason to stay home from school. I try my best, but Mum says she's completely certain a doctor will never write me a sick note for that. And I can't even use my *Bible to the Stars* to get me off the hook because it's still Aries Season and apparently I have to "power on ahead no matter what, with all the boldness and bravery in the world." Thanks for NOTHING, Aries.

School is very awkward. Avoiding Zanna is impossible—I literally sit next to her in homeroom! I soon discover from Mrs. Warren that we *can't* just sit wherever we want. Especially not if we want to sit in the corridor outside. But one thing I *can* do is talk to my friends about being nicer to Morgan and not making her feel like a three-eyed fish! Because who wants to feel like that?

"A three-eyed what?!" asks Lip Gloss Lizzie, pausing her

glossing, when I proudly announce this at the picnic tables on Wednesday. "Ew, that's so gross!"

"So are Morgan's gym socks," says Siobhan, not even pausing typing on her tablet, where her campaign notes are open. "I wonder sometimes if those green hair extensions she wears to those tragic emo gigs are actually just stink lines!"

I cough awkwardly. "Yes, you see, that's actually an example of what I'd really like you to stop saying, Siobhan. Morgan doesn't really like it."

"And?!" Siobhan snaps shut her tablet. "Maybe she needs thicker skin! She is the Givenchy to my McQueen!" We stare at her blankly, and she rolls her eyes. "My RIVAL, fools! Anyway, do you think the Chinese 'liked it' when Genghis Khan invaded their entire country?! He still did them a whole load of good, and managed to win ten Grammys as well. They don't call him the queen of funk for nothing."

"Um . . ." I go, absolutely lost. "Do they . . . call him that . . . ?"

"Well, of course they do," says Zanna smugly. "Just like they call disco diva Chaka Khan the founding father of Mongolia. Right, Siobhan?"

Siobhan frowns, looking irritated. "Well . . . Duh!"

Everyone stares at one another confusedly, and me and Zanna exchange smirks. Then we remember that we aren't friends anymore, so we abruptly stop smirking and Zanna hurries back to doodling lightning bolts. I shake my head: we're definitely getting sidetracked!

"Listen, everybody . . ." I start again. Alison is getting confused because she's trying to stick postcards into her scrapbook with lip gloss, while Lizzie is currently gluing her mouth shut without even realizing. I try not to be distracted—*again*. "I really like Morgan!"

"At least somebody does," says Habiba, and Siobhan snorts.

"*And* I'd really love if you at least gave her a chance!" I blunder on. "It's actually really hard being a girl with a girlfriend and friends who are girls as well . . ."

"Sounds like a dream," retorts Siobhan. "Men are repulsive."

"Uh-oh," says Habiba, biting into her energy bar. "What's Dale done now?"

"URGH," goes Siobhan. "Well, his name may as well be FAIL, considering how useless he is! I spent a whole hour yesterday evening outlining to him the pros and cons of getting back together—which I KNOW he wants!—then it turned out he had his earplugs in the entire time! He always forgets to take them out in the mornings. He did the same moronic thing on our date to the sunflower farm! Men are utterly substandard. Fact!"

Kenna giggles. "Maybe you should be gay as well, Siobhan!"

"That won't be necessary!" I cut in before Siobhan can reply. Lesbians have a hard enough time without Siobhan being on their scene. "But maybe you could just . . . include Morgan more in things? Not calling her a freak would also help . . ."

"Well, I'm sorry, Cat," says Siobhan, which would be a first. "I tried including her when I invited her to your birthday party—and what thanks did I get? She buddies up with that absolute GREMLIN who ruined my dress! So frankly, she can lick rust."

This is not going well, but Alison reaches out and takes my hand.

"I'm sure we can figure this out!" she says, eyelashes aflutter.

"We'd love to get to know Morgan really. I think we're all just a bit scared of her. She's so . . . different! Right, guys?"

Crickets. It may as well be a plague of locusts! Kenna quietly signs at Siobhan "Don't want" (rude) and Siobhan responds with something that leaves both of them snorting back laughter. It's a good thing I've learned to expect literally NOTHING from my friends.

Eventually, it's Zanna who breaks the silence. "Here's a groundbreaking theory: maybe the problem isn't us or Morgan. Maybe you're the one who needs to accept that we don't all need to be friends just because that's what *you* want. I know you usually forget this, but other people have their own thoughts and feelings. Boom. Think about that."

Then she gives me this smile that isn't really a smile, with narrowed eyes and thin lips. She slams shut her planner and stalks off toward the English block without looking back.

I jump to my feet. "IT'S THE WORM MOON, ZANNA!" I call after her. "Neither of us are thinking clearly right now!" She keeps walking. "ZANNA!"

But Zanna, like my faith in this sick and twisted life, is gone.

"Christ on a bike," says Siobhan. "Have you guys been inhaling plastic?"

I think about what Zanna said for a long, long time though. Even when the bell rings and everyone goes to class. Even when I get sent to Mr. Drew's office for skiving class to sit outside in the rain. Even when I'm being told off and asked why I have nothing to say. Even when the school nurse is called because I am "actually worryingly unresponsive."

Am I, the one and only Cat Phillips, really a selfish person?

I know I don't recycle as much as I should. I don't follow back everyone I know on Instagram (I've even blocked a few weird relatives), and I did once lie that Luna was adopted and we weren't in any way related, so as not to damage my social standing in front of Zariyah Al-Asiri.

But for the most part, I've always thought I was fairly decent, by Disney princess standards (which obviously apply to me).

Now it seems I've let Zanna slip away, and I'm not sure *what* I really am. Have I only been thinking about myself this entire time?! I *thought* I was thinking about everyone else, how I could fix things and help everyone get on, but . . . maybe Zanna's right. I am self-absorbed, like . . . wet tofu, or something. And I only did all of this for me.

Perhaps I am the Evil Cousin, and Lilac is the good one! I did pray to Aphrodite (unsuccessfully) for my cousin to slip in her figure skating exam just last week. But I didn't say any prayers for my one truest friend . . .

And as Shakespeare himself might say: therein, mayhaps, lies the problem.

When I'm back at the iPhone Box, I shut all my curtains, turn all my lights off, and lie in the middle of my floor: a true existentialist experience . . . (I think). I feel Zanna-less and alone. When she's gone, how can I even try to go on?

My door creaks open and Luna pokes her head round. "What are you doing? You're not trying to be spiritual, are you? Because that's my thing, Cat, and you'll just ruin the flow of universal energy if you start messing about with it, too."

I glare at her. "You can't just claim spirituality, Luna! I am the one with the *Bible to the Stars,* remember?! And I'm not messing

about with anything—it's MY LIFE that's a mess. So unless you have a solution, please just leave."

Luna hovers annoyingly. She really is the worst person. "Maybe you should become a nudist," she suggests, and I sit right up on my floor. "My friends are thinking about having a nudist weekend at Willow's house this Easter. It's meant to be really mentally liberating and all the extra vitamin D should help tackle seasonal affective disorder!"

I swipe my Jane Austen hardback of *Sense and Sensibility* and throw it at my sister, because sense is something she clearly needs knocked into her. She runs away screaming about "nude-phobia," which is absolutely NOT a thing, and I go back to lying on my floor.

Completely in my clothes, thank you very much.

Chat Thread: The Gang

Siobhan, 8:19 p.m.:
Right crew, Cat wants us to stop calling her pathetic loser girlfriend "freak" so I've thought up some NEW nicknames we can use instead:
Mog-Face (has a dog face)
MORE-GONE (I wish)
Smells-Like DEAD LADY
Morgan Failure
Morgum Sticky Boots
Mooch the Female Pooch

Habiba, 8:25 p.m.:
Morgan Failure LMAOOOO
Girl you're too much, I'm #DYING

Alison, 8:26 p.m.:
We could try her name?
I know it's not as exciting . . .

Cat, 8:27 p.m.:
:(

19
Lesbianism and Idina Menzel

I may not be friends with Zanna anymore, but I still need to know who she's going out with and make sure he's of acceptable quality. What if he's a Gemini or something like that?! But the rest of the week has passed and she still won't talk to me. So in my desperation, I do something I've never done: *call* Lip Gloss Lizzie. Like, on the phone.

It's fine: I'm only at the supermarket with Mum.

Lizzie tells me that his name is Freddie, but he's not a Labrador. He's a sixteen-year-old who is okay with being called that. Very curious. He plays *Animal Crossing*, this tragic game Zanna is obsessed with, so he's probably a bit funny all round. They met while picking digital fruit in the same digital village, and while I have no idea what any of that means, they apparently really hit it off and have been talking on Discord ever since.

"It all sounds kind of creepy and somehow illegal?" Lip

Gloss Lizzie lips away at me over the phone. "But apparently it's not, and he actually is who he says he is."

My eyes widen. "He's a teddy bear in a green Hawaiian shirt?"

"No, honey, he's a sixteen-year-old boy from Southampton," says Lizzie. Mum is waving a block of shrink-wrapped cheese at me, asking if I "like blue." Is she having a senior moment?! She *knows* my favorite color is orange! I flap her away so I can listen to Lizzie.

"I made Zanna text me throughout the day to make sure she didn't get abducted," Lizzie says. "Although I turned off the sound when I was in the spa . . . I needed a break from doing Siobhan's PR and I'd maxed out my loyalty card for a free mud bath. I figured I'd sense it in my pelvic floor if anything went wrong."

Then she starts glossing on about her coccyx massage, which I could really do without, to be honest. I never have to put up with such heebie-jeebie-fests with Zanna. Zanna always knows what to say. She knows I can't cope with swearing, sex scenes, or bodily functions, and in return, I know she can't handle sentimentality, children/childbirth, or pom-poms. Does she really not miss me at all?!

•★.✦˙★•

"Stop checking," says Morgan on Wednesday, swiping my phone out of my hand and pocketing it in her leathery black trench coat. "Just wait until Taurus Season. Zanna will calm down and we'll all feel more grounded again. But the debate is *tomorrow*, babe. I need you to focus."

Forlornly, I pass Morgan the spray paint. We're in the backyard of the iPhone Box, adding the finishing touches to Morgan's campaign banner. Mr. Drew has this horrendous idea (he called

it a “vision,” so maybe he’s sucked too much ink from his ballpoints?) that the candidates can put a banner behind them in the hall when they debate.

“Just whatever represents you to your best,” he told Morgan with a wink.

It’s a good thing I’m not running for Head Girl and having to represent myself on an enormous piece of cardboard. My banner would be awash with depressing grays and weepy blues. Which is Zanna’s whole vibe, to be honest.

Morgan’s spraying her entire banner emerald and is currently painting the words *DARE TO VOTE DELANEY FOR A GREENER, BRIGHTER FUTURE* in white. It looks like something that Extinction Rebellion would make, so of course Luna and Niamh have insisted on joining in. Will I ever get my girlfriend to myself?!

“I think we should have a day where we wear tie-dye for Tibet,” says Luna, emerging from the back wall (glass sliding door) with a trayful of herbal tea. She’s wearing these bin-bag-floppy trousers and looks blitheringly bizarre.

I’m just opening my mouth to announce that I will never, for any reason, wear tie-dye, when Morgan says, “That’s a cute idea, actually. We should be showing our awareness for global issues, as well as ones that affect us locally.”

Luna turning our house into a hippie commune is an issue that affects us locally, but I don’t see Morgan adding *that* to her manifesto! I roll my eyes as they ramble on. Then Niamh rises out of the shrubbery. “I think you should pitch putting a community garden behind the tennis courts,” she dreamy-sighs. “Imagine all the opportunity for garden-based learning.”

Gooseberries galore. I actually cannot cope with this nonsense anymore. I stand up from the grass and zip toward the kitchen, but Morgan calls me back. "Where are you going, babe? Everything all right?"

I turn around with my face bolt-gunned into a smile. "EVERYTHING IS PERFECTLY SPLENDID, THANK YOU, HAHA!" I say, and Luna and Niamh exchange worried glances. "I WILL BE RIGHT BACK, GOOD DAY."

"Why are you walking like a malfunctioning robot?" Morgan asks. "Cat, are you actually okay? Did you mix up your toothpaste with your antifungal cream again?"

"I DON'T HAVE A FUNGAL INFECTION!" I scream, then I take a deep breath, because I may slightly be overreacting. But I also cannot tell Morgan how I absolutely hate the Head Girl campaign, because that would be unsupportive. "I just have lots of lines to learn," I say levelheadedly. "And right now, my ears are hurting from Head Girl drama. I'm also friends with Siobhan, remember . . ." Niamh winces. "And she is . . . Well, you know . . ."

"Awful?" suggests Morgan.

I frown. "Um, not exactly . . ."

"Bit of a megalomaniac?" Luna chips in.

"Capable of real-life murder?" Niamh offers. "Like, have you seen her arms since she started golfing? I've seen her crush a cactus with her bare hands."

I think we may be getting sidetracked, so I give Morgan a pleading look. I am quite good at that, seeing as I'm "so obviously desperate for affection," according to Zanna. Sappho-NOOO, now I'm thinking about Zanna again! Will the torment never end?!

Luckily, Morgan catches the hint. She always has been a really great catcher, as well as a really great catch. The only thing I'm likely to catch is "on fire"—there's a good reason my parents have "Cat-proofed" the kitchen. Anyway, Morgan drops the green spray paint and swashbuckles over to me. Even when I'm stressed, she doesn't stop being dreamy.

"Let's forget about Head Girls for now," she says, and my breathing regulates. "And let's think about the school play instead." Instantly, the horror returns. Gooseberries galore. If it's not one disastrous storyline, it's another! "I actually brought the DVD of *West Side Story*. The musical from 1961? I thought it could be useful."

Useful for dozing off perhaps! However, if it's between a musical or more Head Girl hullabaloo, I'll probably have to bite the bullfrog for now. Or at least gently nibble it.

Morgan Delaney being a film nerd is one of the grooviest things about her. We basically have *Desperately Seeking Susan* to thank for our entire relationship! Dad's just impressed Morgan's persuaded me to watch anything made before the OG *Mean Girls*. But the sixties?! I worry Morgan is really scraping out the ballerina's bottom for this one.

"So how exactly is this relevant?" I ask as Morgan slides in the DVD for *West Side Story*. We snuggle up on the sofa together, which would be really romantic if my parents weren't sitting a few feet away at the dining room table. I tried to exile them, but since the entire house is one enormous room, unless they go to bed at eight o'clock (we can hope: they are almost fifty) there's nowhere for them to go.

I glare at Mum and she waves merrily back. URGH.

"I know how you feel about old musicals—" Morgan begins.

"Lacking in lesbianism and Idina Menzel," I confirm, and Morgan nods.

"But this one is more interesting," she says. "It's based on *Romeo and Juliet*, but it's set in fifties New York, between two gangs from two different cultures, white American and Puerto Rican. It shows how timeless this play actually is."

I'm not convinced that anything containing the word *thou* can be timeless. But I'm hardly going to reject the opportunity to have Morgan's arm around me for two hours, so I settle down and Morgan hits play. The beginning is very strange. I've no idea how it'll help me to watch a group of Captain Americas clicking their fingers. But Morgan tells me to be patient. Hmm.

Two hours later, I am completely falling apart. The hero (Tony) dies in the heroine's (Maria's) arms and with him, my heart dies, too. The credits roll and I leap to my feet. "MAAAAAAAAAAAAAAAARIAAAAAAAAAAAAAAAAAA!!!" I sing at the top of my lungs as my parents flee upstairs. "Morgan, did you see Maria's dress at the dance?! The white one, with the little red belt? Did you see it, Morgan, did you see it?!"

"I've seen the film before," says Morgan. "So yes."

"MAAAARIA, MAAAARIA, MAAAARIIIIIIIIAAAAA!" I skip over the coffee table and pirouette. I actually pirouette right into Mum's potted cactus and have to pause for five minutes to pull the spikes out, but the only thing that's really pricked is my INTEREST, my love and adoration, for *West Side Story*. "MAAAARIAAAAAAAAA!!!!"

Luna appears at the top of the stairs. "Did you *have* to teach her that song?"

"I'm really sorry, honey," says Morgan, but the rest of her apology is drowned out by me going "MAAARIIIIII-AAAAAAAAAAAAAAAAAAAAA!!!!!" again.

"And I get to *be* her!" I sparkle breathlessly. "I get to be Maria, Morgan, in the white dress! Did you see the dancing?! Wasn't it amazing?! Did *Romeo and Juliet* really inspire all that, with their breaking windows and *yonder*s?! To think that Siobhan says the only good things to have come out of Italy are pizza and her cream Cavalli trench coat!"

Morgan narrows her eyes. I know what she's thinking. How could Siobhan not credit Italy with Lady Gaga? But before I can explain that as a straight woman, Siobhan simply does not have the same level of taste that we lesbians do, Morgan says, "I'm so going to enjoy destroying that girl in the debate tomorrow."

I gulp, my blossoming urge to go "MAAAARIIIIAAAAA!" again dropping like a Gemini's standards. (Although not Morgan's standards; those are obviously VERY high . . . Ahem.) My stomach goes all wriggly like an eel in a plastic bag, and I don't think it's just because I ate too much of Mum's spinach soufflé.

Chat Thread: Siobhan Collingdale

Siobhan, 11:03 p.m.:
HOROSCOPE. SCORPIO. NOW.

Cat, 11:05 p.m.:
Ummmm yes ofc!!!!!!

Jupiter is in Aries THANK SAPPHO

By which I mean ummm you need downtime!!! It's very important!!! So don't just lie on the floor, your house of wellness is at stake, Siobhan!!! So maybe go easy tomorrow . . . ?

Siobhan, 11:09 p.m.:
JUPITER CAN SUCK A SQUASH

Do you think I HAVE to go with Head Girl or can I call myself Queen's Creative Director? Also I want to change our school's name to McQueen's. UNRELATED obvs . . .

20
Someone Is Going to Ohio

Thursday morning, I wake up and discover I am still alive. So we're already off to a bad start. The moon is also in waning gibbous, meaning we are encouraged to "soften and surrender" . . . Has the moon ever MET Siobhan or Morgan, for Slender Sappho's sake?!

I'm looking forward to the debate even less than Mum's Monday Mozzarella and Mango Macaroni—if that's possible. I think I'd rather eat Dad's slippers! I trudge to school in a state of absolute despair. Which means I am in mental anguish, not Ohio or somewhere.

When I trudge into homeroom, Zanna is already fully prepped to spend the day ignoring me, headphones in and reading *Twilight*. She really must be angry if she'd rather read a vampiric straight-fest than talk to me! I trudge over to Alison Bridgewater instead.

"Gosh," says Alison, hand on her heart. "You don't look very happy. Did Disney give Elsa a husband or something? You'll always have your fan-fic, no matter what."

"If that happened, I would be in the hospital, probably receiving oxygen, and not at school," I reply. "No, Alison, I am thinking about the debate today. Where's Siobhan? Beating up a piñata of my girlfriend or something?"

"No, that's scheduled for the weekend," says Alison. "Babe, it's going to be fine! Siobhan said it's *highly unlikely* the debate will end in physical violence. And it's just a silly school campaign—not a big deal. We're all friends at the end of the day!"

I stare at Alison, wondering what it must be like to live in a world where everyone makes daisy chains together, and children genuinely help old people across roads, and flowers have faces and sing. I sometimes worry she is a few leaves short of a salad.

Then the door comes crashing open and Siobhan appears with her bright red megaphone. She marches in, swipes Augustus Ming's bag from the carpet, and drop-kicks it out of the open window.

"WHO'S READY TO KICK SOME EMO BUTTS TODAY?" she announces into the megaphone, and everyone erupts into thunderous applause. Augustus Ming even hands over his gym bag, eyes shining with pride, so Siobhan can drop-kick that as well.

I clap my hands so that Siobhan doesn't drop-kick *me*, but inside, the only thing that's clapped is my peace of mind. I shuffle back to my seat and silently pray to Aphrodite that my girlfriend will still be alive by the end of this dismal day.

The hall is more packed than a rich kid's stocking. This must be the first assembly ever that no one wants to miss! I take a seat between Lip Gloss Lizzie and Alison, which is when I notice that

Miss Ward has brought actual popcorn with her. She's snacking away with Miss Spencer in the corner.

Mr. Drew comes northerning onto the stage in his usual boring, suit-and-tie way. He gives a long speech about golden opportunities and how exams will be here before we know it because time flies, although you wouldn't know it from his speech. Then he says, "Now, I want everyone to remember that we also have a Head Boy debate . . ."

"BOOOO," goes Imaran, and Jasmine McGregor hoots loudly.

"CAT FIGHT, CAT FIGHT, CAT FIGHT," the Lad Friends start chorusing, and I exchange frightened glances with Catherine Cahill from seventh grade. Mr. Drew nervously adjusts his tie, grimacing at Mrs. Warren, whose arms are folded in absolute boredom. All she does is roll her eyes and check her watch.

Before Mr. Drew can finish boring us to death, Siobhan steps up to rapturous applause and swipes the mic from his hand. She flicks her hair over her shoulders, catching Morgan right in the face, who lets out a surprised sneeze.

"And that's the sound of someone who's allergic to perfection!" she announces. "Let's hear it for my super *brave* competition, Miss Morgan Delaney!"

Everyone applauds and Mr. Drew apologetically hands Morgan a second mic.

"I don't need applause, Siobhan, but thanks," says Morgan, and I realize I am holding my breath. Mainly because Alison is nudging me and asking why my face is blue. "I only need a few moments to show everyone why I'm the better candidate—trust me, I won't need longer. Why don't you go first?"

Everyone goes, "Oooooo . . ." Siobhan doesn't flinch though, just flicks her hair again and strides to the front of the stage. "Thanks *so* much for asking me to go first, Morgan. It's probably a good idea you learn how it feels to come second, right?" She smirks again as everyone sniggers. "Friends, I'm going to keep this short, like Kenna Brown. You already know who I am: a natural leader who's not scared of anything. Someone who will take what you want right to the top and put senior staff into headlocks . . . Not literally, of course, unless you ask nicely."

Everyone laughs again and Siobhan flicks her hair. Then Morgan raises her mic. "And what does everyone want, Siobhan? Why don't you enlighten the room?"

The laughter fades, and so does Siobhan's smile. Only for a moment. "Well, duh!" she says. "I was obviously just coming to that, Mogs. People want learning that takes them outside the classroom. We need more school trips to engage us and create new memories!"

"That's nice," says Morgan, nodding. "For people who can afford school trips anyway. But what about people who can't? We shouldn't be putting our funding into stuff that'll only look good in a graduate's yearbook. Wouldn't taking measures to tackle period poverty, and cutting the cost in the school cafeteria, be more valuable than some glittery vanity project?"

There's murmuring through the ranks. Then Lip Gloss Lizzie whispers, "Babes, what's vanity? Is that where all the veins in your hands start showing?"

"Look in a mirror," mutters Zanna on Lizzie's other side, and I snort.

Up onstage, Siobhan looks flustered as a flamingo. She raises

the mic again. "Um, well, totally! And as someone who works in a food bank, I know all about that. Diversity is über-important and Queen's should cater to everyone! Even freaks like Jasmine."

"YOU SAID IN SCIENCE YOU THOUGHT POTASSIUM WAS AN ICE CREAM FLAVOR!" Jasmine bellows.

"You're right, Siobhan. Queen's *should* cater to everyone," Morgan continues. "So why, on that health and safety training day, were we only taught CPR on male mannequins? And why are twice as many boys receiving learning support than girls? We need to look at gender bias in this school and smash it down."

People are clapping and nodding. Even Lip Gloss Lizzie looks like her brain has switched on, a very rare sight indeed. Yikes on egg yolks. Morgan is killing it! It's actually very, very . . . attractive. I sit up in my seat, my heart all wuthering-heightsy.

The debate rages on. Siobhan stumbles over school trips, Morgan proposes discussing trans identities in health class. Morgan says we should have gender-neutral bathrooms, Siobhan says Morgan should try *taking* a bath. Morgan suggests allocating three mental health days to each student. "We need to end the stigma around mental health," she says. "We're teenagers and we have to go to school five times a week. Obviously we're miserable."

Everyone giggles for Morgan *again* and Siobhan's smile noticeably tightens, like a homicidal rubber band. "Well, my dad is a psychotherapist, actually!" she cuts in, swanning in front of Morgan.

"ARE YOU HIS FAVORITE PATIENT?!" Jasmine yells, and hooting ensues.

"No heckling, Miss McGregor!" Mr. Drew interjects, but the damage is already done. The whole school is sniggering away, like

a mosh pit of mockery. Siobhan's face turns completely Scarlett O'Hara, her dignity gone with the wind.

Then Morgan puts her hand on her hip. "School culture's toxic, guys. Everyone's scared. And when you're faced with Siobhan every day? I can't blame you . . . But we *make* this school. Without us, they can't even open their doors, so let's use that power to boot Queen's into the twenty-first century. That, as we say in Ireland, would be mother-crackin' class!"

I have no idea if they really say that in Ireland, but in the name of Mary Quinn's big clock, I'm convinced! Everyone stands to applaud, and that's when Morgan lifts her mic and drops it like Barack Obama. It's very dashing and divine.

Even as I'm clapping though (I am a very supportive and amazing girlfriend), I notice Siobhan, eyes wide like an entire apocalypse is happening at x3 speed in front of her. And my stomach twists like a sweaty spaghetti. Because they can't both win. One of my special amigas is going to end the day in a state of extreme disappointment.

And no, I'm still not talking about Ohio.

Everything is awkward at the picnic table. More awkward than just alligators, actually. This might even be the Awkward Appalachian Mountains. The only sound is Habiba slowly peeling back the wrapper of her energy bar. Siobhan is like a statue. Or a gravestone, given how grim her face looks.

"This is really bad," she murmurs at last. "Mr. Drew even told me after that I'm not taking this campaign seriously. He doesn't like any of my ideas!"

"What about the mandatory skiing lessons idea?" asks Habiba.

"Not even that one." Siobhan sighs, and Habiba gasps. "*Moron* Delaney has a Vegan Meals Initiative, thanks to my TRAITOR of a sister. And her Hairstyles Don't Affect Education proposal. *And* she wants to make the bathrooms gender neutral! What do I have?"

I try not to react to Siobhan calling my girlfriend a moron, and Kenna opens her clipboard, clearing her throat efficiently. "You have . . . Um, well, we scrapped putting a DJ booth in the library . . . And we shelved the more-cooks-less-books proposal after you found out that the cafeteria's head chef is writing a novel . . ."

"What are the chances?" Siobhan scowls.

"You've still got some amazing charity fundraiser ideas! Bricklaying for Black Lives Matter and . . ." Kenna squints. "Wall-building for Water Aid. Although aren't those actually . . . Well, aren't those the same activities?"

Siobhan makes a shrugging gesture. "My uncle is a builder. Well, he employs builders. Well, he owns a lot of buildings. Whatever, okay?! I was low on inspiration!"

"Sorry," Alison chips in delicately. "How exactly is it for charity, Siobhan? If we're building walls for your uncle, aren't we, um . . . Aren't we just working for him? For free?"

Siobhan blinks a few times. Then she grabs Kenna's clipboard and Frisbee-hurls it onto the roof of the art studios. "I NEED GOOD IDEAS OR I AM GOING TO LOSE! WHY ARE NONE OF YOU HELPING?! ARE YOU ALL UTTERLY USELESS? KENNA, STOP WHIMPERING. HABIBA, WILL YOU STOP EATING THOSE ENERGY BARS, THEY'RE NOT EVEN GOOD FOR YOU, THEY HAVE REALLY HIGH SUGAR!"

“Hey!” protests Habiba. “Leave the energy bars out of this!”

Siobhan looks like she’s ready to throttle her. Then she just closes her eyes and says, “You’re right. That was uncalled for. They sell those energy bars in Waitrose and I actually . . . really . . . like them . . .” Then she turns on her heel and dithers away, wavering all over like a distressed spirit in stress.

Kenna scurries after her and I glance round the remaining members of the gang. (Minus Zanna, who I think has actually gone to the library to avoid me.)

“Um . . .” I drum my fingers. Then I grin. “Did anyone else notice how Gucci, Prada, Dolce and Gabbana Morgan looked when she was owning the stage though?”

“I’m not a lesbian, Cat,” says Habiba quickly. Then her eyes glaze over. She chews her energy bar in thought. “Although actually, now that you mention it . . .”

“I’m just going to say it,” says Lip Gloss Lizzie. “I would totally consider letting her come on to me sometime, maybe. Like, if I wasn’t with Lawrence.” Then she frowns at me. “Babe, do lesbians kiss the same way straight people do?”

I smirk back very smuggy-in-a-buggy indeed. “No, Lizzie,” I tell her, with all the confidence of a Capricorn girlboss. “We kiss much, much better.”

New Post From @OffishialSkinnydippers

@offishialskinnydippers:
WASSAAAAP Mini Skinnys!!! This is yo frontman roadman skillzboss JAMIE and I got some SKINNY-AF newz!!! As y'oll know, FEMINISM is at the EPICCENTER of EVERYTHING we do as Skinnys. Because women are WHAT? FUNDAMENTAL TO THE SURVIVAL OF OUR SPECIES! (As well as great in stacks of other ways). That's why we're superman excited to announce we now have a GIRL in our band!!! Her name is BROOKE, she's a singer, stinger, downright ginger (in a really good way) and also the ruler of my heart ;) To celebrate this moment of empowerment, please enjoy our freshest jam, by Brooke and me, MY EYES SWELL (inspired by FEMALE-created song All Too Well by Ms Taylor Swift!) #SkinnySkinnySKINNY!!!!

Comments (6 of 29):

@owusuperman:
So hyped!!!! #womenaregreat

@kieran_wb:
Solid one mate #womenaregreat

@a.bridgewater.xox:
Exciting for u guys!!!xoxox

@graceowusu:
Very Proud of my Grandson. Love & Kisses.

@morgan.mp3:
we love to see it

@m.marcus.jpg:
ayoo, someone tag taylor

21
Just Your Type on Tinder

Jamie put Brooke the Crook in his band?! Personally, I wouldn't have thought it possible to make the Skinny Dippers more embarrassing, but lo and behold, Jamie has found a way. Oh well—Easter break begins tomorrow, so hopefully, I can pause my ongoing crescendo of humiliation and have lots of cute dates with Morgan, and lots of very SEPARATE cute dates with the gang. Life's not all Cold Moons and misery.

But when I arrive at school, ears aching from Luna and Niamh's nonstop Mongolian throat-singing, I notice Siobhan's seat is empty. What the beetroot?! Siobhan has missed school ONCE, ever, and that was only because she got suspended. She once said that illness is "for spineless amateurs who mollycoddle their way through life like tissue-wrapped rose petals."

It's a dismal day without Zanna OR Siobhan to bounce off. Literally bounce off, considering we're playing tag rugby in PE. Siobhan will be sad to have missed out.

Unusually bruise-free, I ghost-drift to rehearsals for last period, where I'm instantly assaulted by Brooke, squirreling on about how she swallowed a bath bomb last night—I use up my Brooke tolerance for the day in about five minutes flat! As a result, I'm thoroughly ready to be daggered to death by the time Rich Elizabeth marches into the studio, head held high. Which is pretty easy, considering she's nearly nine feet tall.

"Hey, chicka," she crones, her snotty girl gang pouting about over her shoulder. "Think you'll know how to act today?"

I scowl. "I'm not in the mood, Elizabeth."

"Oh, she's not in the mood!" Elizabeth chortles. "I wonder if Meryl Streep is in the mood every single shoot. I wonder if Saoirse Ronan ever says to Timothée Chalamet, 'You know what, hun? I'm not feeling it today. Let's hold up EVERYONE and get lunch.'"

"Well, she might if she's hungry!" I reply, and Elizabeth goes all frowny.

Anyway, rehearsals are THE WORST. Miss Spencer spring-beaning about, the Goldilocks Gang sneering away at me, and Elizabeth (who, to her dizzying disgust, is put on lights when I'm running through the balcony scene with Brooke) adjusting the brightness all the time so that I get distracted and forget my lines.

Eventually, Miss Spencer claps her flippers, actually looking disappointed. Which is a miracle, considering her beam is pretty much bolt-gunned into place. "All right, let's take a break," she yaps. "Cat, I need you to learn these lines."

"But Miss," I protest, floundering in Elizabeth's direction. "The lights kept—!"

"No excuses, Cat!" Miss Spencer interrupts. Everybody stares, like lizards at the theater. "Listen, you lot—I want ENERGY!" She does a random handstand, presumably to demonstrate. "This is a story about CONFLICT! And PASSION! When two groups are forced to CLASH and confront their discomfort with one another! And how they overcome that for the sake of TRUE LOVE!" She pirouettes. "So, next rehearsal, I don't want to see mumbling and stumbling and chewing food that you think I can't see . . ." Brooke hastily hides her chocolate bar. "BEST FEET FORWARD, my young thespians! Now, go home."

I've been waiting ALL DAY for those precious words. But now that Miss Spencer has bestowed them upon me, I am Elsa-style FROZEN. Because I *am* Juliet. Juliet is me. For real! Siobhan is the Capulets and Morgan is the Montagues and Luna is very annoying, but I don't suppose that's relevant to this. I'm just thinking about how very wise I must be, to have spotted this symbolism, when someone nudges my arm and I notice Morgan has materialized.

She smiles in a very cool and breathtaking way, then says, "We're gonna go hang to celebrate that school's out for the next two weeks. Come with?"

"Sure!" I chime, trying to reboot my robot. We link arms and follow Maja and Marcus into the corridor. I'm just thinking it's actually very Romeo-romantic that Morgan came to pick me up after class when I notice Brooke is going in the same direction and a much more worrying worry comes to mind. "Um, Morgan?" I ask. "Who exactly is 'we'?"

Well, this is not how I wanted to celebrate the start of Easter break. I'm trudging down some rural roadside with Morgan,

Maja, Marcus, Millie, Brooke, and Jamie—who has a very worrying, guitar-shaped bag over his shoulder. Sappho strike me down, preferably quickly.

I tug Morgan's sleeve. "Um, babe, where are we going?"

Morgan is flicking peanuts into her mouth while walking. Which is very cool in its disregard for health and safety, but also means she isn't paying full attention to me, so harrumph. "Oh, just the Plow," she says, and before I can ask her what in the name of Shaun the Sheep she's on about, Maja switches on some obnoxiously loud music with her portable speaker and Morgan goes, "I LOVE THIS SONG, HECK YEAH."

It is a song I don't know from a band I've never heard of. It could be by the Skinny Dippers for all I know.

We tramp on until we get to this weird gap in the hedge by the road. Then, to my utter astonishment, Maja starts climbing *through* the gap, leading the way into the dark and dingy trees beyond.

"C'mon, babe," says Morgan, dragging me through the twigs. She doesn't seem to notice the heavy resistance in my every move. "This is the plow. It's cool."

I gaze around. Beyond the hedgerow, there are some scrappy-looking trees and a clearing. And an abandoned Land Rover. There's also a huge, rusty piece of farm equipment, which Maja and Marcus and Millie instantly jump on to lounge about looking edgy.

"This is the plow?" I repeat, gulping.

Maja snorts, rolling her eyes. "We hang out here, like, all the time, Snow White. Don't sweat it. No one's been murdered here . . . Yet." Then she reaches into her rucksack and pulls out a four-pack of Coke cans. She yanks one off and says, "Catch."

I'm still gazing at the abandoned truck.

"What?" I say, then—*WHAM*—a can knocks me right on the forehead. Startled and flat on my back in the muddy leaves, I'm reminded why Siobhan made me sign a written contract to promise I'd never audition for the netball team.

"Oh, Christ," Morgan mutters, crouching. "Cat, you all right?"

"I said catch," Maja points out unhelpfully.

I glare at her, rubbing my forehead, feeling anything but romantic. Not helped by the fact Brooke and Jamie are already being all gooey and gross, feeding grapes to each other on the hood of the truck. I feel like I'm in an episode of *Skins*!

"Do we HAVE to hang out here?" I hiss at Morgan.

She looks confused. "I thought you wanted to hang out more."

I gesture around. "But Morgan, we're in a field in the middle of nowhere."

"It's not about the place," Morgan says, kicking back and lying among the leaves like it's not damp and brown and soggy. "It's about the vibes. Relax, okay? I'm here."

Then she smiles in this really easy, squeeze-me-round-the-waist kind of way, and I'm ogling her freckles again like a truly muppet-struck microscope with a crush. I shuffle closer and she slings her arm around me. I still glare some more at Maja though.

"I didn't fall!" I call to her. "I meant to sit down all along, actually."

Maja sips her weird, neon-colored energy drink. "Sure thing. Did you mean to forget all your lines in rehearsal, too?"

Marcus cackles and I scowl again. "That wasn't my fault! Elizabeth totally sabotaged me! You saw her messing around with the lights! Just because she's jealous—"

"Well, you are WAY more blond than her," says Maja, smirking.

I frown. "Of my role, Maja! Not my hair."

Marcus makes eyes at Maja and Millie. "Never gonna get it . . ." he murmurs, and they all break down sniggering like poltergeists in too much eyeliner.

"Elizabeth is evil," Brooke interjects, crossing her legs on the truck's hood. Jamie inhales a grape and begins choking and spluttering, but nobody pays him any attention. "She only hates you because of Siobhan. She's into Kieran Wakely-Brown, but he won't go out with her because he's scared Siobhan will skin him like a dalmatian. I overheard him telling Imaran when I was hiding in the air vent above the boys' bathrooms."

I blink at Brooke in alarm because *what*?! Jamie keeps on wheezing.

"It's so disappointing when girls blame other girls instead of the lousy-ass men who hurt them," says Morgan, stroking my shoulder. "It's not Cat's fault."

Maja snorts. "They're all just Barbie Brigade Basics, Morgan. I don't know why anyone's surprised when they backstab each other. Siobhan Collingdale cares more about Ariana Grande than she does about any of her actual friends."

"LOL," says Millie Butcher. "True."

I feel prickly. And *not* just because I walked into a holly bush before.

"Actually, that's not true," I say, shrugging Morgan's arm off me. Which hopefully shows how truly annoyanced out I am

becoming. "Siobhan cares about her friends, too. How many people would hire a hot-air balloon just to find a lost glove? Yes, she probably should have checked Alison's pockets first. But she still goes that extra mile. Well, one thousand three hundred sixty-eight miles, actually, if we're talking all of Kent."

"Oh, whatever," says Maja, tracing a tear down her cheek. Which Kenna Brown will confirm is NOT even the right sign for "sad." "She dated a guy called Dale Collins and never even noticed his name is her surname backward."

Marcus pipes up. "And let's not forget Alison Bridgewater reacted with genuine shock when she found out Hugh Grant was British because she watched *Notting Hill* dubbed in Hindi by mistake and believed he was genuinely Indian."

Morgan bursts out cackling, and that's when I stand up and brush off my skirt. It's supposed to look assertive and such, but it doesn't help that my enormous hair gets tangled in some nearby branches. Once Morgan has successfully extracted me, I try again.

"Alison is really caring, actually," I say, heart thundering. "She looks after rescue hedgehogs in her yard and it's actually quite endearing how she never remembers what day it is but always remembers your birthday." I nod. Awkward alligators galore. "Anyway, um, I might go home . . . I'd rather read a real book than listen to you read my friends."

Everyone goes a bit quiet. The edgy music edge-shuffles on. Jamie finally coughs the grape back into his hand and the Triple M's give Morgan told-you-so eyebrows. Brooke just looks evil and excited. Morgan turns a bit pink. "We're only joking, babe," she says as my heart sinks into my unmentionables. "But don't stay if you're not in the mood."

I hover there looking stupid. Which is quite an achievement when standing so close to Jamie Owusu, still thumping his chest from that stupid grape. Both our eyes are watering, but for very different reasons. I pick up my bag and say, "Fine, then."

Mum has told me frequently that I am very good at flouncing. So I put all my flouncitude into practice at once and stomp toward the road. Behind me, I hear Morgan scramble to her feet. She calls, "Cat, wait," but I do not wait. I am flouncing.

I flounce through the hedge and onto the road. I am about to flounce all the way back to Lambley Common, but then I hear a screech, I turn around, and OH MIGHTY APHRODITE, THERE IS A CAR SKIDDING TOWARD ME, and then Morgan grabs me by my shirt collar and yanks me into the hedge.

We fall into a ditch with a splat.

The driver does some rude hand gestures, but Morgan does worse ones back, and they screech off looking dazed. Then she says, "Idiot. What's next—you'll get hit by a plane?"

"Well, EXCU-U-USE ME," I exclaim, yanking a thorny branch of blackberries from my hair. "I was a bit distracted, actually, by how attacked I felt back in that dodgy scrapyard."

"Yeah, all right." Morgan sighs down at her black Doc Martens. "Look, I don't want you to leave. Come back. We can chill. Maja just has a weird sense of humor. She's totally down to get to know you."

The wind catches our hair and it blusters poetically about our faces, tangling together like ivy. Morgan has very beautiful eyes. Pale blue, like sunlit glass. I open my mouth.

"Morgan, where are you?" Maja's voice comes calling. "I've

found someone who's just your type on Tinder if Curly doesn't work out."

I stare at Morgan. Morgan stares at me.

"She doesn't mean that," Morgan says, but I am already walking away. After way longer than acceptable, she calls, "Cat, just text me later, okay? We can sort things out?"

I *almost* pause my flouncing—although it's actually more just sad walking by now. But I manage not to, and I hear Morgan vanishing back into the hedge, like that Homer Simpson meme. Pitter-pattering through the drizzle, I take out my phone and listen to it ring.

"Why are you CALLING?!" Siobhan barks without even saying hello.

"H-hey!" I stammer. "Um, no reason, I just . . . missed . . . you . . . ?"

Siobhan says, "Don't be a sap." Then she says, "What's up, then?"

Chat Thread: Morgan Delaney

Morgan, 11:15 a.m.:
Morning . . . Can we call today? I think we should talk about things

Cat, 11:39 a.m.:
Sorry Morgan but today is the waning crescent moon when one should withdraw and refresh. It's important that I consciously carve out time for this reflection as I am usually v busybusybusy like a bee so will maybe have to raincheck talking for now xx

Morgan, 11:42 a.m.:
Are u serious? Cat you can't raincheck bc of the moon

Anyway I'm leaving for Ireland soon

Cat, 12:20 p.m.:
Well then we can call after the cosmic reset of the new moon when we have fresh perspectives!! Toodle-oo till Tuesday!!!

Morgan, 12:25 p.m.:
That's next week???

Cat come on

We both know you only say toodle-oo when you're rlly, rlly mad

Cat, 12:27 p.m.:
TOODLE

OOOOOOOOOOOOOOOOOOOOOOOOOOOOOOO
OOOO

22
Buzzing in Solitude

I have two weeks off school for Easter break: the perfect length of time to forget everything I've learned this semester. But upsettingly, I don't really feel happy . . . I'm like a Gemini who has just agreed to be in a committed relationship: full of regrets.

And Morgan seems to be living up to the stereotype daily!

Not only are things very UN-McQueen with my girlfriend (as Siobhan phrased it), but this will be the first school holiday where I won't be going to Zanna's house because we're not talking. Usually, it's because I can't be bothered to take the bus. But it's very sad. And worse, it's coming up to Taurus Season, where everyone will be staying stubborn and true to themselves. So Zanna is unlikely to soften up anytime soon . . .

Luna comes into my room. "What are you doing, lying on the floor like that?"

I lift my head to scowl at her. She really is highly annoying.

"I'm trying to stay grounded," I explain. "It's almost Taurus Season, you know."

"Don't be ridiculous," says Luna. "You're obviously just sulking about Morgan and Zanna again. And don't throw another Jane Austen hardback at me! You know I'm right."

I lower my copy of *Northanger Abbey* and glower. Luna being right really is the most heinous thing. She looks at me expectantly, as if I'll suddenly have all the answers.

I stroke my imaginary beard to see if it will make me feel wise, which it doesn't. Who decided beards make you smart anyway?

Eventually, I sigh a tragic sigh. "Sometimes, people grow apart, Luna. Like the lunar cycle, people in our lives come and go. We have to accept that winds change and that life is as short as the falling of snow."

There's a pause. Probably as Luna processes the deep poetic nature of what I just said. It's heavy stuffing indeed, to have proclaimed such wise and philosophical truths as that.

"What in the name of Rupi Kaur's milk glands are you on about?" Luna says, staring at me like I'm completely out of my mammaries. "That's literally the stupidest thing I've ever heard you say. Have you been listening to Coldplay again?"

I sit up, scowling. I should have known Luna would not be cultured enough to understand. "Coldplay actually has some *very* impactful lyrics, Luna—" I begin, but my Gandhi-sidepiece sister isn't done.

"Firstly, I wouldn't let Dorian be rude about my friends." Luna folds her arms. "It would be very anti-feminist of me. And

second, how long have you known Zanna? Ever since she untangled your hair from that fan in kindergarten, you've been best friends. The most empowering and feminist thing you've ever done is stick together through thick and thin—or thick and thick, considering how stupid you are—and now you're going to throw all that away because you've got make-out buddy problems?! That's truly pathetic."

Then she stomps off, muttering about meditating the ineptitude out of her system with Niamh. I've no idea what Neptune has got to do with anything, but I wish Luna would just leave me to car-crash all my relationships in peace. Morgan is really waxing my gibbous right now—and it's Zanna's loss if she doesn't want to be my friend anymore . . . !

It might also be my loss. Sigh.

No, no, and no again—Luna is completely wrong. I don't need Zanna to have a good time! I have other friends, like Kenna and Alison, who invite me with them to Hashtag Browns, the coolest café in Lambley Common, one boring-as-brown-hair holiday afternoon when Siobhan has gone off the grid and Habiba is doing a triple triathlon, Sappho save her soul.

But you know who they don't invite? Zanna. Luna says that's probably because Zanna's in Poland, not because they like me more. But who cares what Luna says? I still make sure to post loads of group selfies on Instagram to show Zanna who's boss.

Hashtag Browns really is the überest of cafés. Their drinks are cool and hipster, like Shoreditch in the Ice Age. They even make waffles shaped like hashtags! And since waffles are shaped

like hashtags already, it's really very smart. We all order from the #SundayFunDay menu, then lounge around on the emoji-face beanbags by the window.

It's a very proud moment, actually, like a sidekick spin-off series! We're dandy as dandelions without Zanna *or* our Queen Bee. We are just fine buzzing in solitude.

Kenna keeps checking her phone between every sip of her Apple Skin and Cinnamon Sprinkle Peach Iced Tea though. She doesn't seem to be listening at all to my and Alison's hilarious conversation about Kieran Wakely-Brown using the black thumbs-up emoji on Instagram even though he's whiter than Swedish toothpaste.

Eventually, Alison puts down her Beetroot and Brazilian Walnut Coffee-Free Cappuccino avec Glacé Cherry and says, "Who are you texting, Kenna? Is it a guy?"

I anxiously stir the straw round my Skinny Strawberries and Cream Iced Hot Chocolate, crossing my fingers and toes that we're *not* going to start talking about Alison's newest new crush, Max from math.

Kenna flicks her screen on and off. "No," she sighs sadly. "I haven't heard from Siobhan since the debate. Do you think I ordered the right drink? She's not replying!"

"Gosh," Alison says, hand on her heart. "I hope she's okay. I don't think any of us expected Morgan to do so well. I honestly thought she was too moody for public speaking. It's like when Billie Eilish went blond! No one saw that coming . . ."

That's when I notice a flash of orange over Alison's shoulder and I almost spit my drink! Brooke the Crook has clattered into view on the street outside. For the love of Aphrodite and all her

chubby cherubs, can I never escape that girl? I try to slide down my beanbag and out of sight, but almost get swallowed by the heart-eyes emoji.

Kenna signs something shocked-looking as I flap about like an ostrich in quicksand. "Is that Brooke the Crook?! Oh my days, and Maja Vidmar. She's wearing her *nose ring*, too!"

Alison scrambles to save me from the cannibal cushion. The comatose hipsters of Hashtag Browns have actually woken up to laugh and point at me! Not ideal. "I'm sure she's perfectly nice, Kenna," Alison says, heaving me up. "People with nose rings can even adopt kids nowadays. They can basically lead nice normal lives, whoever they're with!"

"Not everyone with a nose ring is bisexual, Alison," I say, dusting myself off, and Alison frowns in surprise. "But she's *not* perfectly nice. In fact, she probably has that nose ring because she's a complete cow."

"Are they going into *Boots*?" Kenna flaps. "There's no way either of those two do skincare. I bet you my edible nail polish recipe that they're up to no good."

"Oh, well!" sighs Alison merrily. "There's no way of knowing *what* they're doing!" She beams around the beanbags. "Should we order cherry Bakewells?"

Me and Kenna exchange glances.

Thirty seconds later, we're scurrying out of Hashtag Browns on a stalkathon, Alison whimpering that she should've just gone to brunch with her Sunday school friends. Shockingly for England, it's sunny and warm today, so we all have sunglasses in our bags. Me and Kenna even have brimmed hats, so we put them on for maximum disguisability.

"Guys, I think more people will notice us if we crawl!" Alison whispers as we scamper in and dive behind the first makeup counter. I peek over the edge.

"You see what?" signs (and mouths) Kenna impatiently.

I narrow my eyes. "Some middle-aged people," I report back. "Lots of beige."

"Maybe Brooke and Maja aren't here?" Alison says hopefully, and that's when I spot them, Brooke's crescendo of orange hair visible in the cosmetics aisle.

I gesture to Kenna and Alison and we scuttle over like beetles. We poke our heads in height order round the corner: Kenna at the bottom, then me, then Alison. Brooke and Maja are browsing the eyeliners. Which isn't overtly wrong, even if I think Brooke's more likely to eat makeup than wear it. Then—oh my googly goodness—it happens!

Brooke swipes two mascaras off the shelf and mumbles something to Maja. They're totally going to steal them! I nudge Kenna and she fumbles with her phone. Alison's dewy eyes widen into planets with their own orbit. Kenna zooms right in on Brooke and I hold my breath, ready for the moment we finally catch her ginger-handed . . .

"'Scuse me, ladies," a gruff voice interrupts. "What do you think you're doing?!"

Kenna jumps so hard, the top of her head thwacks into my chin above her, and like dominoes of Easter Island heads, I jump right into Alison until we're all stumbling about the place like bowling pins.

"What the . . . ?!" I hear Maja mutter, and oh, gooseberries, this is awkward.

There's a security guard in a gray suit that's stretching at the seams squinty-eyeing us. He's built like a fortress! Kenna always becomes helpfully nonverbal when in panic, so she falls completely silent, her beautiful brown eyes quivering in alarm.

"D-doing?" Alison stammers. "Well, um, we're not doing anything!"

The guard glares down at us. "Were you filming customers?"

Brooke and Maja are gawping, the mascaras are still in Brooke's hand, and Kenna's phone is still in camera mode! This looks sticky as Mum's hand creams. We need a genius excuse! I open my mouth and . . . "Um, we're doing a project!" I blurt out. Oh, for the love of Ohio. "Kenna's making a documentary about, um, redheads' shopping habits."

We all blink at each other. Kenna sign-mouths, *"WHAT?!"* but I've said it now! And suddenly, Alison is panic-nodding along. "It's true!" she vigorously agrees. "We're calling it, um . . . 'Red and Ready to Shop till We're Dead'!"

"And we're learning that their spending habits are, like, red hot!" I babble, hopping about ridiculously. "Would you agree, as a redhead yourself?"

"I'm bald!" roars the man. "What are you talking about?"

"But you're quite sweaty!" I blunder on. "And is that a touch of sunburn . . . ?"

He's getting redder by the second, too. That's when Kenna realizes that Siobhan isn't here to rescue us and, shockingly, finds her voice. She steps between me and the man before I can dig our graves any deeper. (We might actually be in New Zealand by now.)

"LISTEN! Mr., um . . ." She squints at his badge as we gaze in awe. "Um, Stanley. This is all just a misunderstanding. We know

these girls from school and we were just, um, joking about those other things. Hahaha . . ."

Stanley looks about as ready to see the funny side as a homicide detective. Clicking his neck, he turns to Brooke and Maja. "Is this true, ladies?" he asks them. "Do you know these strange young women?"

We grin at Brooke and Maja hopefully. Maja rolls her eyes, but before she can answer the question, Brooke puts on her most crooked smirk and says, "Sorry, Stanley, but no. I have never seen these girls in my life."

I could *throttle* her. After everything she's put me through—THIS?!

Stanley glares back around. Alison lets out a genuine whimper. Then Kenna panic-shrieks, "I DON'T WANT TO GO TO JAIL!" and swipes a packet of cotton pads, throws them right at Stanley, grabs my hand, and runs.

The pads bounce right off Stanley's shining head, but there's no time to think! I barrel after Kenna out of the automatic doors, Alison squealing on my heels as we rush out . . .

. . . straight into someone else walking in.

I barely have time to register that it's *MRS. WARREN* before I've crashed right into her.

She stumbles back into the street and falls over a dustbin.

WHAT YOU NEED TO KNOW ABOUT KENNA BROWN

- She is Leo loyal galore and will literally do anything Siobhan asks. Sadly this includes demonstrating how to kiss with tongues and seductive dribbling. That was one sleepover I *really* could have done without.
- She won an award for having the most beautiful eyes in school when we had our Queen's Golden Globe Awards in eighth grade. Siobhan now makes her blink in all their photos together.
- She's just gotten her first proper hearing aid. It's purple, and for some reason I'm unsure about, we've named it Monica. Kenna wears it full-time at school now . . . although I'm sure I've seen her switch it off around Siobhan.
- Her sign name is Brownie. For ages, I assumed chocolate was involved, all very drool-a-licious. Then I found out it's Brownie as in GIRL SCOUT! How disappointing is that? Then she said one of her Deaf friends is stuck with the sign name Doorbell, so hmm. Brownie is probably quite safe actually.
- She once had an existential crisis because Siobhan went on holiday and there was no Wi-Fi at the hotel. Siobhan had to mail her a handwritten list of things to think about when alone. One of the things on the list was "hummus."
- Kenna has loved hummus ever since.

23
A Slap to the Face with a Blobfish

If you're going to knock anybody into a dustbin, it may as well be Mrs. Warren. She's able to smooth everything over with Stanley, who it turns out is an ex-pupil of hers from many moons ago, and we're all able to leave without any charges being brought against us.

We bought her an Influencer Apology smoothie from Hashtag Browns to say thank you (it included "lying lychees," "gushing goji," and "insincere Indian figs"!) but I'm not convinced it won her over. I suppose she will just punish us after Easter break.

But worse than that, it turns out Loudmouth Jasmine McGregor was having a mani-pedi in the beauty parlor next door, and she saw the whole ordeal! By the next day, *everyone* in Lambley Common and their aunts seems to have heard how I "decked Mrs. Warren into a bin." My phone is exploding! Almost literally, given Siobhan's passion for capital letters. She tells us to NEVER *EVER* AGAIN MAKE THE GANG LOOK STUPID IN FRONT OF MORON DOOLALLY AND HER KNOCK-KNEED FRIENDS!!!! I AM TRYING TO FIND MYSELF RN AND I CAN'T BE NANNYING YOU SWIVEL-EYED SLUSH-BRAINS 24/7!!!!! PULL YOURSELVES TOGETHER!!! KENNA, THE BLACK BOOTS WORK BETTER THAN THE BROWN ONES.

Radio Zanna is still silent salamanders though. I try to distract myself by learning my lines for the school play, but end up just forlornly watching from my window, not a yonder in sight, as Mum and Dad throw away another perfectly good day nailing together their greenhouse. Then my phone buzzes: an incoming video call from Morgan.

Oh, gooseberries. I forgot about the new moon deadline! Do I really want to talk to Morgan now?! We've barely spoken since the plow. Maybe I can delay until the waxing crescent instead . . . ? Then I remember Luna's judging face when I told her this morning that I still hadn't talked with Morgan *or* Zanna. She'll get frown lines if she's still judging me by dinner.

I take a breath, mutter a quick prayer to Aphrodite, and accept the call. Then I scream because I completely forgot that I was doing a face mask. I look like the moon emoji, all my hair scraped back into an almost invisible bun. Morgan, of course, looks goose-level divine, in full eyeliner with dark green hair.

"Morgan!" I beam very normally and hope she won't notice my face. Probably a bit of a lost cause since we are on FaceTime. "How's Ireland coming along? Or, um, how's Ireland? Since it's not exactly under construction . . . Right?"

"Hey," Morgan says. "Ireland's boring as usual, but I just wanted . . ." Then she looks at the camera and double-takes. "Christ on a cracker. What's that all over your face? Where's your hair gone? I'm getting a Danny DeVito vibe."

I scowl. "I'm doing a face mask, Morgan! And my hair is just tied back. Anyway, um . . . How are things feeling under the new moon? Any fresh takes?"

What should happen now is that I sit back and bask in the glory of being rightly apologized to. But instead, Morgan says, "I've just been talking to Maja, actually. She told me about you and your friends stalking her the other day."

I sit up quickly, shooketh and surprised. At least my face mask is masking my blushing cheeks.

"Um, would we call it stalking?" I nervy-laugh. "I'd say it was more heroning, actually. Get it, Morgan? Like, because a stork is a type of bird . . . ?"

But Morgan just frowns. "Cat, I'm trying to get my friends to like you. I thought that's what you wanted? How am I supposed to though if you keep pulling stunts like this?"

Now it's me who turns frowny. *Trying* to get her friends to like me? Everybody likes me! Habiba even called me "not the worst" in a recent Instagram livestream.

"Morgan, are you joking? Maja doesn't like anybody! She probably doesn't even like you. Anyway, you should have been there. Then you'd know that they were actually shoplifting! We almost caught them redheaded."

Morgan just groans. This is going badly, plague-on-both-your-houses badly. Morgan hasn't even acknowledged what happened before the break, and now I'm being accused of all these things I didn't even do? And some things I did?! It's utterly unacceptable.

"Cat, you have SUCH a vendetta against Brooke," says Morgan, before I can point out the many reasons she's wrong. "She's *not that bad*. If you actually got to know her, you'd see that. But as usual, Siobhan's opinion is biblical—"

"*Siobhan's* opinion?" I glare at the camera. "Morgan, Brooke gives me quite enough reasons to dislike her all by herself! Unlike you, I've known her since sixth grade. She's always been a crook and I doubt she even knows what makeup is, so why else would she be browsing it unless she was stealing?!"

"Because Maja was helping her get ready for her first Skinny Dippers gig?" Morgan says. "*Because* she's never worn makeup before, I asked Maja to help her out."

I blink at the camera a few times because, gooseberries, that actually sounds worryingly believable. Hmm. I consider backing down. Then I say, "Asking Maja about makeup is risky though. I mean, does Brooke *want* to look like a zombie blobfish?"

Morgan tilts her head. "You know, when you say things like that, I wonder if I'm dating you or one of your Regina George–knockoff friends."

Well, ouch in a kangaroo pouch. That stings quite a bit.

"If that's really how you see me, Morgan, then maybe you were right before," I say after a hiccupping silence. "Maybe we aren't going to work."

Morgan stares at me through the camera, her comatose cool finally faltering. At least she looks surprised. Then she does the worst thing ever.

"Right," she says judderingly. Although that might be the

rubbishy Irish phone connection. "Well, I'm going to have to talk about that later. I've got lunch with my grandparents now. Enjoy the face mask."

Then she hangs up. I actually gasp, like a new moon in shock. The disrespect! She may as well just have smacked me in the face with a Maja-shaped blobfish! I'm so annoyed that I hurl open my window and launch my phone right out of it onto the lawn.

Unfortunately, there's a shiny new greenhouse on the lawn, so I watch with wide-eyed horror as my phone smashes right through the fresh pane of glass and the whole left-hand wall collapses. FIZZLESTICKS! Dad comes rushing out into the backyard, blustering and waving his arms about like a slapstick cartoon builder.

"Christ!" he splutters. "What the devil happened?! CAT, GET DOWN HERE NOW!"

I quickly shut the window. Although he's right to be angry, I suppose. His stupid greenhouse better not have broken my phone!

Well, there's nothing like a trip into town to buy a new phone. Mum makes her thin-lipped face all the way, wittering on about how I have no respect for anything, that I don't know how lucky I am, that there's a wasp on my arm, look out. Wait—WHAT?!

I wave my arm and the wasp buzzes off out the car window. Which gives Mum the perfect excuse to rave about why I shouldn't open the windows because the air-conditioning won't work. She really is outstandingly boring.

"At least I can get a new phone number," I grumble as we

pull into the multistory parking garage. Tragically, we've had to drive all the way to Maidstone for this. "I'm basically afraid to switch my phone on since Lilac put my number on a website for selling feet pics!"

"Oh, darling Lilac!" Mum sighs as I shrug in hopeless despair. "Did she tell you she's just passed her Gold figure-skating exam? I don't know why you two haven't gone skating together. It would be such a lovely family outing!"

"Of course she didn't tell me!" I gesticulate as Mum locks the car and starts walking toward the shopping center. "We don't talk because WE HATE EACH OTHER. If I went ice-skating with her, she'd probably cut my throat with the blade of her ice skate."

"Lovely Lilac," Mum carries on. I give up. "It'll be so nice to have the whole family together again this weekend—"

I stop in my tracks. "Mum, the weekend?! What are you talking about?"

My heart rate rises until it's knocking planes out of the sky. Because I was really hoping I wouldn't have to see my evil cousin until at *least* Gemini Season, when she throws one of her lavish family birthday parties in London (although why anyone would want to celebrate Lilac having lived another year, I've no idea).

Mum rolls her eyes. "Why do I ever tell you anything? You never listen to a word I say!" True, but hardly relevant. "Easter Sunday, Cat! Rose, Hillary, and the girls are coming for lunch—it's been on the calendar for months! That's why your father *wanted* the new greenhouse to be ready . . ."

Considering Auntie Rose and Uncle Hillary got married in

Kew Gardens, which has glasshouses the size of Kendall Jenner's ego, I'm not sure why Mum thinks a greenhouse from IKEA is going to impress them. Especially since our house is practically a greenhouse already! But that's parents for you: illogical and irrational galore.

"But Mum!" I whine, racking my brains for ANY excuse to get out of having to see my insipidly twisted Gemini cousin. "Morgan is back by Sunday! I don't want to spend time with Lilac when I could be spending time with someone who isn't a sociopath."

"Well, invite Morgan for lunch!" Mum quips, and I almost vomit out my skeleton. "I'm sure your cousins would be delighted to meet her . . ."

She whitters on about asking Morgan's mum along, too, as I turn queasy. We're in the shopping center, the phone shop right ahead. Probably best I *don't* annoy Mum now, or else she might make me pay for my own phone, or something equally barbaric!

But inviting Morgan to lunch when our relationship is on the rocky horrors?! I can't possibly! Then again . . . if Lilac gets even a *sniff* that things are far from honeymoon, she'll parade it over me forever. She still taunts me to this day that no one gave me a Valentine's card in kindergarten. (There was an odd number in the class, okay?!)

Mighty Aphrodite, what do I do? "I . . . don't think Morgan will be back in time!" I babble, panic-flapping my hands. "Or . . . She might have a cold by then!"

Mum looks utterly confused. "But you just told me she is . . . !" Then she closes her eyes and puts her fingers on her temples.

I'm treading on very thin ice—and I would guess I weigh a little more than Elsa with her Disney hips. "Well, invite her or don't, Cathleen—it makes no odds to me. But you're spending Sunday with your family. End of discussion!"

I make squeaking noises, but all she does is mime zipping her mouth (if only) before she marches into the shop to buy me a new phone. What an absolutely heartless person she is.

THINGS LILAC WILL ALMOST DEFINITELY SAY IF I BREAK UP WITH MY GIRLFRIEND AFTER ONLY FOUR MONTHS

- "That lasted, didn't it?"
- "Glad to know my latest jar of organic peanut butter outlived your relationship . . ."
- "Don't be sad, Cathleen, the first breakup is always the hardest. Once you've been dumped, like, five hundred times, you won't even feel it . . ."
- "Oh, baby! Did she update her glasses prescription?"
- "Oh, cry me a river . . . No, seriously. I want to watch."
- "That's just a TRAGIC shame. It'll be hard finding someone else. I'd recommend an app, but what chance does someone like *you* have online? Or in real life . . ."
- "LOL."

24
Sucked Wisdom from Your What?!

Even though we're technically arguing, I text Morgan from my brand-new whiter-than-Rylan's-teeth phone to inform her that if we're even still together, she's invited to lunch on Sunday. She's all distant and bristly, but she *does* agree to come. Maybe this means she *does* want to work things out? I wonder what phase the moon will be in by then . . .

Anyway, Sunday *has* to go well, or we really are pancake-doomed, so my Virgo Moon better not mess this up for me! Morgan being there will prove to Lilac that I really do have a properly überliscious girlfriend. I'm still not sure she believes it! Convincing Mum was hard enough. After walking in on me making out with Morgan back in January, she called my relationship "a genuine Christmas miracle," which is a bit insulting, actually.

Speaking of miracles, I am outside in the yard, and not just because my parents have forced me to be there. It's sunny and hotter than Jodie Comer in a pantsuit, and I am searching for four-leaf clovers on the front lawn, since I could do with some luck. Just as I am deciding that yes, it probably counts if you stick an extra leaf on with eyelash glue, a black taxi pulls into our driveway. The door opens and my jaw drops like a Taylor Swift album as Rich Elizabeth ballet-steps into view, carrying a potted plant! What in the name of Bella Hadid's homeboy hash-up can *she* want? Does she want to buy my house?

Her limousine legs mean she reaches me at alarming speed. Then she's peering down at me, still crouched on the lawn like a *Peanuts* cartoon. I probably look like a dog who's been sent out to pee. "Good afternoon, chicka," she says. "Why are you squatting in the dirt?"

I hastily jump to my feet. "Um, Elizabeth, how unexpected and frightening! I was, um, well, I was just searching for four-leaf clovers! I wasn't weeing or anything like that."

Elizabeth wrinkles her nose. "Oh, wow. Gross. Well, I can see you're busy, so I'll be brief. Cat, I feel I've been unprofessional. As an actress and future Golden Globe winner. I wanted to be Juliet and allowed myself to get jealous, like some sort of second wife. But we have lots of scenes together and I intend to really shine as"—she gulps shiveringly—"Juliet's nurse. So I'm here to offer an olive branch."

Then she hands me the potted plant. It's actually quite heavy. I grunt in surprise and almost fall right over. "Um . . . !" I wheeze. "Is this a whole olive tree?!"

"Yes, I've just come from the garden center. They're not complicated: just water it twice a week. Oh, and Bubble Wrap in winter. Tomato-feed fertilizer works best." She adjusts her

enormous sunglasses. "Anyway, I'll leave you to it. Adios!"

She turns toward the waiting taxi. I'm still staggering about beneath the weight of the actual tree I'm holding, so the moment is not as life-affirming as one might think. I heave the pot onto the ground, gasping for breath. "Elizabeth! Wait!"

She turns and I shake out my arms. Gooseberries, I've probably pulled a muscle!

"Um, I didn't expect to be Juliet, either," I explain. "And I'm really sorry you didn't get the role you wanted when you're, well, you. I'm not an actress, but I'm doing my best—when I'm not dealing with relationship drama, that is . . ." Gooseberries, STOP OVERSHARING. "I even watched *West Side Story*! And if you have any tips for learning lines, I'd really appreciate that, because I don't really know my *aye-me's* from my eyes and, um . . . knees."

Long pause. Elizabeth sniffs. "Do you have any elderflower cordial?"

I blink. "Um . . . we have cranberry juice and some tiny cocktail umbrellas?"

Elizabeth smirks, then turns back to the taxi. "Apollo!" she calls. "You can go."

"How do you know your taxi driver's name?!" I ask, wide-eyed, as the driver salutes Elizabeth goodbye, then scoots off down the road.

Elizabeth lowers her sunglasses to frown. "Chicka, that's the family taxi. Apollo's been with us for years! Now come on—we have *oodles* of work to do . . ."

Well, I did *not* expect to spend my afternoon with three of Rich Elizabeth's very long fingers stuck into my mouth, but here we

are. She screams bizarre sentences at me, which I have to repeat back with her entire hand still there. It's a good thing she tastes like luxury marzipan.

"THE L*A*DY G*A*VE ME A PL*A*TE ON FR*I*DAY!"

"GLE-LEGGEE-GEME-APLAY-ONG-FRIGAY!"

"THE CH*I*LD SM*I*LES ALL THE T*I*ME!"

"GLE-HILE-CHLILE-ALLE-HIME!"

"Speak from your chest!" she raves on, sandwiching me between her hands then pumping me like a lesbian accordion. "Feel the language like a howl of passion or pain! This isn't just dialogue, it's poetry! Enunciate and elongate those vowels! What did your elocution teacher even teach you?! THE LI*TT*LE GIRL WAS A*BS*OLU*T*ELY CER*T*AIN!"

She makes me scream the lines, then hiss them, then sing them. I recite Juliet's verses over and over and Elizabeth shrieks, "AGAIN! AGAIN! AGAIN!" Mum peers around my bedroom door like she's afraid of what she might see. "YOU ARE A THESPIAN LESBIAN!" Elizabeth roars. "TELL ME WHAT YOU ARE!"

"I AM A THESPIAN LESBIAN!"

"And we're so proud!" Mum chimes tearfully.

"GO AWAY, MOTHER!"

Then we launch into the scenes we have together. I've never seen Rich Elizabeth so impassioned about something you can't buy with a platinum member's club card.

"How stands your disposition to be married?" she says, haughtily regarding me down her nose. She's having to switch between the Nurse and Lady Capulet, which is actually quite amusing.

"It is an honor that I dream not of!" I reply.

"An honor!" Elizabeth gasps, changing her voice completely. "Were not I thine only nurse, I would say thou hadst suck'd wisdom from thy teat!"

We stare at each other for a good long second. Then we both burst out laughing like professional SCROL artists. Elizabeth throws the script at me.

"Sucked wisdom from your what?!" I giggle.

Elizabeth sniffs theatrically, although she's smiling as she sips cranberry juice from beneath her cocktail umbrella. "See? This is why I'm way out of your league when it comes to acting. I'd *never* be so immature. It's *Shakespeare*, you child."

"Hey!" I protest. "Have some respect! I'm Juliet, remember?"

Elizabeth narrows her eyes. For a moment, I'm worried she's about to diva-meltdown on me. Then she says, "You're, like, loco for the stars, aren't you?" I nod. "You see, this really is the play for you, baby girl. O, swear not by the moon, the inconstant moon, that monthly changes in her circled orb, lest that thy love prove likewise variable."

I gaze at her. Gooseberries galore! The words sound amazing when Rich Elizabeth enunciates them all in the right order. "That's beautiful!" I breathe. "What is that?"

"Your line, Dumbo," she says. "Act two, scene two. Remember?"

Then we both giggle again. It's actually very ridiculous and wonderful how quickly someone can go from being the most annoying person in the world to someone you actually might consider inviting to your house again. Morgan is going to SCREAM when I tell her.

If we ever speak again, that is. Aye, me.

• ★ . ✦ ˙ ★ •

Darkness has actually fallen by the time Elizabeth goes home. It's almost nine o'clock and I have been babbling in Shakespearean for seven entire hours! How doolally is that?

I gargle with salt water for five whole minutes (an essential practice for a budding thespian flower like myself) before returning to the script in my room. Shockingly, I've really enjoyed my Elizabethan afternoon. Focusing on the play (at last) means it's probably, actually, the longest I've gone in weeks without worrying about Morgan, Zanna, or the lunar cycle.

Then again . . . What phase is the moon in now? I'm just edging away from my script toward my *Star Bible* when my ears are assaulted by the tinkling wind-chiming of my chakra-smooching fool of a sister with her new-age relaxation music.

"Luna, turn that down!" I shout like some forty-five-year-old killjoy. But can you blame me?! Sometimes I feel like I'm living in some woodland yurt, not a house. "I'm about to run through my lines and I don't want to go into a trance!"

It seems Luna is too comatose to hear me. Scowling, I stomp round the corner, but before I can barge into her room and tell her *exactly* where she can hippie-dip herself next, I see Luna and Niamh through the slightly open door.

" . . . and are kaftans really that bad?" Niamh is sniffling as Luna pats her back. "I feel like I can't do anything right. Siobhan just looks right through me like I'm not even there."

"Well, she's stupid," says Luna, stroking a tear off Niamh's cheek. "Because you're here and I see you! With my eyes *and* celestial energies."

Suddenly I am overcome with Piscean dramatics. Zanna doesn't even have my new number. What if she fell over and got

hurt? How would she contact me so I could laugh at her and ask if there was CCTV? Luna leans forward to give Niamh a hug . . . then she notices me hovering.

"Urgh," she says. "What? Are you here to hate on my dream-hop again?"

"NO!" I blurt, crossing my arms. "Although dream-hop isn't a genre." Then I pause. Hmm. "Niamh?" I say eventually. "Have you heard about Black Moon Lilith?"

Niamh frowns. "Like, in astrology?"

I nod. "My *Bible to the Stars* says that Lilith represents our shadow side, which is, um, kind of cool and edgy, right? Basically, it reveals what's inside us that we're ashamed about, or maybe even scared of, like, um . . . being jealous or . . . cobwebs."

Niamh and Luna exchange puzzled frowns.

"Okay, let's not get sidetracked!" I interject. "What I'm trying to say is, Siobhan's Lilith is in Leo. Which means that even though she's popular and charismatic, she's also scared of being forgotten and, well, not being liked. Marilyn Monroe was a Leo Lilith, too! They're like magnets who are afraid of losing their, um . . . magnetyness! I don't think Siobhan hates you. She's just, um, a bit dented, ego-wise." My heart clenches in sympathy. Or possibly in fear: I'd be deader than a Tuesday night if Siobhan overheard me *acknowledging she has feelings*. "She's scared you don't like her."

Niamh nods slowly and I blush even rosier. "Thank you for saying that, Cat," says Niamh. "And, um, thanks for being cool with me staying. You guys really are my second family."

Thank Aphrodite that Zanna isn't here to witness this: the sentimentality would probably kill her! Luna says, "Niamh, I'll

always be your soul sister, okay? No matter who comes or goes. You're never going to be sisterless."

When Luna pulls her friend into a hug, she actually *smiles* at me over Niamh's shoulder. For once, she looks like she doesn't think I'm a complete idiot. Not that the feeling is mutual. I smile as non-weirdly as I can, then return to my room.

Luna may be as cringey as her grassy salads are green (and disgusting), but I like the idea of having a soul sister.

Actually though, I *do* have one . . . or I did until recently, anyway.

I scroll through a certain Slavic someone's socials until my eyes are stinging. It seems no rising sun or shiny new friend can kill my envious moon. I will stay sick and pale with grief forever.

Chat Thread: Zanna Szczechowska

THURSDAY

Cat, 10:29 p.m.:
Zanna, Zanna, wherefore art thou, Zanna?

Apart from Poland ofc

I have a new phone number!!!! NOT that you care

But in case u do this is my new number

Cat, 11:50 p.m.:
I GUESS YOU DON'T, THEN. FINE.

BYE FOREVER. AGAIN.

IDC AT ALL. I MEAN IT!!!!!

FRIDAY

Cat, 10:03 a.m.:
Actually I do care a little bit actually

STOP EATING RAW BROCCOLI and reply!!!

Please? With a glacé cherry?

Cat, 4:30 p.m.:
My parents are rebuilding the greenhouse I broke. How ridiculous is that??

Luckily my parents won't let me near glass so don't have to help :)

Cat, 7:31 p.m.:
Driving back from the hospital. Dad's finger is attached again. Yay!!

Cat, 10:51 p.m.:
Are u upset about the broccoli thing? I have decided to reconsider,,, if it means that much to u. I can perhaps even grow it in the new greenhouse we now have

Cat, 11:56 p.m.:

I really am serious, Zanna

I will eat raw broccoli for u :(

SATURDAY

Cat, 6:06 p.m.:

Are we really never going to talk again?

Cat, 11:07 p.m.:

Wrote this for u:

There is a girl called Zanna. All her clothes are gray.

She's really kinda edgy, 'cause her bestest friend is GAY!

She's probably a Vampire, but that's okay with me,

'Cause Lesbians stand with Vampires in solidarity!

I guess her clothes are not ALL gray; some of them are black,

And all I want for Easter is for her to text me back!!!

25
A Ghastly Gathering of Geminis

Oh, most horrifying of horrors, today is the day. I wake up shivering, a cold and sinister trickling sensation running down my spine. It might be because I left my window open last night to soak up all the self-improvement vibes from the waxing crescent moon, and then it rained. But it also might be because evil is steadily approaching.

Lilac Victoria West is all kinds of wrong, and not just because she's a Gemini. She spends all her time doing evil, icy things, like figure-skating and straightening her hair, even though it's already straighter than *Love Island* and everyone who watches it. She recently started growing Venus flytraps in the upstairs greenhouse of the family mansion. She poses with them on Instagram like a botany-based butcherer of innocents.

Because she absolutely hates me for no reason, Lilac

never misses a chance to criticize. It's always, "You chew so loudly, Cathleen," and "You should really consider a stronger deodorant," and "I can't believe you melted my handbag in the microwave—it's Givenchy!" She thinks she's completely perfect, and mostly she is, but it's extremely disturbing that she literally only wears white: a truly Narnian narcissist.

What should *I* wear though? Morgan is coming today, and it's imperative we rekindle our romance in time to rub it in Lilac's face like one of her limited-edition moisturizers. I try on everything in my wardrobe (except for the tutu) before picking the right EGGshell-blue dress. Luna says she doesn't get the joke. I think I'm being deeply and Easterly humorous.

Meanwhile, Mum spends the whole morning caterwauling around the house in a panic. I watch her vacuum the same bit of floor five times. Then she does this awkward thing where she lies on her back and cleans the underside of all the tables. It's really very embarrassing.

"You could help, you know!" she yaps as me and Luna gaze at her in awe. "Look at the state of the place! I still haven't bleached any of the taps and your father's got so many windows left to clean!"

They probably should have thought of that before they bought a house made entirely from glass. Why are my parents such clowns? I don't have time to help though—I'm far too busy thinking up ways to insult Lilac's relationship when she arrives. She's going out with this sad specimen who I call Has-to-Be-Hypnotized Henry. He goes to her snotty private school and his Instagram profile picture is him shaking hands with some yeasty-looking former prime minister. Exactly.

But oddballs enough, I haven't actually heard from Morgan yet, and she's supposed to be here in half an hour! She had better not be late AGAIN—at this point I am beginning to lose track of which of us is more annoyed with who! Soon enough, we will just be standing opposite each other going "AAAAAAA" until our heads explode at all the convolutedness. And there's no way I'm going to give Lilac the satisfaction of seeing my head explode. Since Lilac will be here any minute, I stay cucumber-composed and text Morgan again, then nervously apply a second layer of mascara.

"Dorian's here!" chimes Luna, swanning into my room at five to twelve. She's dressed in astonishingly normal clothes, not a repurposed tote bag in sight. (Dad won the negotiations by promising he wouldn't use Amazon for a month, so she finally caved.) "Where's Morgan? Is she still coming?"

I scowl, applying a *third* layer of mascara. "I don't know, okay?! She was supposed to be here ages ago! I hope she's not arguing about Scarlett Johansson on Twitter again."

Luna checks her phone. "Nope. She was last online fifteen hours ago, calling out biphobia in the gay community. Which is both valid *and* important—"

I lean over to swing shut the door, but before I can, there's gravel crunching outside and we rush to my window. A sleek black Mercedes has arrived.

"Gooseberries!" I breathe as Luna gulps by my side.

Lilac, the Empress of Everlasting Evil, is here! And Morgan Delaney, as o'freaking usual, is late.

I've never seen a table so full of food I can't even name. Mum has clearly just panic-bought everything the Waitrose deli counter

had to offer. There's an enormous roast chicken, which might actually be a turkey, and more bowls of dried fruit than I know what to do with.

"Would anybody like some figs?" asks Mum, as if anyone might want figs ever.

"What a delightful meal!" Auntie Rose gasps, shoveling couscous onto her plate. "It's so exciting to finally be visiting! We were all so disappointed to miss the scheduled viewing at Christmas. I'm glad to see you're once again celebrating those natural curls, Cat!"

Everyone laughs good-heartedly as my cheeks turn rosy-rouge. Gooseberries galore. You set fire to your house with hair straighteners ONE TIME and no one will ever let you forget it! Slowly, I glance at Lilac, who's fluttering her lashes around her icy-blue eyes.

"Well, I for one am *so* looking forward to meeting Cathleen's new beau," she drawls, forked tongue flicking insidiously as she smiles her slickest fake smile. "Though I must confess, being late for an important family lunch doesn't send the *best* message."

What an absolute harpy, pointing out something so utterly true! I clatter down my fork. "Morgan's on her way, okay?! She's only late because . . ." I rack my brains. "Because she's dropping off some Easter donations at a charity shop!" I snap my fingers victoriously. "Yes. She's raising money for, um . . . Well, all sorts of causes. I can't name any of them right now, but, um . . . Yes." I gulp back my annoyance. "Children and . . . horses! That's one."

Niamh frowns. "Is that for children? Or for horses?" she asks, and I shrug.

"Well, she's clearly a very charitable person," says Lilac. "If she's dating you."

I make a fist, already suppressing a strong desire to launch a plateful of avocado sushi directly into her smug-as-a-Siamese-cat face. Also—sushi for Easter?! I'd say Mum must be out to lunch if we weren't eating lunch in our house at this very moment.

"Aren't we lucky," chuckles Uncle Hillary at Dad before I can start hurling starters, "to have such quick-witted daughters! Eh, David?"

"The last time Cathleen tried to be witty, Gatwick Airport nearly went into lockdown," scorns Lilac, tittering disgustingly. "Who jokes about explosives at passport control?"

"I was talking about Dad's really loud sneezes!" I retort through gritted teeth.

"All right, girls, let's calm down!" chortles Auntie Rose, rolling her eyes lovingly at Mum. My younger cousin, Harmony, is currently yanking fistfuls of handkerchiefs out of her sleeves but no one is paying her any attention. Clearly she's not given up on her magician's ambitions. "Let's just enjoy that we're finally together as a family!"

I actually SCROL because I assume Auntie Rose must be joking. But then everyone looks at me very strangely, so I go back to nibbling my ricotta-stuffed pastry triangle.

At which point the doorbell rings. FINALLY! I leap to my feet before anyone can stop me and skid to the front door, which I swing open with my biggest, sunniest smile splattered on, like a gunshot of clown paint to the face. Then I see my girlfriend, and the paint-smile slides off my face and onto my glittery-pink toenails with a shocked splat.

There is an entire branch in Morgan's hair, floating there like a weird smell. And there's also a weird smell. Morgan is very red-faced and shiny and there's a tang of barnyard coming from somewhere. Gooseberries galore. Did she sleep in a pigpen?!

"Hey," she says, stepping breathlessly into the house before I can stop her. Which I really should do before Lilac sees! Unfortunately, Lilac already has seen, thanks to the ridiculous open-plannitude of our house . . . Her mouth delicately pops open in a gasp. Then her eyes light up like sniggering jack-o'-lanterns. "I'm so sorry I'm late," Morgan carries on. "I had, um, a complication . . ."

I am completely speechless. Morgan has shown up to my house looking like a zombified crypt keeper! Mum quickly jumps to life like a clockwork soldier. "Morgan, you made it! Why don't you sit down and tuck right in? Better late than never!"

Is it though? I ghost-drift back to the table and Morgan takes a seat between me and Niamh, still panting like a fugitive. Even Luna has been shocked into silence, which deserves an award, to be honest. When is Luna quiet? Dorian sniffs, then looks like he regrets it.

Finally, Lilac clears her amphibian throat. "Hello," she coos. "You must be Morgan Delaney. I've heard *so* much about you."

Morgan gives a tight smile. "Yeah, that's me . . . It's nice to meet you all."

"Is that an Irish accent I hear?" Auntie Rose says, which would be a good icebreaker if she weren't literally holding a napkin over her nose! What *is* that smell?! "Cat has probably

told you already that my sister and I come from a proud Irish mother!"

I certainly have not told her that. Siobhan told me that you should only ever discuss family history if a date is "failing harder than Zoella's advent calendar." Morgan cranks on a very believable smile though. "Yeah, dead on. I grew up in Northern Ireland, actually . . ."

"Did you walk from there this morning?" interrupts Lilac, and everyone goes quiet, then stares at Morgan expectantly, as if she might actually say she has. I want the ground to digest me. Morgan *knows* Lilac is a blue-blooded conversation killer. What was she thinking, showing up like this?! She's handing Lilac the victory on a gold-plated platter—and Lilac has nearly as many of those as Siobhan does.

"Sorry I'm late, Ms. Phillips," Morgan says to Mum. "I really rushed to get here."

"We can tell," Lilac titters.

"I think you might have a branch in your hair, young lady," Uncle Hillary says, chuckling in this slightly frightened way, and I have to bury my nose in my couscous.

To my absolute aghastitude, Morgan slowly drags the stick out of her hair, then places it next to her knife and fork on the dining table. Sappho strike me down, bury me alive, and set fire to all my worldly possessions.

"Are you an outdoorsy type?" asks Auntie Rose, doing her best to smile. "You look like you must have spent all morning wonderfully al fresco! I do miss the lovely fresh air in London. Not so much the twisty lanes and, well . . . the smells!"

Morgan goes a bit redder. "Sorry. I think I trod in something."

Lilac lets out a little snigger of glee and even Harmony has stopped crafting a circus tent from salad leaves to watch the mortification unfold. Then Morgan wipes her hand down her jeans and her fingers come up brown. Auntie Rose coughs water back into her glass.

"Ew," whispers Niamh. "What is that?"

"I have an idea!" Mum cuts in before Morgan can answer, thank Sappho. "Cat, why don't you take Morgan upstairs and find her a change of clothes? I can't imagine she wants to eat lunch wearing . . . Well, dressed like that."

"Yes, Morgan, what *is* your style, exactly?" asks Lilac, scanning her up and down with her icicle eyes. "Would we call it 'grunge' or 'grime'? Or just greasy, perhaps?"

"I can think of a few things I'd call *you*!" I hiss back, but Mum loudly clears her throat, then gives me those wide *I'm almost annoyed* eyes that she does. I will have to save my insults for later. Possibly when I have my "Lilac Insults" memo up on my phone.

I grab Morgan's wrist and yank her to her feet, then march toward the stairs in a way I hope shows Morgan that I am really not impressed at all. Unfortunately, I trip right over the glass-topped coffee table. Mum has cleaned it so well, it's become invisible! Laughing apologetically as everyone watches, I swivel on my heel and walk smack-bang into the spotless mirror opposite the staircase.

I really hope no one thinks this is an accurate reflection of who I am.

They probably do though.

LILAC INSULTS

- Lilac has lizardy hands.
- Lilac has lizardy feet.
- Lilac is a lizard.
- The dead sea was alive until Lilac went swimming there.
- Lilac is why Noah built the ark.
- Lilac's full name is Lilacking-In-Vitamin-D.
- Or Lilikes-Licking-Feet . . . (She probably does as well.)
- Lilac is why Jesus won't come back.
- Lilac makes Snow White look tan.
- Lilac once ate snails in France. I can't believe she's a CANNIBAL as well!
- (That's more of an insult to snails actually . . .)

26
Blame It on the Scorpios

UN-BUNNY-EARS-BELIEVABLE. After escaping the ghastly gathering of Geminis, I'm very much not in the mood. Aries Season is supposed to be about determination and keeping driven, but the only thing it's driven me is off a cliff. I am NEVER going to look good in front of Lilac, no matter how much mascara I wear.

"Why *are* you wearing so much mascara?" asks Morgan as I panic-apply a fifth layer in my bedroom mirror. She's currently taking off her clothes, which would be extremely sexy and amazing if her clothes didn't smell like a sheep's morning breath, and if she weren't having to do this on a hefty layer of plastic bags. "You already have really pretty eyelashes."

"Don't try to butter me up!" I finally snap, accidentally stabbing myself in the eye with my mascara wand. Wincing painfully, I whirl round. "Morgan, I'm really very upset by this. This isn't school—you can't just show up an hour late for no reason! And why do you look like a junkyard?"

Morgan steps toward me. "Cat, listen . . ."

"Don't stand on the carpet!" I gesticulate, and Morgan steps back.

"Sorry. Look, I really didn't mean—"

"Were you late because you were too busy sumo-wrestling a donkey?!" I explode, dithering round my bedroom like a flustered pheasant. "What in Old MacDonald's name happened to you? You look like you've been E-I-E-I-O-ing all over the nearest farm!"

"Cat, will you stop?!" Morgan butts in. "I was with Brooke!"

That shuts me up quicker than a cow goes moo. Suddenly, I am all shivery in my timbers. And not in a good way. "So the reason you're late to my very important family lunch . . . is because you were hanging about with Brooke the Crook? *Again?!*" Suddenly, I'm bubbling with Siobhan-like rage. "Morgan, do you care about me AT ALL?! Do you even want to be together, or would you rather be skateboarding around with—"

But Morgan cuts me off. "Of course I want to be together, Cat, I was doing it for you!" She presses her muddy fingers to her forehead. "But I might have messed up, okay? Like, really."

"More than I messed up when I invited you to this lunch?" I ask icily.

Morgan nods, and I gasp. "Look. Remember your rehearsal with Elizabeth Greenwood? How she messed with the lights? Well, Brooke suggested we reclaim your honor. And after that phone call where we argued about Maja and Brooke and stuff, I was worried, and I wanted to smooth things over, so we went to this field and, long story short . . . Brooke stole a cowpat and dumped it on a certain someone's birthday Porsche."

I ogle Morgan, my skin turning jittery as the horror sinks in. "But Morgan, I've *just* made up with Elizabeth! Please say you are joking!" But Morgan doesn't reveal a hidden drum kit to badoom-tish. Oh, Ohio, Ohio. "You vandalized her car?!"

Morgan shrugs. "Not directly . . . I just helped Brooke climb over the wall. And then I watched her smear it all over the windshield. Which makes me more of an accomplice, right?" She groans, clawing her hands down her face. "Look, I had good intentions . . . I thought it was just a prank and we'd . . . drop it on her driveway or something! But Brooke took it way too far."

Truly, I am speechless apricots now. I stare into space like I am Saoirse Ronan acting a very serious moment. Then the lava-gates OPEN. "You think *Brooke* took it way too far? Morgan, I've been telling you for *weeks* that Brooke is bad news! There's a good reason Siobhan doesn't invite her to stuff, but you've just ignored every red flag! If Elizabeth finds out about this, it'll make everything worse! And you could get in proper trouble! People will call you Morgan the Menace or Morgan the Manure Spreader or—"

"Cat, I didn't mean—" Morgan tries stepping toward me again and I squeal.

"STAY ON THE PLASTIC BAGS! My rug is very white and fluffy!"

"Sorry." Morgan stays trapped on her tiny plastic island. "I just hate seeing people left out, okay? I know Brooke can be a lot. But I thought if someone gave her a chance and didn't treat her like a freak for once, she might turn out okay."

I cross my arms. I'm still a good three feet away from

Morgan and she can't come any closer. "Morgan, do you actually believe that?" I ask. "Do you really want to be friends with Brooke? Or do you just want Siobhan to be wrong so much that you're willing to completely crash and burn just to make a point?"

Morgan seems to swallow her words. "Um . . . Is that . . . how it seems?"

I goggle her. "Just a bit." I sigh resignedly. "Look, I've made an effort. But you and your friends are giving nothing back! I'm sorry my friends aren't all edge-queens like Maja—who *has* been horrid, by the way, about me, right to my face—but Morgan, they're my friends! Siobhan may be furious all the time for no reason, but she actually was trying to include you before you decided to disrespect her in her own Hoxton Square."

Morgan frowns. "Her what?"

"It's what she calls her living room," I explain. "McQueen reference. But Morgan, what I mean is that you're being more difficult than they are! Really, I'm starting to wonder if Siobhan is right. Maybe you do want to be Queen McFreak of All Things Weird."

Morgan almost steps off the plastic bags again, but I give her a very stern look. My heart is going boom-shaka-laka galore. It's weird, being on the moral high ground. Usually, it's me who messes everything up. Literally, if blenders and soup are involved. But this time, I'm pretty sure I'm right. Like Greta Thunberg.

"You're not wrong," Morgan says eventually, and I resist the urge to soccer-punch the sky. "I've probably pushed back too hard, but when I saw Siobhan throwing Brooke out,

I remembered how it felt, you know? And I heard the stories about Brooke being . . . Well, a crook. About the missing Bunsen burners and how she fried the school goldfish . . ."

I grimace. "That was a dark, dark day . . ." If only Alison's tears possessed healing powers. She could have revived the fish . . . and every other fish who's ever perished, actually.

"But sometimes I think I'm like a bull," Morgan continues. "I see a red flag and charge toward it. Blame my Scorpio Rising, I guess. Things got way out of hand."

Out of hand and out of foot, too, from the sounds of it. I consider this for a moment and then, very strangely indeed, Zanna pops into my head, like a Slavic mirage. Gooseberries galore, my best friend really is wiser than the three wise men and all their beardy brains combined. I suddenly understand everything she's been annoyed about.

And it really wasn't about the raw broccoli at all.

Slowly, I shake my head. "Morgan, I think if our relationship is going to work, we need to make a very important change. We need to stop blaming the stars. I have been a useless friend and my Virgo Moon has nothing to do with it. And we cannot blame this on the Scorpios either . . . Even if most things really are their fault."

Then we stare at each other, like I've just said the most biblical and moon-quaking thing. Which I have, actually. Morgan studies her mucky socks. "Yeah, sounds about right. Been a bit of a dickhead, haven't I?"

"Ew," I reply. "And yes. But I have been . . . not completely adequate myself, so it's okay. We all make mistakes . . . Look at the mistake my aunt and uncle made!"

Morgan frowns. "You mean . . . your cousin?" I nod solemnly and Morgan snorts a laugh. "Yeah, she seems like a piece of work. Tell you what. Why don't I sort myself out and we go back down and make her miserable? Will that cheer you up?"

It definitely will, and I feel quite Aquarian and mushy. When I nod, Morgan smiles, and this enormous weight is lifted off my shoulders. Possibly because my cardigan has just fallen off, but I am also very relieved. Morgan reaches out a hand and I am just about to take it when . . .

"Hmm," I say. "Morgan, don't take this the wrong way. But I think you should possibly take a shower. Especially now that I know there's cowpat on your jeans."

Morgan gives me a salute, and I go to fetch her a towel.

I've had an epiphany! And for once, it wasn't brought on by Luna's intoxicating incense. After Morgan has showered, we go downstairs holding hands like everything is okay again, which it is, for now. I'm not sure what will happen when we go back to school (apart from the standard desire to drop dead of course), but for now, we're worry-free.

Lilac's foul feline eyes flicker to Morgan the moment we reappear. She's draped over the sofa like a panther. Our parents are drinking wine and Luna, Niamh, and Harmony appear to be making a human pyramid that Dorian is photographing. Hmm.

"Gosh," Lilac drawls at Morgan. "I don't envy you. The *last* place I'd want to be when I need a change of clothes is Cathleen's house."

Morgan inspects herself. She's wearing leggings and my

stripy bumblebee T-shirt. "I don't know, Lilac, it could be worse," she says, raising an eyebrow. "I could also have gone gray at age fifteen. That must be really hard for you."

Lilac's knife-edge jaw drops. "I'm very pale blond, actually," she hisses as I giggle into my hair. "I have Norwegian blood. *Royal* Norwegian blood, as it happens. From my father. Cathleen doesn't have any."

"Sounds very special," I gasp. "Don't drink it all at once."

Morgan lets out a cackle and Lilac growls, then grabs her phone and starts pouty-texting again. Probably issuing a death warrant in our name to her vampiric brethren.

Shockingly, the rest of the day goes okay. Mum and Dad do their clownish tour of the iPhone Box, even subjecting Auntie Rose and Uncle Hillary to a viewing of the brand-new greenhouse, Aphrodite save their souls. Then Auntie Rose gives us each an Easter egg from Harrods, like some sort of millionaire. Although Lilac "accidentally" put mine on the radiator, so it looks like a Picasso painting gone rogue. It's a good thing I've already bitten the ears off her chocolate bunny.

When Harmony is performing *Phantom of the Opera* before they all poodle on home, I notice I am touching Morgan's amazing knee and she is not touching mine back. I'm ready to be offended, but she actually looks quite worried, freaky-frowning into the digital fireplace.

I nudge her. "Hey," I whisper as Harmony hits a high note. "I know it might seem risky, singing opera in a completely glass house, but Mum tested with a Kate Bush CD earlier and she's pretty sure it's totally safe!"

Morgan rolls her eyes, but I get one smile out of her. "Sorry.

But what do I do about Brooke back at school? I've never ended a friendship before. And I need to talk to Maja about how she's been. I'm already feeling like, well, a massive cowpat about it."

I close my eyes. "Please don't say 'cowpat' in my presence, Morgan. You know how I feel about bodily functions. But it's going to be totally okay. And I'll be right there with you, even if it isn't! That's the amazing thing about having a really clingy girlfriend."

Morgan smiles and it's a very gooey moment. Not even Lilac, sneery-staring at us from across the room, can water away the happy non-digital flames inside me. Then Morgan whispers, "Cat, about that phone call. Bit of a wake-up call . . . Literally, since it was on the phone . . ." I give Morgan *a look* and she blushes. Morgan, blushing! Now I've seen everything. Then she says, "I'm genuinely so crazy for you. I don't want to lose you. I really want us to work because . . . you're kind of my dream girl, actually. Just saying."

My atoms completely separate and clatter back together again. My heart does eighteen thousand loop-the-loops. Approximately 746 million miles away, Saturn gains an extra ring, and I mentally compose a love sonnet about this very moment on the spot without even blinking. What a perfect, lovely feeling.

It's very Morgan, to say something like that in this super-casual-in-leather-pants way, but I am not going to let her off the hook. I kiss her fully on the lips in front of everyone.

Chat Thread: Morgan Delaney

Cat, 11:08 p.m.:

Good night (but in a hello way)!!!

I should have said hello actually

HELLO

I was just thinking that I don't want us to not communicate again.

So in case we ever have nothing to talk about, here are some ideas for how we can text!!!!! We can . . .

Write alternating lines of a poem!!!!!

Play AD LIBS together!!!

Learn a language no one else knows so we have OUR OWN COOL LANGUAGE . . . maybe Halq'eméylem?? then test each other on the vocab :)))

I'M THINKING OF AN ANIMAL THAT BEGINS WITH . . .

Let me know what u think!!!!! Xxx

Morgan, 11:17 p.m.:

Omg, omg

You're so adorable

We're not gonna be doing any of those things

Also loads of First Nations people already know that language

But you are totally the cutest xxxxx

Taurus
SEASON

27

A Potato Sack—Literally

Now that I understand my many mistakes, I need to find a way to win Zanna back, and Taurus Season, when absolutely everybody is pining to go back to their roots, should be the perfect time. But Morgan doesn't think I can catch a thousand doves, either. She says I should keep it simple and maybe "write her a poem or something."

It will definitely have to be "or something." Zanna once told me that if I ever write another poem, she will "find the Other Mother from *Coraline* and walk right into her arms." And although I think Zanna would really suit button eyes, I don't want that.

"You could just talk to her," Niamh says when I am pretending to meditate with her and Luna. I am actually in Luna's room because I want to breathe in some oak-scented incense fumes. Who knows what amazing ideas may come to me when I am hallucinating?

"Yeah," agrees Luna. "You know, like a normal person."

I scowl. What would Luna know about being a normal person? She's literally wearing a dress made from Dad's old shirts! Apparently, throwing out clothes is wasteful and fashion needs to be more sustainable. Personally, I'm not sure life is worth sustaining if it includes wearing Dad's shirts. But before I can vocalize any of this, the doorbell rings.

"URGH!" Luna exclaims. When I frown at her in confusion, she explains, "The doorbell breaks the metaphysical feng shui, because it throws an electric sound wave into the fluid tones of our spirituality. Now we've got to start the meditation cycle again!"

"So inconvenient," sighs Niamh, rolling her eyes.

I'm suddenly wondering if Zanna's onto something, skipping merrily into her button-eyed future, but then Mum calls up the stairs, "Niamh! You have a surprise waiting for you! It's in my lovely new greenhouse outside!"

She sounds excited, like she always does when the new greenhouse is involved. But we all frown at each other with suspicion. Niamh has a surprise?! We hurry downstairs and into the backyard.

The new greenhouse is offensively huge. It's even bigger than the one I broke with my phone, and as Luna slides open the door, I'm wondering if it's actually more of a BUNKER. Then I see what's *inside* the greenhouse-bunker monstrosity, and my thoughts completely evaporate with the built-in misting system.

The whole greenhouse is illuminated with tea lights, in true fire-hazardous fandangle. There is a horrendous tie-dye green banner (which looks like a repurposed bedsheet) saying COME HOME, NIAMH hanging across the tomatoes, and in the middle of the room is Siobhan Deidre Collingdale, dressed in a potato sack—literally.

It has balloon sleeves and she's tied it in at the waist with her Alexander McQueen belt.

Gooseberries galore. She doesn't even look angry! She's not wearing makeup though, so that helps. Siobhan is the only girl I know who shapes her brows to look like they're glaring.

By my side, Niamh lets out a whimper-that-could-be-a-laugh. Mum appears with this massive beam on, which makes her look like some sort of murderer. "Isn't this lovely!" she glitters. "I always say no problem is unsolvable once you've had a proper heart-to-heart! What do you say, girls? Time to bury the hatchet?"

She really is very embarrassing. I give her a *look* and she sighs, then trudges back outside. Possibly to dig up more hatchbacks, or whatever she's talking about. Then I turn to my friend.

"Siobhan!" I say, since no one is speaking. "Um . . . How are you?"

Siobhan scowls. "Christ on a bike, Cat! You know how I feel about small talk. We're not at the freaking opera. Where's Niamh?"

"Um . . . I'm right here?" Niamh says, and Siobhan startles.

"Christ," she says again. "I saw all that linen and assumed you were Judi Dench or someone. Why are you dressed like one of those old ladies at a charity shop?" Then she seems to remember herself. She takes a calming breath. "Um, sorry. Namaste. You look fine and, as you can see, I'm *trying* to show respect for you." She gestures down at her potato-sack dress and I grimace. She is braver than me. "Niamh, I'd like to talk to you."

Niamh glances at Luna uncertainly. "Do you have to?"

"YES!" Siobhan shouts, and Niamh jumps behind Mum's potted cactus. Siobhan groans exasperatedly. "Niamh, I chose the greenhouse because I know nature is, like, your church or whatever and I haven't even brought my water pistol to threaten you. Please just hear me out."

Slowly, Niamh creeps back into view. "Siobhan . . . Did you just say 'please'? Did Mum pay you to be more polite again?" She gazes round, eyes wide in disbelief. "The greenhouse does look nice. Maybe it even symbolizes the growth our relationship needs to heal?"

Siobhan looks visibly ill at that. But she gulps down hard, then gestures us over. Slowly we approach, like she's liable to explode at any moment. And she is. She's Siobhan, and she's wearing a potato-sack dress. But finally, we're all gathered round the tomato vines.

"Listen," Siobhan says to Niamh. "I want you to come home. I . . ." The words seem to catch in her throat, like she's actually on the verge of retching. "*I miss you.* Christ, I hate how that sounds out loud. Like I'm desperate or something."

"You were saying, Siobhan?" I intervene quickly. "About how much you miss your sister? Who has been living with us for over a month?"

"Yes," says Siobhan, shutting her eyes. "Right. Niamh. I'm not used to losing. I'm not like Cat here: I'm a winner." I open my mouth to protest, but Luna taps my hand and subtly shakes her head. Siobhan trumpets on, "Girls are always asking me how they should dress, what they should say on dates, what's the quickest way to knock someone unconscious if they're about to tell your boyfriend you've been cheating on them . . . Well, that was just one time. And it's always, always about going for the side of the neck . . ."

"Siobhan," I interject.

"All right, whatever!" She rolls her eyes. "Everyone wants to be me, okay? Fact! But then you, my actual sister, don't even want me to be Head Girl. And you wear ridiculous clothing like you're living in some Nepalese monastery and you don't care about makeup or hair or how you look or smell . . ."

"I wouldn't say I don't care—" Niamh tries, but Siobhan isn't done.

"And it's frustrating, okay?!" Siobhan snaps the bamboo cane she's gripping and we all jump. "Because of everyone I want to think I'm amazing, which I *am*, you are the person I care the most about impressing. My baby sister, of all people, *should* look up to me, but you don't, do you? You think Cat's wacko girlfriend is the coolest queen since . . . I don't know. Genghis Khan?"

"Zendaya," says Luna. "She's a good example of a queen, Siobhan."

We all sigh and nod in agreement. Then Siobhan says, "So I'm sorry I freaked out and made you leave home. But I'm going to lose this rat race anyway probably. And I've lost my dunder-headed excuse of a relationship, too. Me and Dale have called it off for good."

I gasp. "Siobhan! Did he insult Ariana Grande?!"

Siobhan rolls her eyes. "It's not always about Ariana, Cat. Although he didn't appreciate her enough, it's true. No, he just told me I was annoying and it turns out his earplugs were in on purpose?! What an absolute lichen-licking loser . . ." Then she

shakes her head. "It's whatever. But Niamh, I'm losing things. And I don't want to lose you as well."

Luna looks properly Piscean, all watery and emotional. She lightly elbows Niamh, who readjusts her Celtic ring. "I might not dress like you or talk like you," says Niamh quietly. "Although I do really love what you've done with that, um . . ."

"It's a potato sack," says Siobhan matter-of-factly. "And I hate it."

"Right." Niamh takes a deep, steadying breath. "And, well, I might not agree that Ariana Grande's ponytail holds the secrets to the universe . . ."

"Even though it does," Siobhan cuts in.

"But I still look up to you. I think you're really brave and beautiful and it's super impressive that you can make anyone cry within fifteen seconds. I wish you'd be more vegan sometimes. It really is good for the planet. But I still love you, Siobhan, even when you're slapping me awake with slices of mortadella just to mock my beliefs."

I nod at Siobhan in admiration and she smirks in acknowledgment. Then she takes a breath. "Well, I guess I love you, too, or whatever." A genuine shudder of discomfort ripples through her body. "My skills are super transferable though. I can help you organize a *real* protest. With signs that hurt people's feelings. Like, 'Change your busted look, not the climate.' So . . . Will you come home? Or are you going to stay here like some blithering Bohemian freak show?"

Niamh and Luna exchange glances. Then Niamh says, "I'll pack my things."

Suddenly, Mum comes somersaulting through the

greenhouse door like a Slinky with Niamh's suitcase. "No need!" she sparkles, beaming like a tennis ball. "I've already packed all your things for you! Isn't it lovely to forgive each other? Not that I was listening outside! Do make sure you blow out all the candles before you go . . ."

How utterly embarrassing my mother is.

Subject: Your Online Shopping Delivery
From: theonlineshop@classycomestibles.com
To: cathezodiaclown@genericemailprovider.com

Dear **Car Phillops Cat Phillips**,

Your online food shop was successfully delivered to **Zanna Szechwan** at **29 Orchard End Road** at 11:43am today. Thank you for shopping with Classy Comestibles.

Receipt of Items:

3x Fresh Broccoli

1x Fresh Purple Sprouting Broccoli

1x Pocket Mints

TOTAL: £7.95

28
Brushing Out the Chimneys

Luna laughed when I told her my plan. She said, no matter the moon, I couldn't in a million years successfully transport a dining table, two chairs, genuinely breakable crockery, and fifty-seven tea lights across Lambley Common to host a candle-lit apology dinner for Zanna in the street. (And she was right.)

Instead I'm here, outside Zanna's house with my *Bible to the Stars* under one arm and my heart in my throat. Well, still in my chest, thankfully, but I'm quite nervy. It's a scorching day, the air as dry as Dad's elbows. But I've waited until sunset for dramatic effect.

Zanna lives in an ordinary house with actual walls and rooms. It looks the same as every other house on the street, but luckily, I've been here before, so I know which house I need. Well, after I've peered through an old lady's window and almost given her a heart attack anyway. Once I've helped clean up the dinner tray she dropped, and fetched her inhaler from the upstairs bathroom, I'm whistling my way to Zanna's, peaceful as a pear.

I kiss my pebble for luck, then throw it at her window. It's really very Shakespearean! With perfect aim, the pebble hits the glass and bounces into the shrubbery. Then I stand with my *Star Bible* under one arm, a beam ready and waiting on my face.

Then I wait some more. My smile fades a bit.

Hmm. I didn't prepare for this. Should I have checked that Zanna was in? What if she's downstairs and not in her room?! Gooseberries, I really didn't think this through. Also, why did I only bring one pebble?! Then the light comes on in Zanna's room. I gasp. SHE LIVES! But I'm still out of missiles . . . What now?

Hastily, I stand on one leg and pull off my boot. It's got a heel, so my legs are suddenly different lengths, but apart from that, very resourceful scenes. I swing the boot once, twice, then launch it at the window. Marvelous! There's no way she won't hear that . . .

Then the window opens and Zanna pokes her head out, frowning. The boot smacks her right in the face, she lets out a squeal, and she collapses back into the room with a thud. I gawp in the street like a goon. Gooseberries, gooseberries, gooseberries! Did I knock her out?!

"Zanna!" I call. "Are you okay?!"

I hear a groan from the open window. Then Zanna crawls back into view. I breathe a sigh of relief. I didn't kill her! Which is a really good start to making amends. Then Zanna sees me and my heart deflates like a shrink-wrapped avocado. She doesn't look happy.

"Zanna!" I greet her brightly. "Um, sorry to . . ." Oh, gooseberries, don't. "Sorry to put my . . ." DO NOT SAY IT! "I'm sorry to put my foot in the door like this." Then I let out a nervous

giggle. It is quite funny though. "Or my shoe in the window, anyway . . ."

Zanna actually closes her eyes like she's in pain.

"Good grief," she murmurs. "That's the stupidest thing I've ever heard. Look, Cat, I don't have time for this. I'm about to make dinner and if you don't get why I'm upset by now, I think we should just leave it."

"But I do get it!" I squeak, and Zanna pauses closing the window. I hop about on my longer leg and try to think of the right words. "I understand why you've been mad and I am really monumentally sorry, and if you'll just hear me out . . ."

But Zanna rolls her eyes. "Cat, words mean nothing. Calling me your best friend and actually *being* my best friend are two different things. I'm not happy being the Kenna to your Siobhan. I don't feel important to you."

"But you are!" I say, and that's when I reach into my tote bag and pull out the lighter. Zanna frowns. "You are more important to me than the sun, the moon, and all the stars combined. And you're right! I need to stop blaming the stars."

"Cat, is that a lighter?" asks Zanna, suddenly nervous. "Please be careful. You know that you and fire is a worse combination than pineapple and pizza."

"Well, firstly, Zanna, I tried pineapple pizza in secret once, and it was surprisingly okay," I say. "But that's not important. I am going to prove to you that I can change!" I flick the lighter and a flame springs to life. Then I dangle my *Bible to the Stars* toward the flame. There's a slight breeze and my hair falls into my eyes, so I brush it out of my face. This is my moment, my stepping-stone into a future of self-control, accountability . . .

"CAT, YOUR HAIR IS ON FIRE!" Zanna screams, and OH GOOSEBERRIES GALORE, SHE'S RIGHT, WHAT THE PINEAPPLE PIZZA?! I drop my *Bible to the Stars* and then I'm hopping about like a kangaroo on a pogo stick and Zanna is screaming and I am screaming and—OH HOLY APHRODITE, WHERE'S A WEEPING PISCES WHEN YOU NEED ONE?!

Suddenly, everything goes black. I am being suffocated and thrown to the ground like a sack of slightly singed potatoes! But the screaming stops and the crackling dies down and then I am blinking into the dreamy pink sky, smoke curling up into the clouds.

Next to me, panting in relief, Zanna drops her hoodie to the asphalt and collapses onto her back next to me. We stay there, panting and gazing at the sky, together.

"This hasn't entirely gone entirely to plan," I sigh, gazing at myself in the mirror of Zanna's bathroom. I look like someone's used me to brush out a chimney.

Zanna rinses out the washcloth in the sink, then hands it back to me so I can dab at my scalp again. "So you *didn't* mean to set fire to your hair?"

Zanna is actually smirking like a slaphappy arsonist, and I scowl. "No, of course I didn't mean to do that! I came here to apologize, Zanna. You really could try to appreciate my efforts! My heart was in the right place . . ."

"You threw a boot in my face," Zanna says. "It's hardly what I'd call a dazzling apology. Is it your lifelong wish to give everyone you know a black eye? Are you going to hit Siobhan in the face with a shovel on Monday?" She gazes into the middle distance. "Can I watch if you do?"

I squeeze out the washcloth. "Would you consider being friends again if I hit Siobhan in the face with a shovel?" It's valid to consider all possibilities, right?

Zanna raises one eyebrow. "Oh, so we're not friends?"

My eyes fill with tears. Chim-cheroo, where was all this water when my actual head was on fire?!

"I've really missed you, Zanna Szczechowska. And although it's amazing having an überliscious girlfriend, it's not the same at all as having a Zanna. And I'm not a magpie! I shouldn't just go for the newest, shiniest thing. You are rusty and maybe a bit moldy as well, but like blue cheese, you truly have a place in my emotional fridge . . ."

Zanna nods slowly. "You are so annoying and stupid and I absolutely hate you. But I have unfortunately missed you, too. I should really go to therapy and work out why that is, as you really are outrageously awful. It makes no sense that I should want you in my life . . ."

She trails off and I do my best Bambi face. "But . . . ?"

Zanna rolls her eyes. "I want you in my life . . . and I can't afford therapy anyway. Also I sometimes need your astrology knowledge so I can blame the stars for being emotionally unavailable or whatever. Let's just live-laugh-hug and get over it, okay? Quickly, before this gets uncomfortable."

After I have hugged Zanna for five entire minutes and she has cut the burned bits out of my hair, we go to her crypt (bedroom) and Zanna finally spills the boy-beans about Freddie Hepburn. He isn't related to Audrey (I do check) but he does have slightly long blond hair and really nice teeth and pale gray-blue eyes that make him look like a serial killer.

"He could bury me in cement under his patio any day!" I gasp. He really is quite smoldering and smoochable, actually. Thank Sappho that Morgan is gay.

"I know, right?" Zanna replies. "He even has a pet snake. It's very, very snexy."

Then she tells me about her date, from when they explored a graveyard together (Zanna enjoys calculating the average age of death in every graveyard she visits) to when he kissed her on the cheek before she got on the train. We eat an entire tub of cookie-dough ice cream while we're talking, like ravenous racoons on a bender. Later, when I am groaning in pain on her sofa, Zanna models two potential outfits for her next date with Freddie.

"The first one," I say, and Zanna smirks, then nods in approval.

"I knew it," she says. "I knew Lizzie was wrong."

"Well, she is a Taurus . . ." I begin, but Zanna gives me a look. I carefully brush a singed curl out of my face. ". . . but obviously, Zanna, that doesn't *ever* excuse poor taste."

That said, it's still fun to look through Freddie's star chart. He's a Cancer, so you can't be too careful: a responsible zodiac expertesse must always do a full astrological screening before letting a water sign near anyone they love. And when it comes to Zanna, I must confess, I love her quite ferociously.

WHAT YOU NEED TO KNOW ABOUT LIZZIE LEESON-WESTBROOKE

- It's very lucky that Lip Gloss Lizzie prefers to be called Lizzie, because her name is also Elizabeth, and one is bad enough. Her older sister, Vaseline Verity, is the only person who doesn't call her Lizzie. She calls her Duck Face instead. I'm not sure what her older brother, Dry-Lipped Damian, calls her.
- She has a killer body. Literally. Last year, she sat on her hamster, Horatio, and it was instant curtains for her chubby-cheeked chum. We all had to attend a funeral in her backyard. But Lizzie actually buried her *other* hamster, Horace, by mistake, who wasn't actually dead. Although he was by the time she dug him up again. So Lizzie is basically the Glossy Grim Reaper of hamster world. Yikes!
- But she's also got a standard-issue killer body, tanned to perfection, which is why Siobhan always crops her out of pictures. Lizzie is the only girl Siobhan is jealous of, because Lizzie could have literally any guy she wants.
- Despite this, she only wants Gloss-Guzzling Lawrence. They have been in love since first grade, when he gave her a thistle on Valentine's Day. We once asked her if she thought they'd ever break up and she burst into tears for three (VERY exhausting) hours. Lawrence had to fly

home from Ibiza to calm her down! They are clearly very committed. It's probably a Taurus thing.

- She really is obsessed with lip gloss. She has a fridge magnet that says, 'True balance is gloss on both lips.' Very strange. I blame her Libra Moon.

29
Balance in My Boondoggle

Oh, happy days! Who knew Taurus Season, when all the most boring people are born, could be such a fruitful and plentiful time to be alive? Zanna is my friend again, Morgan is chucking Brooke the Crook, Siobhan has gracefully made peace with her probable Head Girl defeat, and Dad reversed the car into Mum this morning when she was taking out the trash bins, which was hilarious to watch. All in all, on the first day back to school, I'm feeling elevated elephants galore.

Before the bell, Mrs. Warren's classroom is abuzz with holiday gossip. Habiba broke up with Imaran after he accidentally called her Hayley mid-smooch. Augustus Ming discovered that he's allergic to latex. (I really don't wish to know how.) A girl I know from art named Hamisha Chowdhury came out as bisexual on Instagram (her nose ring did make me wonder), and Posh Josh O'Conner came out as "actually quite middle-class." The shock!

Then the door crashes open and Jasmine McGregor appears, with red train-track suspenders and her foghorn sidekick,

Cadence Cooke. This grabs everyone's attention because Jasmine isn't even in this class! (Something I am grateful for every single day.)

"OMAG," she hoots, tsunami-crashing over to Siobhan's desk. Siobhan positively recoils in horror. "OH MY *ACTUAL* GOD! Guess what I just overheard in homeroom!"

Siobhan is mid-hair-brushing and doesn't look impressed at the interruption. She glares Jasmine into the ground. "The last time I gave a grape pip what you have to say, Mrs. Warren was still in the womb. What in Aladdin's fez are you doing here, Jasmine?"

Jasmine McGregor takes an enormous breath, which is saying something, given she's got lungs like a toucan's beak. Then she bellows, "YOU'RE GOING TO BE HEAD GIRL! Morgan Delaney stole Elizabeth Greenwood's car and set fire to it in the woods with Brooke the Crook and EVERYONE IS TALKING ABOUT IT! She might get EXPELLED!"

There's a moment of apocalyptic silence as every other piece of holiday news is paper-shredded from our minds. Then the whole world explodes into Charleston-dancing chaos. People are bellowing questions, Jasmine is absorbing attention like a thirsty paper towel, Alison Bridgewater is weeping for no apparent reason. Even Zanna is elbowing me and saying, "What the actual freaking armadillo?!"

In fact, there's such a red-rioting racket that no one notices the bell ringing. Siobhan is trying to shake more details out of Jasmine (literally, by her collar), and me and Zanna appear to be shaking each other when a high-pitched whistle slices through the sky and everyone covers their ears.

Mrs. Warren has materialized in the doorway like Siberian snowfall. She lowers her whistle and glares around the classroom. "Tell me, ninth graders. Was the Easter break truly so long that we have entirely forgotten all appropriate school decorum? Has there been another outbreak of nits? Has a wasp's nest fallen from the ceiling? What possible reason could there be for such unseemly and raucous behavior?"

"MORGAN DELANEY'S BEEN EXPELLED!" Jasmine McGregor hollers. "MISS, IT'S THE CRAZIEST THING SINCE SOMEONE MARRIED MR. DERRY!"

"Silence, Miss McGregor," Mrs. Warren cuts across, raising a finger. "Don't you dare raise your voice in my classroom again!"

"She can't help it, Miss, that's just her voice," Cadence Cooke chimes in, but trails off once Mrs. Warren has fixed her with a glacier-crushing frown.

"Miss McGregor, Miss Cooke, return to your group at once," Mrs. Warren instructs, and the two of them skedaddle like megaphones with scuttling feet. Mrs. Warren marches to her desk and drops her folders with a thud. "I am aware of the situation regarding two students who have made unfortunate choices over the holidays, but I shall not entertain speculation and gossip—"

"You're not really going to expel Morgan?!" I blurt, and everyone's eyes judder in their sockets. Interrupting Mrs. Warren! But what kind of Amazing Aquarius Girlfriend would I be if I stayed silent? "It wasn't even Morgan's fault!" I blunder on. "Brooke is the bad one—she took advantage of Morgan's sexy reckless side! She shouldn't be expelled for trying to be a good friend!"

Everyone gawps like terrified tabby cats. But bizarrely, Mrs. Warren doesn't guillotine me on the spot. "If you are quite done with your outburst, Cathleen." She clears her throat in warning disapproval. "Nobody is being expelled." There's a murmuring around the class. "However." Mrs. Warren pauses. "This is a very serious matter. And in light of these circumstances, the school is indeed assessing Miss Delaney's suitability for the role of Head Girl. Miss Collingdale, Mr. Drew will see you at lunchtime today . . . God rest his soul."

Then Mrs. Warren sits down at her desk and reads the attendance like she hasn't just dropped the biggest bombshell shocker since the Skinny Dippers reached ten followers on Instagram. Morgan could be kicked out of the race? Her Aries North Node must be quaking.

The rumors have flown completely out of control. By morning break, the story is that Morgan and Brooke drove a stolen tank through Rich Elizabeth's nine-section bay window, then set fire to her butler. What's worse is that everyone's staring at me like I had something to do with it! As if I'd ever be savvy enough to actually steal a car . . .

I go to the tree outside the art rooms in search of my green-haired goose, but Morgan is nowhere to be seen, and the Triple M's aren't, either. Which is usually a good thing where Maja's concerned, but I want to know where my girlfriend is! What if she's upset? Weeping out her Gemin-eyes like some sad and soggy spring buttercup?

Okay, I can't exactly imagine Morgan *weeping*. She might be brooding though, and that's not fun, either! We've all read

Wuthering Heights (unfortunately). I can't find her anywhere, not even in the boys' bathrooms. Although all the panicked screaming means I can't search the cubicles as thoroughly as I'd like . . .

When I glance through the doors of the library, Mrs. Bullock ogles me from the desk like she wants to blender me into smoothie form then flush me down the toilet. But before I can escape, I notice . . . Gooseberries galore! Is that Siobhan?!

Hiding behind a hefty rugby lad, I scuttle in and smuggle my way to the back table. Sure enough, Siobhan is sitting there all by herself, shuffling through papers covered in manic scribblings. Is she trying to invent a new conditioner?

I clear my throat and Siobhan jolts in shock. Then she glares at me, her angry eyes readjusting. "Christ on a bike, Cat! What are you—some sort of aspiring pickpocket? Don't sneak up on me like that!"

"What are you doing here?" I ask, wide-eyed. "You call this place a nerd cemetery!"

"Am I wrong?" she barks back. "Everyone in here is basically contracted to die alone." She sighs, jerking her head toward the spare seat. I quietly take it. "Go on, then. Spill. Do you think I'll make a decent Head Girl?"

"Of course!" I say breezily. "Although do you think this whole Elizabeth conundrum could really swing the votes? I suppose it's not over yet. Anything could happen!" I meet Siobhan's frown and my stomach oopsie-daisies. "Couldn't it?"

"It's over, Cat," Siobhan says, shrugging down at the tabletop. "I had my meeting with Goody Drew Shoes. Morgan's withdrawn, so I've officially 'won' the race." I watch as she

screws a sheet of paper into a ball and flicks it into the back of a sixth grader's head. "Didn't Morgan tell you already?"

"I can't find her, actually," I say, and Siobhan rolls her eyes, like my failure to track Morgan down is somehow offensive. "I thought you'd be happier?"

Siobhan's eyes widen. "Are you dense?! Of course I'm not happy! Winning by default is *not* winning—I couldn't be more apoplectic! Look at all these hideous ideas!" She grabs the sheets of paper and flings them into the air. They rain down around us and people turn to stare in fear. I can't blame them. Siobhan has flipped tables before. And chairs. And Miss Graham, the PE teacher, for giving her a red card. "I am disgusted with myself, Cat! Finally, I know what it's like to be you."

"Um, I wouldn't say I'm *disgusted—*"

"Will you shut up and listen?! I'm trying to hold myself accountable!" Siobhan's nostrils flare and I mime zipping my mouth. She puts her head in her hands. "Morgan was right, okay? My policies are substandard. My campaign stinks of elitism and lavender . . ."

"I *would* love having incense in the changing rooms," I assure her.

"It's just utterly shameful," Siobhan scoffs. "I deserve to be beaten till I bleed, then feasted upon by foxes for thinking I could win with this absolute dross. And now I'm actually going to be Head Girl? This whole process is just paper-pushing boondoggle!"

Once we have established that *boondoggle* is indeed a word and not another of Siobhan's Scrabble-based bamboozlements, we sit in uneasy silence. Well, Siobhan orders some sixth graders

to pick up the papers she threw everywhere, but apart from that.

"Siobhan," I say carefully. "You know I love you, don't you?"

"This isn't the time for spineless statements, Cat," Siobhan mutters. "We're not making greeting cards here! Love is good for absolutely no one. It's a disease."

"Um . . ." I shake my head. "No, Siobhan, what I mean is, please don't, um, hurt me for saying this . . . But you're right. Your campaign wasn't good enough. And Morgan knew you wouldn't prepare properly and she used it against you. But you are the same person who organizes parties and keeps the gang together and organizes mass blockings on Instagram!"

Siobhan sniffs. "Jasmine totally deserved that. She shouldn't have posted that photo of me standing next to Lizzie. Everyone knows the rules about that, Cat. *Everyone*."

"What I'm saying, Siobhan, is that you get things done," I explain, and Ohio my goodness, this is all coming out shockingly well. I'm even persuading myself! "I completely believe you can be an amazing Head Girl if you put in the effort. You really are the most . . . Um, the most! I mean, not physically. Although you're tall. Well, healthy. Moist. Most! Not moist. Not that I'm saying you're dry! I'm sure you're soggy in all the right places. Um . . ."

Well, I had a good run. Even though Siobhan now looks like she wants to sink into the Mariana Trench just so she can unhear that last part. Eventually, she says, "You know what? You're right. I know you're not used to hearing that . . ."

"Only in math!" I squeak.

"But you're right." Siobhan smacks the tabletop. "I am going to fix everything. Just like I did at that pitiful event Habiba had

the audacity to call a 'party.' Remember? With those repellent green napkins?" I grimace and nod. Siobhan slides her blazer back on, then stands up. "Well, mustn't dillydally. I have a really important meeting to prepare for. Thank you very much and all that. I know exactly what I need to do." Then she marches out of the library, pausing just one time to drop all her notes in the recycling bin.

Well, she actually drops them all over the floor again, but I think she was *aiming* for the recycling bin, so credit where credit's due.

NEW POST FROM: @ITSHABIBABABY (HABIBA QADIR)

@itshabibababy:
HEY MY HABABYS, HOW ARE YOU? Did you remember to #hydrate today? ☺ My weekly #HabibaLive livestream is happening TONIGHT (who is excited?) where I will be revealing the #WinnerWinnerFitterNotThinner from my #fitstagram #giveaway and talking all things #POLITICS with NEWLY appointed Head Girl AND FOREVER appointed #GURLBOSS, @siobhan.dc! #StayTuned and #StayHydrated! Hbb xxx

Comments (10 of 74)

@siobhan.dc:
urgh. did I actually agree to this???

@owusuperman:
Love to see #women killing it in the workplace!

@siobhan.dc:
@owusuperman SHAME THEY *DON'T* LOVE SEEING YOU.

@kieran_wb:
@siobhan.dc miss u babe

@siobhan.dc:
@kieran_wb WELL DUH. GET USED TO IT.

@a.bridgewater.xox:
So proud of you babes wow!!!!!!!!!!!!!!!<3<3<3

@dalecollinsgolf:
nice, congrats @siobhan.dc

@siobhan.dc:
@dalecollinsgolf GO SUCK A GOLF CLUB

@z.szcz:
z deszczu pod rynnę

@siobhan.dc:
@z.szcz ZANNA WHAT DOES IT MEAN. TELL ME. NOW!!!

30
What Palace of Dim Light Is This?

Very strange and suspicious scenes in rehearsals. I shuffle in five minutes late and everyone goes quiet, like a theater of silent salamanders. Rich Elizabeth is swooning about on the makeshift stage with her snooty sidekicks and they all give me stink eye. Which probably smells like Armani luxury perfume, in their case.

"So ungrateful," catcalls Ella or Eliza.

"So," agrees Eliza or Ella.

"So," agrees Un-Alliterative Abigail.

Rich Elizabeth says nothing. Just studies her nude manicure and doesn't even look at me. I sigh tragically, then walk over. Which seems to take her girl gang by surprise. They all mime pinching their noses.

"Elizabeth, I'm sorry about your car," I say, and she finally deigns to meet my eye. "I absolutely did not have anything to do with what happened! I was really goosed out when I found out what Morgan and Brooke had done. I really liked rehearsing with you and I hope we can still be friends. Even if just for the play."

Elizabeth rolls her expensive eyes. "There probably isn't even going to *be* a play, chicka. Brooke's been suspended. Can't do *Romeo and Juliet* without Romeo."

"So inconsiderate of her," says Ella.

"So," agrees Eliza.

"I suppose the difference between Romeo and Brooke is that Romeo didn't have to worry about CCTV when he broke into people's gardens and lamented them under the moonlight." Elizabeth sighs. "Insulting to think we wouldn't catch her."

"*So* insulting," agrees Abigail.

But I am too flabbergasted to process. No play?! All because of Brooke?! I learned all those sucky-lipped sonnets . . . FOR NOTHING?! I might actually hit the roof. Or get Rich Elizabeth to hit the roof for me, since she's probably the only one who can reach it.

But before I can say anything, the studio doors creak open and Miss Spencer pads through like an unhappy Christmas elf, shuffling along in her sad white sneakers. We all gawp at her in shockaholic surprise. Miss Spencer has been in the room for five entire seconds and she hasn't done one backflip yet. She must be on death's door!

"Morning, gang," she deflates. "I won't say *good* morning, as I'm sure you've heard the news. We've lost our lead with just one week until curtains! Oh, it really is sad. I'm not sure there's ever been a story of more woe than this. Ironic, under the circumstances . . ."

"Has Brooke really been suspended, Miss?" Marcus asks.

"I'm afraid so, Marcus." Miss Spencer nods. She then extracts

a very wet tissue from her sleeve and hoots into its damp folds. "My hands are tied, even more than they were in my years as a magician's assistant. And as Brooke's should be, too, for the mess she's left us with. Oh, it's very sad . . . You've all rehearsed so beautifully. Even you, Cat . . . !"

"Then why don't we do it?" I say, standing up grandly.

Everyone gawps at me. Maja goes, "How?"

Hmm. I should probably have thought of my grand and masterful master plan *before* I made a whole Banquo banquet out of this. I grimace at Rich Elizabeth, who raises a well-plucked eyebrow. And then . . .

I snap my fingers. Which hurts a lot, and needs practice, but Ohio well. "Elizabeth can do it!" I announce. "Miss, Elizabeth knows this play outside in. She can quote random lines like some sort of nerd!"

Eliza, Ella, and Abigail all blink around at their Drama Queen in surprise. Rich Elizabeth's cheeks turn a rich shade of pink. "That's not true," she says quickly. "I just picked up some lines when the private jet got delayed and I was stuck in a public airport for sixteen hours! You know, for fear of that, I still will stay with thee, and never from this palace of dim night depart again! By which I mean Starbucks. They had a power outage."

Miss Spencer's eyes sparkle. She leaps to her feet. "Romeo!" she gasps. "Act five, scene three! Elizabeth, you know the lines! Is this a magical opportunity I see before me?! The handle toward my hand . . . !"

"That's the Scottish Play, Miss." Elizabeth rolls her eyes. "Everybody knows that."

"No!" Miss Spencer glitters. "No, they don't, Elizabeth! Most

teenage girls would *never* bother learning the words to a *male* lead in a Shakespeare play! This is just wonderful! And it would show dazzling range when you apply to theater school!"

Elizabeth's eyes ka-ching like dollar signs. "Range?" she repeats as I grin victoriously. "Did you just say *range*?! The only thing more valuable than money?! Wowzer's trousers, Miss, do you really believe I have what it takes?"

Maja rolls her eyes. "Jesus wept, Elizabeth, she's only asking you to be a man. Isn't that, like, already the easiest job on the planet?"

"Not all men are cis-het, babes . . ." Marcus murmurs, and Maja groans.

"I'LL DO IT!" Rich Elizabeth announces, jumping to her feet and narrowly avoiding headbutting the projector. "Marcus can take over as the Nurse. He's already essentially a comedy character, so it shouldn't take much. I will be Cat's happy dagger!"

And then she actually smiles at me. Gooseberries galore . . . Did I just save the days, the gays, and the whole school plays?!

It seems the reason I couldn't find Morgan at school today is because she wasn't at school today. She's at home in Marylebone Close. Which also means I got a detention for smuggling myself into the staff room on the tea cart for nothing—SO annoying.

Anyway, I skedaddle round to Morgan's after school. It's a great excuse to not walk home with Luna, who's so heartbroken about her Vegan Meals Initiative dying with Morgan's campaign, she's actually considering chaining herself to the cafeteria's oven instead. I asked if she'd consider climbing *into* the oven, but she didn't seem too amused by that.

I think I was being very hilarious though.

What's not hilarious is Morgan's mum's face when she opens the blue front door. Caroline is usually quite merry, but today she looks very grave. Like a gravedigger, in fact. She says, "Oh, Cat, it's you. Why don't you come in? We could do with a laugh."

I'm not sure what she's implying with that. I open my mouth to say so, but then I trip over the doormat. Quite impressive, considering I'm standing still. Then, like a true citizen of Ohio, I catch my blazer on the door handle and rip my entire sleeve open. *Sigh*.

"Morgan's upstairs," says Caroline. "She's been there all day . . ."

I peer up the murky staircase into the gloom, like one of those idiot murder victims in horror movies. But Morgan is my girlfriend and murder is a risk I'll just have to take.

Morgan's door is shut and I can hear Lana Del Rey playing. So we're already off to a rocky start. I gently knock on the door, then I wait. Then I wait some more. Then I push open the door and peer around like a nervous mole.

All the curtains are drawn, making Morgan's dark red walls look cavernous, yawning black. Avril Lavigne is gazing at me sullenly from the wall above Morgan's bed, but I can't actually see Morgan. Frowning, I step into the room. Then I notice a foot sticking out from under the duvet, wearing a green bed sock. I clear my throat.

"Morgan?" No response. I cough louder. "Morgan, is that you?"

"No," says Morgan. "I'm dead."

How very TV lesbian.

"Oh," I say. "Is there anything I can do?"

"Can you reverse death?"

"I don't think even Zanna can do that," I admit. "And she's very efficient."

"Then there's nothing," says Morgan.

We go back to being silent salamanders. Carefully, I sit down on the bed. Lana Del Rey drones on. "Could we maybe change the music, Morgan? I feel like it might not actually be helping. We could listen to Cher! You know, so you can SCHNAP OUT OF IT!"

But not even my Cher impersonation gets Morgan to take the pillow off her face. These are truly dark times. Forget Rich Elizabeth in Starbucks in a power outage. What palace of dim light is this?!

"What about ABBA?" I suggest. "Or some Gemma Collins quotes?"

Morgan moves the pillow off her mouth. Progress! "Do you know what this song is called, babe? It's called 'Cruel World.' And next is 'The Blackest Day.' And before this was 'Born to Die.' So I think this music is just cracker, to be honest."

Is Lana Del Rey okay? Has anybody ever asked? Also, do Irish people really say *cracker*, or has Morgan just stolen that from *Derry Girls*? Many, many questions in my Curious Aquarius Mind. But none of them are going to make Morgan feel any better.

"Do you want to talk about it?" I ask. "Talking can help, although not usually for me, because I talk too much. I ended up telling my dentist that I have a secret phobia of one day mistaking a grape for an olive. Like, can you imagine? They're such different flavors and textures, but they're both green balls, so are any of us safe?"

Morgan says nothing and my panic rockets to Babble Level 2.0.

"I probably should have waited until he'd taken his hands out of my mouth," I ramble on. "I accidentally bit him three times! But it's so awkward having to lie there in silence. He told me he was going to reconsider his position on freedom of speech, all because of me. How embarrassing is that? I said I didn't even realize we had to pay to talk . . ."

"Babe," says Morgan, and I hush. She moves the pillow off her face so I can finally see her eyes. They're a little blotchy, but still very swoony and amazing. Seeing them so sad turns me Piscean. Morgan takes a breath. "Can we just lie here, maybe?"

I nod quickly. "We can do that! It'll be like going to the dentist. Well, not exactly the same. If my dentist called me 'babe,' it might be weird. But . . ."

"Can we lie here . . . and *not* say anything?"

I nod again. I should probably stop talking about dentists. I take off my blazer and then lie next to Morgan. She puts her arms around me. It's very safe and swoony. Even if Lana Del Rey is still trying to hypnotize me, like Has-to-Be-Hypnotized Henry.

Chat Thread: Mumulous Maximus (Mum)

Cat, 6:15 p.m.:
Morgan very sad. Can I sleep over?

Mum, 6:27 p.m.:
Typing . . .

What does Caroline say?

Cat, 6:28 p.m.:
She is fine!!! Dandy in fact, o mother of mine!!!!

Pleeeeeeeease? She really is in a Sylvia Plath Plateau

Mum, 6:42 p.m.:
Typing . . .

Okay.

Mum, 7:07 p.m.:
Typing . . .

No funny business, Cathleen. Don't think it doesn't count because you're both girls.

Cat, 7:09 p.m.:
MUM!!!! EWWWWW!!!!!! WT-FANDANGO!!!!!

GO AWAY!!!!!

31
Taylor Swift Trashes the Kitchen

What fresh hell is this?! I wake up (in Morgan's bed, Ohio-la-la) to the horrifying news that the Skinny Dippers got retweeted by TAYLOR SWIFT. Apparently, she "couldn't stop laughing" at Brooke and Jamie's cover, "My Eyes Swell," in which Jamie catalogs his struggles with hay fever, and now the entire planet is obsessed with them!

Overnight, Jamie Owusu has become the most famous person I know, with over eighty thousand new followers online. TikTok stars are inviting him onto their podcasts. Harry Styles says he and Jamie "should jam sometime." Melissa McCarthy called Brooke a "comic genius." Has the entire world been knocked senseless by a bus?! Here I am, a stalker-level Swiftie without so much as a toenail from Taylor, and Jamie Owusu is suddenly the coolest guy in Queen's. And in Kent. (Probably.)

Morgan can absolutely NOT find out about this. For Brooke's star to rise just as Morgan's sun, moon, AND stars are all descending into total eclipse . . . It's too much boondoggle to bear. My girlfriend might genuinely slip into a Lana Del Rey coma and never wake up! So I do what any gracious girlfriend would. I cut off Morgan's access to the outside world and steal her phone and hide it with mine in the fridge. Thank Aphrodite her mum has gone to work!

Next on my list of Ways to Save Morgan's Day, I call the school and tell them that I am sick.

"Hello," I say into the phone. "Um, I am sick."

"Who is this?" the lady says. "What grade are you in?"

"Oh, um, sorry, I'm Cat Pillips. I mean, Phillips!"

Some typing. "And what are you sick with?"

"Um . . ." Oh, Sappho's sniffles, why do I never plan in advance?! "I have a bladder infection," I blurt, then wince. WHY THAT?! "It's really quite serious, Miss. My wee is coming out in these great brown gushes, like tar or something . . ."

"All right, all right," the lady interrupts. "I really didn't need to know that. Get well soon! Definitely don't come back until your . . . um . . . problem is sorted. Goodbye!"

Fake bladder infection or not though, I can't just sloth about. What can I do to positively kick off Morgan's day?

That's when my eyes fall on a hardback book titled *Easy Peasy Lemon Squeezy: Cooking for the Non-Cook* propped against the wine rack on top of the fridge. Perfect! I can make Morgan a romantic breakfast in bed. I swipe the book down.

Then the wine rack COLLAPSES. Bottles rolling in more directions than Harry Styles would know what to do with. A

weight-bearing recipe book?! COME ON! Glass shatters all over the tiles and before I know what's happened, I'm standing in a pool of red. Morgan's kitchen looks like a murder scene! And it will be—mine!—if I don't clean this up. But cleaning takes forever—and it's also boring. And what about Morgan's surprise breakfast?! I will just have to cook quickly, then clean up afterward. Everyone knows cooking is a *bit* messy.

I find an omelet recipe labeled "Skill Level: Lemon Squeezy," and then I find an electric cake mixer under the sink—since I can't find a whisk, it'll have to do. I break three eggs into a cereal bowl. Then, biting my tongue, I plug in the cake mixer and advance toward the eggs . . .

The mixer roars like a power drill when I flick the switch, and before I can say *idiot sandwich*, the *bowl* begins spinning like a merry-go-round. It launches off the table and smashes right into the microwave.

I gawp in gut-wrenching horror at the mosaic of egg mix and smashed glass. Hmm. Perhaps cleaning is more important than making the perfect breakfast after all? I hop from foot to foot in panic.

Oh, why didn't I listen when Mum tried to teach me how to mop a floor?!

Never mind—that's what the internet is for. Or I can call Zanna! She'll know what to do.

My phone is in the fridge . . . but as I rush over to retrieve it, grabbing the door handle in my sweaty, egg-splattered hands—FIZZLESTICKS! THE WINE!

I slip and land flat on my back. Then I watch, with glacier-collapsing terror, as the fridge door crashes open, bulldozes the

nearby crockery shelf, and drowns me in a rainstorm of shattering mugs and plates. The last thing I see is a Nigella Lawson hardback, spinning toward me like an unnecessarily stylish boomerang.

There is screaming in my dream. Lots and lots of screaming.

Then I frown—wait! I'm not dreaming! My eyes flicker open. Morgan is shrieking at me from the kitchen doorway.

"OHHHHH JESUS FREAKING WEPT!" howls Morgan, her knees almost giving out beneath her.

It's then I realize that coming downstairs to find your girlfriend lying motionless on the floor in a pool of red liquid and broken crockery probably does give off a bit of a vibe.

I sit right up. "Morgan, I'm alive! It's fine!"

"WHAT THE ACTUAL FRICKING HELL, CAT?! I THOUGHT YOU WERE DEAD OR SOMETHING, JESUS CHRIST!"

Morgan's eyelashes flicker and she suddenly seems to notice the rest of the kitchen. Smashed crockery. The microwave door. Egg absolutely everywhere.

"What happened?!" she whispers. "Look at the place!"

Okay, Cat, it's time for some quick thinking. "Um, I don't know!" I blurt. "I just came down and found it like this! I think a burglar stole our phones as well!"

"But that makes no sense!" Morgan pushes past me and surveys the kitchen. "Why would a burglar come in and just wreck the place?! Is that egg all over the wall? Why is that frying pan on the stove? Was the burglar making omelets?!"

I study the smashed microwave door, sweat and wine running down my forehead.

"IT WAS TAYLOR SWIFT'S FAULT, OKAY?!" I shout before I can stop myself.

Morgan frowns, even more confused. "Taylor Swift trashed my kitchen?" Her eyes shift to the wide-open fridge. "And . . . put my phone in the fridge?"

I avoid Morgan's eye. Even as she slowly, painfully, turns to face me, and then folds her arms. I clear my throat. "Would that be better . . . than if I had somehow done it . . . ?"

Well, cleaning the kitchen together is not exactly what I had planned when I said I wanted to treat Morgan like a queen and make her breakfast. She's surprisingly understanding about my attempts to keep her safe from the news about Taylor Swift and the Skinny Dippers and doesn't seem to mind that cleaning up my mess takes almost the entire day. An experience that teaches us both that liquid *can't* just be vacuumed away.

"So we've got to get a new microwave, new plates and mugs . . ." Morgan hangs her head in her hands. "And a new vacuum cleaner as well. How dead am I when my mum gets back? Like, on a scale of one to, I don't know, a Skinny Dippers gig."

"Um . . ." I grimace. "Are we remembering that they might be famous now?"

Morgan closes her eyes. "Jesus. No. I totally forgot about that. Life is wild."

We are sitting on the kitchen floor in rubber gloves, a mop propped across our legs.

"Well, you've definitely kept me distracted today," Morgan says. "That's what you wanted, right? I mean, I can think of a few more fun ways to do that, but this worked."

I blush. "I'm just trying to be a good girlfriend!"

Morgan eyes me. "I think it's me who needs to try a bit harder, babe. Karma really came for my backside. When I was in Mr. Drew's office with my mam, I thought Brooke would stick up for me but . . . all she did was fake-cry and tell everyone that I *dared* her to trash the car. That's why we're both getting punished the same."

Morgan notices my shockaholic-ed expression. She takes my hand and squeezes as we both gaze ahead in void-like disbelief. Then she just snorts with laughter.

"You know what's funny? I felt bad for her because I thought Brooke was, like, less fortunate, you know? But it turns out she lives three doors down from Elizabeth Greenwood. Her mum is a film producer and, apparently, never shuts up about how great an actress Elizabeth is going to be one day. Brooke's had it in for Elizabeth ever since."

I'm a little speechless. Although, Sappho slap me silly, I have a LOT of questions. Like, what *is* Brooke's actual star sign? What does she spend her stolen-swan-egg money on if she's already rolling in it? What if it's hair dye? IS SHE EVEN A NATURAL REDHEAD?!

"But according to her mum," Morgan continues, "*I'm* a bad influence. Brooke is as crooked as you told me . . . and then some. I can't believe Siobhan was right."

Her final statement hangs in the air. It's like Siobhan's Armani perfume has just shadowed the entire kitchen. Morgan looks so deflated . . . All my questions will have to wait. I have a much more important job to do: general clownery and mood-lifting.

"Well, you are a slightly bad influence," I say carefully, and

Morgan actually looks worried for a moment. "You did turn me into a lesbian."

Morgan cackles in relief. "Because you were *soooo* straight before, Mrs. Bridgewater."

We gaze at each other for a while. A very satisfying pastime. We might even be about to kiss. But then I say, "You know, Brooke may have no morals, but Siobhan always sticks by her friends. And she's not going round school gloating!"

Morgan sighs. "You mean the same Siobhan who literally made me into a piñata?" I um-uh for a moment. "I do follow her Instagram, Cat."

I shuffle right up to my girlfriend. "Morgan, this isn't *Romeo and Juliet*. We're not dead and the Montagues and Capulets are going to have to get over themselves in the end, because life goes on and . . . We do the Hokey Pokey and we . . ." I gulp. Uh-oh. "We turn around and . . . that's what it's all . . . um . . . about."

Morgan nods slowly. "You might actually be in danger of sounding wise."

I gulp, trying to maintain a mind clear of Aquari-chaos. "All I mean is that I know it's going to be weird. But you'll have to go back to school and Siobhan will be Head Girl and that's just how the crumble has, well, crumbled. But I still love you and we're going to be fine. It's not like we're Virgos!"

Morgan tilts her head. "What did you just say?"

I frown. "I said we're not Virgos, Morgan. You know, because they're quite boring?"

"No, before that." Morgan smirks. "You said you loved me."

"Oh." I feel myself crimsoning over. "Yes, well, I suppose

I did. Um, is that okay? I mean, I can't do much about it if it's not . . . I could try to be a bit more Scorpio, I guess. I don't think they feel emotions like the rest of us . . ."

Morgan raises an eyebrow. She really is beautiful, even without any makeup on. But she's also a little more real than when I met her. She makes mistakes, just like me, and not just because her Venus is in Gemini. Somehow, to me, Morgan's mistakes make her even more wonderful . . . but I will probably keep that to myself. She'll never let me see her without eyeliner again if she thinks she's being vulnerable.

"I love you, too," Morgan says. "But I think you already know that. Since you've literally trashed my kitchen and I'm not even mad about it."

I distract her with a kiss at this point. I am sure Taylor Swift would write a very swifty-swoony song about us, actually. But she's probably too busy trashing kitchens elsewhere.

My Eyes Swell

by Jamie Owusu & Brooke Mackenzie

I'm stuck in my room again,
It's hot outside.
Can't even breathe; I got itchy eyes
And I left my nasal spray in my school locker,
So I woke up this morning with one hell of a blocker.

Oh, the pollen is high,
And my eyes are red.
I sneezed on my girlfriend when we were kissing in bed.
Tree pollen falling down right into my hair—
I took medicine this morning, but my nose don't
care . . .

And I know it's just summer, and sure, it's a bummer,
But my nose is streaming like a marathon runner, on
and on . . . !

'Cause here I am again, in a field, half-blind,
Sniffing so hard, I might blow my own mind,
Here comes a sneeze, then a wheeze,
Can't even see you, 'cause my eyes swell . . .

Went out with my girlfriend
One pollen-high day,
She wanted a picnic, and what could I say?
She packed sandwiches and salads, strawberries and cream,
Arranged in a basket, thought she'd be eating with me.

But I was long gone from the moment I woke up that day,
'Cause as freaking usual, hay fever got in my way!

There I was again, with eyes so swollen,
On the kitchen floor, where I had fallen—
Could not see, nose runny,
Cannot go out, 'cause my eyes swell . . .

32

Fearful in My Best Dress

I really am a very amazing girlfriend. But then I am an Aquarius, so what else would Morgan expect? Although Morgan's mum isn't too impressed when she learns that "the milkman asked to use the bathroom and somehow accidentally broke the microwave and all the crockery."

"I didn't realize Lambley Common even had a milkman," Caroline says as we shamefully shuffle our feet. "Didn't your mum say Luna scared him back to Dundee?"

"That's probably why he was in such a frenzy . . ." I reply. "It was blind panic!"

Luckily, Caroline doesn't ask too many questions, so I think we completely fool her. Then she gets distracted by Fran and Mum going gaga in their tragic WhatsApp group over Jamie's newfound fame.

"The Skinny Dippers are going international," he tells everyone on Wednesday at the picnic tables, where Siobhan has

INVITED JAMIE to sit with us, Sappho slap me asunder. "'My Eyes Swell' is a smash. It's been viewed three hundred thousand times, and the numbers are still climbing."

This may be true. But they will never climb as high as my utter astonishment and disbelief that this has happened. Zanna says, "Well, Brooke won't care she's been suspended if she's literally dating a celebrity like yourself, Jamie." She smirks at me as I burst another vessel in my eye. "I mean, *everyone* is going to fancy you now."

Jamie slicks a hand through his still-too-short-to-slick-back hair. "Well, actually, me and Brooke have decided we don't want to mix business with pleasure. We called off our relationship last night, like . . ." He narrows his eyes, nodding wistfully. "Like a broken dream, flying through the clouds like a plane never destined to land . . ."

Lip Gloss Lizzie stares at him. "Wow," she says. "That was, like, *so* poetic."

"If I weren't so against written material, in solidarity with my dyslexic friend Kenna, I'd say you should write a book," says Siobhan as I goggle in disbelief, because she absolutely should *not* put that idea into Jamie's head. "Every sad-fest excuse of a person is writing a book nowadays. Even when they have nothing of substance to contribute to society."

"Jamie should write poetry," pouts Lizzie. "Like Cat!"

They all witter on, with Jamie asking Kenna to teach him the sign language for "coolest guy in the world," until the most shocking thing happens:

Siobhan says, "Cat, is Morgan okay?"

We all go silent salamanders. "Um . . ." I say, eyeing the gang nervously. "Well, she's upset about being suspended. And the Head Girl race. But she'll be okay! Um, why?"

Kenna's eyes are very wide, like she's bracing for an incoming explosion, but Siobhan says, in a very normal voice, "She texted me, actually. We had a conversation. She said sorry for some of her foolish choices and that I'm going to make an exceptional Head Girl."

Zanna frowns. "Did she really say *exceptional*?"

Siobhan glares. "YES?! Well, she implied it. I asked her if by *really decent*, do you mean *exceptional*, and she said, why not. Which is basically the same thing. Fact! Anyway, it was brave of her, considering she's practically been ostracized from society. So I invited her to the aftershow party on Friday. Which I hope you appreciate."

I cannot help but smile and tell Siobhan I appreciate that McQueenly. I could point out that Morgan was already invited to the aftershow party on Friday, because it's at my house and I organized it with Elizabeth. But why dampen the moment?

Thursday *and* Friday are taken up with dress rehearsals for the school play. Sadly, we actually have to be *in* the dresses for these rehearsals (I do check), so there's no getting out of this now. I'm going to be Juliet, onstage, in front of humans with eyes, and one of those humans will be Jasmine McGregor, who is apparently practicing how to hoot with such volume and intensity, I will wet myself onstage from fright.

"Don't worry, chicka," sighs Rich Elizabeth. "Jasmine always heckles us on show night. It's basically just tradition at this

point. Although I heard she's been inspired by Siobhan to smuggle in a megaphone this year, so that's a fabulous new addition."

Moody Maja is tying up my corset. We're all in the studios getting ready to see ourselves in costume for the first time. It *should* be a bonding moment, but she says, "Everyone will be laughing at you too much to listen to Jasmine anyway."

Marcus snorts and that is when I snap, like a riled-up rubber band.

"Right!" I whirl round. "You two, listen. Morgan is my girlfriend, so you can like it or, um . . . dislike it. I am not weird and edgy like you. I don't understand your references to Björk or why it's so funny that I have blond hair. But if you are trying to say I'm stupid, well, I'd like to point out that you are *bleach* blond, Maja, which is a *choice*, which makes you even stupider."

Marcus mimes "Ouch," and Maja reddens to the point she finally looks alive. She gestures at me to turn around again, and I do, but with a very smug expression on my face. Rich Elizabeth looks impressed. Which is saying a lot, considering I'm not jewel-encrusted.

"You look cute-McBeaut, chicka," she says. "That's a gorgealicious dress."

Then she holds up a mirror and I OM-Gasp. I actually am quite jewel-encrusted after all! My dress is white and laced with gold thread, with a red belt around my waist. I look so Gucci-good, I'm quite tempted to go, "MAAAAARIIIIIAAAAAAAAAAAAA!" again, but before I can, Miss Spencer comes topknot-bobbing over.

"Looking FABULOUS, Cat!" she yaps. "I couldn't be prouder if I was bribed by the PTA! *But* we're going to have to pause for

lunchtime assembly! Head Boy and Head Girl time, boys and girls!" Then she claps her flippers and cartwheels off.

Marcus frowns. "There was a Head Boy contest?" So at least I'm not the only one who thought it. Most of the boys are scared of Siobhan, so I'm surprised anyone volunteered.

Eye-rolling, Maja steps toward me. "Guess we should undress you again . . ."

But I hold up my hand, grand as a goose. "That shall not be necessary."

We trundle into the hall still in costume, wholly redefining the concept of a grand entrance. Elizabeth, in her scarlet pantaloons, escorts me to my seat and everyone goggles and gasps. I have no time to be fearful in my best dress—I am too busy being amazing.

When the assembly begins, Mr. Drew insists on making some tragic speech! I am ready to switch off, to be honest. But after he's droned on and on about how time flies (although you wouldn't know it from his speech) and announced that Gloss-Guzzling Lawrence, who I didn't even realize was running, has won Head Boy (Lizzie won't stop squealing), Siobhan finally shoves Lawrence aside and marches up to the podium. With new blond highlights as well!

"Oh, gasp," murmurs Elizabeth. "Someone's making bold choices."

"*So* bold," agrees Abigail or Eliza.

Siobhan clears her throat, then shuffles her papers. I know from break that the papers are blank, but she was right: they *do* make her look more efficient. "Thank you for the opportunity

to address my subjec—I mean, constituents. It's been a strange week. Frankly, I didn't think I'd be the one making this speech—"

"WE WISH YOU WEREN'T!" Jasmine bellows.

"But I wanted to assure you that I'm taking this role as seriously as though I am the creative director of Alexander McQueen. My opponent, Morgan Delaney, made some great points at the debate. Therefore, I'd like to pledge my intentions to make the bathrooms gender neutral as she suggested, and to see that Luna Phillips and Niamh Collingdale's Vegan Meals Initiative is made reality. I will also seek Morgan's input on the proposed buddy scheme, a promising idea . . . that *she* had."

The chatter fades. Even Jasmine McGregor has stopped hooting to listen. Is Siobhan serious?! Luna will be growing grass for vegan joy about this!

"I also plan on organizing a fund for students who cannot afford school trips," Siobhan continues. "We should all enjoy equal opportunities, access, and quality of conditioner."

People clap. Siobhan rolls her shoulders, her confidence returning. "I LOVE YOU, MY MCQUEEN!" Kenna shrieks, and Mrs. Warren gives her a stern throat-clearing. *"Sorry . . ."* signs Kenna, silent once more.

Siobhan shuffles the papers again. "Having sent many people to therapy in my life, I'm also passionate about mental health. Although I personally find judo more helpful than talking about boring distractions like 'feelings,' I plan to improve the counseling services, so that anyone who's struggling—anyone who has seen Jasmine McGregor's ugly face, for example—can be supported. I hope this speech has reassured everybody that I am the best woman for the job. So, cheers."

Then Siobhan tosses her hair and marches offstage without even waiting for applause. But we all applaud anyway because we are amazing friends. Also, equal conditioner for all?! You can't argue with a message like that! We clap and clap until our hands are red.

And until Mrs. Warren starts blowing her whistle.

Lots of line-learning back in the iPhone Box. Luna grumbles at dinner that she probably knows the play better than I do. But I say that's *more* than fair, given how much of her dream-hop flow-through music (or whatever) I put up with.

Before sleeping though, I get a call from Morgan. Always very dreamy. "Hey, babe," she butters me down. "Just wanted to say break a leg for tomorrow. I do mean good luck, just to be clear. Please don't actually break any bones. I know what you're like."

"I will not break any bones," I promise Morgan. "But I will probably break your heart, Morgan, so are you sure you want to come? My acting really is so amazing and wonderful, you will probably completely believe that I am in love with Elizabeth Greenwood."

There's a pause. "Well, that's understandable," Morgan muses. "Isn't she a Capricorn? Really long and elegant figure as well. I'd probably be in love with her myself if I weren't completely infatuated with some other idiot I know."

I smile into my phone, my eyes closed sleepily. Morgan really does say the dreamiest-at-the-seamiest things. "And who, might I inquire, are you talking about?" I murmur.

Morgan is smiling back. I can *hear* her. "Oh, you know her

well," Morgan says. "Her name is Lilac Victoria West. I just think she's so freaking hot."

That wakes me right up. I sit bolt upright in my bed and scream a lot at Morgan that that isn't funny at all, it's very offensive, actually, then I hang up without even saying good night. Gooseberries, my girlfriend is EVIL!

I might still smile as I am falling asleep though. Because she's very funny as well.

Group Chat: The Gang

Siobhan, 7:19 p.m.:
Absolute scenes at my place right now. Told Niamh about her vegan meals and she's been blubbering for more than 15 minutes!
Also I just got called an "ally." NO THANKS.

Habiba, 7:21 p.m.:
Awwwww :') Are you sure you're not a LITTLE #FeelingBlessed?
Also Imaran just texted me sorry again . . . :/ should I reply??? xo

Siobhan, 7:22 p.m.:
YES
And NO

Cat, 7:22 p.m.:
Luna just refollowed you on Insta, Siobhan!!! :')))
PROGRESS!!!xxx

Siobhan, 7:23 p.m.:
LUNA UNFOLLOWED ME ON INSTAGRAM???????
YOU CAN TELL HER RN THAT IF SHE DARES PULL A STUNT LIKE THAT AGAIN, SHE WILL END UP ***IN*** THE FREAKING MEALS HERSELF!!!!!!!

Zanna, 7:25 p.m.:
Wouldn't be vegan then, would they?

33
Juliet's Daring Dagger Escape

In fair Lambley Common, where we lay our scene, today is show day! And I am about as nervous as Mr. Drew must be, knowing Siobhan now represents the school.

Between rehearsals and scraping melted chocolate buttons from between the pages of all my books (which Lilac *definitely* put there over Easter, even though Mum *insists* that "anyone could have put them there—you probably left them there yourself, Cat, you forgetful thing!"), the week flies by, and soon enough, I'm in the very important stars' dressing room (well, it's Miss Spencer's office), getting ready and trying to not be distracted by the many vaguely horrific photos of Miss Spencer in her magician's assistant era.

"I can't believe she was telling the truth about that . . ." I murmur, gazing around.

"Daddy's flown in from Italy for the show," Rich Elizabeth drawls as Maja yanks at the strings of her chest binder. With Elizabeth's sugary hair wrapped into a topknot, she actually looks quite dashing, in a tuxedoed Cate Blanchett sort of way. "I assured him he didn't *have* to bring his assistant, but she's so fond of me . . ."

She really is hilariously strange. But I don't hate it nearly as much as before.

More importantly, Morgan is coming to the performance! Which is serious relationship progress, considering I previously didn't even want her to know I was doing the play. It's almost enough to make up for the fact that Mum and Dad are coming, too . . . I am already cringe-jingling! Why do they always insist on coming to things?! It's not like we don't see enough of each other at home . . .

The cast spends twenty minutes doing vocal exercises in the drama rooms until Miss Spencer knocks on the door and gives us a "gentle reminder" that this isn't *The Sound of Music*.

Soon enough though, I am waiting in the wings like a true Julie Andrews. The lights dim and my stomach lurches because, oh, gooseberries . . . This is the moment of daggerdom!

Posh Josh O'Conner snoots through the prologue and Maja wheels the first backdrop into place. Then it's Romeo's first appearance, and Rich Elizabeth swaggers onto the stage. There's a murmur from the audience. Lesbians getting excited probably. Elizabeth really does look poodle-perfect in her red pantaloons. She says something about rejoicing in splendor all on her own and she is absolutely correct. Elizabeth is TALENT!

The scene changes again. Maja wheels on another backdrop and Marcus glides on in full Nurse costume with Eliza as Lady

Capulet. Eliza says, "Nurse, where's my daughter? Call her forth to me . . . !"

Then there's a pause. Some shuffling feet. That's when I realize—oh fizzle-biscuits! I AM JULIET, the daughter is me! I hurry onto the stage in a very inelegant way, stumbling over my dress so everybody in the hall chortles. Not my smoothest start. I'm opening my mouth to say my first line but then I make the mistake of looking into the audience.

OH. MY. GOOSEBERRIES.

Literally hundreds of eyes are blinking at me. I am like an innocent minnow fish that's just swum headfirst into a hammerhead shark. My mind is blanker than a Capricorn's social calendar. Who am I actually kittening, Elle-Fanning about onstage when I still don't even know what *exeunt* means?!

Then I see Luna. She's sitting in the front row like some sort of nerd, and she's making funny shapes with her mouth. Then I realize what she's doing. For once, it's not because she's trying to re-create the "song of the orca"! Luna is giving me my line!

"HOW NOW?!" I exclaim, and the whole hall explodes into applause. I feel myself glowing like a lantern, orange blossom budding through my bloodstream. I am Juliet Capulet and I CAN ABSOLUTELY DO THIS! I turn to Marcus with a beam. "Who calls?"

• ★ • ✦ • ★ •

I actually can't believe how well this is going! The whole balcony scene giddies by in a haze of dizzy delight. I don't get one word wrong! Well, I might accidentally call Elizabeth "fair Montana" instead of "fair Montague," but I don't think anybody notices.

Then it's the fight scene: Romeo, Mercutio, Tybalt, and Benvolio. It's rather satisfying to watch Elizabeth "slaying" Posh

Josh O'Conner. I'm just watching from offstage with Eliza, eating some very necessary donuts, when Eliza nudges me.

"Eliza, there were three donuts," I explain. "They can't be divided equally . . ."

"Um, *so* true," says Eliza. "But look over there. Is that Brooke the Crook?!"

I almost spit my donut. Why would Brooke be here?! But—surprisingly for someone who wears UGGs—Eliza is correct. Brooke is lurking offstage, unzipping a rucksack full of . . . balloons?! In each pocket of her horrendous cargo pants are cans of spray paint, and I watch as she fills one more balloon before tossing it into the rucksack like a villainous one-woman band.

"Gooseberries!" I hiss. "Eliza, her bag is full of paint balloons!"

Ignoring Eliza as she babbles about calling Miss Spencer, I drop my donut and sneak behind the backdrop curtain. I'm hidden from view of the audience—and hopefully Brooke—although sneaking in a ball gown isn't exactly easy . . .

Once I've tripped over the hem of my dress and fallen flat on my face, Brooke spots me.

"Kitty!" she gasps, sparkly eyed. "How nice of you to come to my grand finale!"

Gooseberries, she's said eleven words and I'm already annoyed. "YOUR finale?!" I repeat. "Brooke, I am Juliet, not you! Elizabeth is my Romeo tonight, and if that upsets you, well, you should have thought about that before you trashed Elizabeth's car!"

Brooke gives this infuriating smile. "Kitty . . . You know that Morgan helped, right?! Your girlfriend is no fairy godmother!"

"You took advantage of her!" I splutter back. "Morgan was a

good friend to you and you got her suspended. You should feel ashamed. You really are Bo Peep's evil twin, shepherding your friends into chaos!"

Brooke stares at me. "You should be thanking me for getting you into the play, Kitty. Although I only did that because Elizabeth needed knocking down a peg! And it worked, didn't it? I ruined that glossy giraffe's life for *months*. My mum seeing her in that stupid Nurse costume would've been the chocolate in the brownie, but your Mother Teresa girlfriend and her moldy green hair just HAD to mess that up for me, didn't she?! Standing out like a CABBAGE and getting us caught on CCTV like total amateurs." She mockingly crosses her eyes, sticking out her tongue. As if Morgan could *ever* look as disturbing as that! "So if you're not here to cheer me on, you can get lost, and so can that knock-off Avril Lavigne you're so obsessed with—"

"HEY!" I protest furiously. Only I can make fun of Morgan like that!

"And what are you going to do?!" Brooke retorts. "Get Siobhan to leave me out some more? I'd have to be as desperate and self-absorbed as, well, YOU to want to join the Barbie Brigade! Admit it, Kitty, you have NOTHING! I can do anything I want. And I'm about to go down in history for Jackson Pollock–ing the lot of you!"

"Are you stupid?!" I hiss, prodding her. "Brooke, I've caught you! I'm going to get Miss Spencer. It's over! You are clearly missing a few screws in your plumbing if you think hurling paint over everyone is going to fix ANYTHING!"

Brooke pixie-giggles. "Who said I wanted to *fix* anything? It's going to be FUN!"

Then she grabs a balloon and flings it with alarming force. GOOSEBERRIES! I leap aside and paint Picassos the wall behind me. Then, like a murderous Matisse, Brooke's heading to the stage. Springing to my feet, I grab her, but with eyes like raging red Rothkos, she shoves me away. Desperately, I grab at her shirt, and we both go roly-polying . . .

Right . . . onto . . . the stage.

Everyone freezes. Even Brooke looks slightly shocked-Chagall. Posh Josh O'Conner rushes over, but Brooke grabs a balloon and splats him right across the chest like a Monet water lily. He jumps back in alarm, and then she goes for the spray paint and blasts. Lost in a yellow mist, Josh trips over his own middle-class feet and goes down with a SPLAT.

Maja comes goth-tumbling out, trying to block Brooke—but Brooke expertly splatters her feet with a bright pink. Maja cries, "NOT MY BLACK DOCS!" and Brooke turns to Elizabeth, grinning like a crazed Kandinsky. She's reaching for another balloon! That's when I launch myself into her like Cézanne into Post-impressionism and we both crash to the stage, balloons tumbling from Brooke's rucksack.

"SHE'S GOT A SWORD!" I hear Zanna yell, and a plague on both my horses, she's right! Brooke has swiped Mercutio's sword and she's now brandishing it at me with all the vigor of a Fernand Léger. Then Elizabeth goes, "CATCH!" and launches a blade my way. Like a true king of cats, I'm victorious, grabbing the hilt to stand upright with my sword—

No! Wait . . .

I'm holding a dagger. SERIOUSLY?!

Elizabeth studies her weapon belt and grimaces. "Sorry, chicka! I grabbed the wrong handle!"

So I am now sword-fighting Brooke the Crook with a butter knife. She swishes and I defend with a clattering blow. The audience gasps. Then I trip over my dress (again) and tumble backward, right into a puddle of yellow paint. All the opportunity Brooke needs to snatch a particularly juicy-looking balloon. She swings it once, twice, THRICE, gathering momentum like her name is Vincent van Go-Go-GO . . . By Brooke's hand, I am slain! I'm about to be Dali'd to death!

But Morgan Delaney appears onstage, rushing like Wonder Woman herself at Brooke, whose eyes flash Klimt-gold in alarm. Morgan crashes into her like a sexy cannonball and they roll around like trendsetting tumbleweed, stage left, stage right—right off the stage! I rush to the edge and see Morgan on her back in a daze. Brooke scrambles to her feet, reaching for another balloon . . .

But Siobhan marches over, swipes the balloon for herself, and bowling-ball launches it into Brooke like a true netball-trained ninja. It SPLATS right into her stomach.

Everyone in the hall goes, *"Oooooh!"* as Brooke, caked with red paint, tumbles back into a front-row seat, winded, sneezing and wheezing like a weasel with hay fever. Habiba vaults the seats like lightning in Lycra and binds Brooke's hands behind her with her sports scrunchie.

Siobhan smirks, kicking the spray paint cans out of reach. "That's for my dress, Raggedy Ann." Then she extends a hand to Morgan. "Nicely done, Queen McFreak."

Slowly, Morgan smiles back and takes Siobhan's hand. "Nicely

done yourself," she replies. "You know . . . For a Basic Barbie."

Everyone stands around in a daze as Miss Spencer and Miss Jamison swoop in to lead Brooke away. We're all in a state of shock. Like Texas. (I've heard they have *lots* of hurricanes, truly shocking scenes indeed.) What now?! Do we have to stop the play? My eyelashes flutter in distress. All the line-learning and hard work—and we don't even get to finish?! It's too tragic to be true!

"Um . . . Juliet, my love!" Elizabeth says, and she extends her hand, pulling me back to my feet. Everyone blinks at Elizabeth in surprise. "With the strength of lionesses, but heart of the purest doves!" she rambles on. "Hast thou saved my life?! What slender dances you perform with your happy lover's knife!"

Gooseberries galore. Elizabeth is making up Shakespeare! Is that allowed?! Well, no one's stopping us. I part my lips . . . "Romeo! My handsome king of kings. 'Tis yet not time to pay for young love's sins! Come . . . Shelter me beneath your, um . . . dashing red cape! Yes, tonight you've witnessed, well . . . Juliet's daring dagger escape!"

Slowly, Luna starts clapping. Then Niamh joins in. Then the entire school is erupting like Vesuvius, cheering and whooping and (in Jasmine McGregor's case) hooting. Like true players, we carry on the play—and I don't even slip on the wet paint.

Well, I may slip once, but nobody really notices.

·★·✦˙★·

Epilogue of Explosive Possibility

Stories of woe be dammed. The Taurus sun is glowing and I am drinking elderflower cordial with a gardenful of pals. What more could an Aquarius want? Not even Jamie, rock-starring about with an arm round Cadence Cooke, can kill my vibe. Although his latest Taylor Swift cover, "This Is Me Drying—an Ode to Eczema," might turn my vibe a *little* queasy.

It's the highly anticipated (by everyone except my parents) *Romeo and Juliet* after-party, and the backyard is busier than dilly-dally circus. Some people have even said the iPhone Box is awesome. So they must be confused. But apart from that, everything is Gucci-liscious! Habiba is teaching Millie how to fitspo-squat like a pro, Kenna is asking Maja whether she'd suit a nose ring, Morgan is dancing with Lip Gloss Lizzie (which I am TOTALLY fine with), and Marcus is explaining to a frightened-looking Alison what *pansexual* means. In fact, the party looks exactly how I wanted my birthday to look back in February . . .

"Well, this has turned out remarkably well," says Zanna, materializing by my side in her baker-boy cap. "I never thought I'd live to see *you* throw a party where people actually showed up. Has Siobhan moved to Alaska?" She does her most annoying smirk. "Any chance we could persuade her, if not?"

I scowl. "Actually, Zanna, Siobhan's in the kitchen making vegan snacks with Luna and Niamh. I have finally brought peace to Lambley Common and united both our houses."

"Good grief," groans Zanna. "Are you going to speak Shakespearean forever now? Because that's going to get old. Like, unbelievably fast. Faster than I lost all my respect for you when you told me you listen to James Blunt."

"He's my guilty pleasure!" I protest.

"Some sins only God can forgive," says Zanna.

She really is the worst friend in the world. I'm very glad she's here. What I'm *not* glad about is Dad, striding around the yard in shorts and sandals, like he's fun-loving and casual or something else completely unbelievable. Who does he think he's kidding?

"What's up, Kit-Kat?" Dad says, throwing in a wink for Zanna. "Having fun?"

"I was until you said that!" I splutter, choking on my cordial. "Dad, what do you want? Can't you go back inside? It's creepy that you're out here with us."

"Have you shown your friends the new greenhouse?" he rambles on, gesturing to it proudly. Zanna nods in appreciation, Aphrodite save her Slavic soul.

"No, of course I haven't!" I exclaim, as out of patience as

an empty hospital. "Dad, my friends are not losers like you and Mum. We have much better things to talk about than greenhouses."

"Do we?" asks Zanna, and I glare at her.

Dad chuckles annoyingly. "Maybe later! Anyway, I need to be here to light the fireworks! Gather your chums, Kit-Kat. This is going to be spectacular!"

It would also be spectacular if Dad stopped talking. Unfortunately, we *do* need him (for purely legal reasons). Siobhan brought a firework. It's huge, red, and rocket-shaped, and is officially the coolest thing that's ever been on this lawn after Morgan Delaney. Dad's making a huge song and dance about safety, like over-forties always do, so no one's allowed to touch the firework except for him. He's finally positioned it on the lawn, so everyone excitedly gathers round.

Dad crouches down, which is never attractive, and reaches into his pocket. Then he grimaces. "Ah. Left the matches indoors! Hold your horses, everyone!"

He scurries inside. URGH. My parents can't even organize one festive explosion, can they?! I wish I *had* a horse to hold, but Mum stamped on that dream, too.

Siobhan comes out of the house with snacks—and Luna, who is looking very smug. She's carrying a trayful of tea lights like some sort of pagan. That's when I clock the matches, poking out of the pouch in Luna's kaftan. That explains why Dad can't find them. He's clattering all over the house on a wild gooseberry-picking expedition while all my very important guests are getting bored. I can't have that!

Rolling my eyes, I march over to my sister. "Give me those!" I say, swiping the matches, then crouch down by the firework myself. "Stand back, everybody. I've got this."

"Oh, Christ on a cracker," says Morgan. "Babe, we should wait for your dad . . ."

I scowl. "I can light one firework without blowing myself up, Morgan. How hard can it be? My dad's already set it up—it's going to be fine. Ready, everyone?" I squat down, Habiba-style, to light the firework and the string starts sizzling. I turn around smugly. "See? Told you . . . !"

It all happens very quickly. I'm crouching and I wobble and I stick out a hand to steady myself . . . and knock the firework over. Everyone screams and jumps back and then—*BOOM!* The firework launches right into the greenhouse.

There's a shattering crash. An enormous explosion. The greenhouse blows up like . . . Well, like a firework. Gooseberries galore! Shards of wood and tomato vines rain down all around us and I goggle in amazement at the smoking carnage before me.

Mum and Dad come tumbling out into the backyard, then stand in shocked silence as the flames crackle. Morgan looks absolutely stunned. Luna peels a cabbage leaf off her forehead. Siobhan has dropped the appetizers, and Zanna face-palms in defeat.

I blink in surprise. Well, I didn't expect that to happen. What am I even supposed to say? I know I can't blame everything on pancakes of doom or stars in the sky, but sometimes, there really is no other explanation!

I open my mouth. "Um . . . Blame my Virgo Moon . . . ?"

ABOUT THE AUTHOR

FREJA NICOLE WOOLF has been writing since she was in elementary school, and at the über-ancient age of twenty-four, she finally wrote her debut novel, *Never Trust a Gemini*, as a joyful, romantic alternative to the issue-led LGBTQ+ stories she grew up with. Her writing is absolutely not autobiographical. (Except for the bits that are.) She lives in London and aspires to be a Capricorn. Unfortunately, she's a Pisces.